A
fool
and
his
money
are
soon
parted

- "Pard, did that bunch of cattle strike you familiar?" asked Wess, a fierce expression on his face.

- "I guess so," came Paul's easy reply. "Looked like our own herd. But all cattle look alike to me."

- "Listen, bozo, an' get this into yore handsome tenderfoot haid. The bunch of cattle I jest counted are from **our** own herd! You're bound to a deal to buy yore own stock!"

BLACK MESA, one of Zane Grey's most exciting novels of the American frontier, was originally published by Harper & Row.

BLACK MESA

MESA

Zane Grey

A CARDINAL® EDITION published by
POCKET BOOKS, INC. • NEW YORK

BLACK MESA

Harper edition published September, 1955

A *Cardinal* edition
1st printing.........August, 1960
2nd printing.........March, 1964

This *Cardinal*® edition includes every word contained in the
original, higher-priced edition. It is printed from brand new
plates made from completely reset, clear, easy-to-read type.
Cardinal editions are published by Pocket Books, Inc., and
are printed and distributed in the U.S.A. by Affiliated Publishers,
a division of Pocket Books, Inc., 630 Fifth Avenue, New York 20, N.Y.
Trademarks registered in the United States and other countries.

L

BLACK MESA

1.

FLOWING OUT from the moss-greened base of a bluff under the bold, looming bulk of Black Mesa was a small spring of alkaline water. It was the only oasis in that desolate country for leagues around. The Indian brought his mustangs there, and the squaw filled her earthen olla; the cowboy trailed his lost cattle over the bleak, cedar-dotted divide down to this spring, and the traveler followed the hard-beaten path to eye askance the strange, clear pool. Cougar and cat tracks showed in the soft red sands. The deer and coyote and jack rabbit slaked their thirst there. But the winged creatures of the desert, those whose wide pinions gave them dominance over distance, never visited the foot of Black Mesa.

The spring had been named Bitter Seeps by the Mormons when they forded the Rio Colorado at the Crossing of the Fathers. Noddlecoddy, the old Navajo chief, said of Bitter Seeps: "It is not good water, but it will sustain life."

A great geologist, studying that region, had remarked that the nature of man and beast dependent upon the water of the spring and its forbidding surroundings must partake of its hard and bitter quality.

Two young men sat upon a rock of the cedar ridge that commanded a view of the trading post, the spring, the mesa, and the illimitable desert beyond.

"Paul, yore askin' me aboot this heah place," drawled the

younger, a lean brown-faced, tow-headed cowboy. "Wal, I reckon it's hell an' I wouldn't be caught heah daid."

His companion laughed a little regretfully at this frank opinion. "I'm sorry," he said. "It appeals to me. Perhaps you've explained why."

"Nope," rejoined Wess Kintell, "I shore didn't explain nothin'."

"I think hell is a rather descriptive epithet. If it doesn't explain Bitter Seeps, what does?"

"Wal, come to think aboot it, I cain't say. I've rode a sight of ranges in my day, but never none like this one. An' I'd hev to ride heah awhile before I could tell jest what it is that makes me feel sorta creepy."

"It doesn't lack color, beauty, magnificence," replied Paul Manning thoughtfully. "There is a difference, though, between this and the Painted Desert behind us, or the canyon country beyond. And that difference is exactly what gripped me."

"Hev you been oot heah before?" asked the cowboy.

"Only once. I'd ridden all over before I struck Bitter Seeps. Trying to find a place where I could *stay*. This is it. I was fascinated by that huge mesa up behind the trading post. It seems to stand for the loneliness and peace that pervade this desert."

"Peace?—ah-huh. I reckon I get you," replied Kintell slowly. "I've had my ideas aboot you, Manning. An' if ever I seen a driven man you shore was him. . . . But thet doesn't give me any hunch why you fetched me oot heah."

"I must have some kind of work. Always leaned toward a ranch, cattle, horses, you know. But that always seemed impossible until last November when I inherited a little money. Now I can have what I used to want, and maybe having it will make me want it again. . . . I like you, Kintell. You're the man to run my ranch."

"How do you know thet?"

"I just feel it."

"Wal, if I'd turn oot true to past performances you'd hev the wrong man."

"Kintell, you hinted once before of a shady past. You can tell me what you've been and done, if you choose, but I'd rather you didn't. I'll gamble on you."

"Did you hev this in mind when you got me oot of jail an' mebbe saved my neck?"

"My memory is hazy on that point. I remember my trouble seemed so unendurable that I wanted to help some other poor devil. And I got you out of your fix. Then came my drunken spree, about which I can recollect but little. After that, then, the idea grew, and finally I brought you out here."

While Wess Kintell pondered the matter, Paul watched him unobtrusively, conscious again of a return of the warm feeling the cowboy had stirred in him. No other person or thing had roused such a semblance of warmth in Paul Manning since the shock that had changed him. And he wanted to hold on to it. He yearned to recapture the old significance of life, the hope and joy that had been his, the love of adventure, the ambition to become a writer, the undaunted challenge to the future, to all that he had been before. . . . But at the moment he could not bring himself to again think over the long ruinous story of his relationship with Amy, and he shut the painful memories out of his mind.

This Texan, if he could be won over, appeared to be a man to tie to. He was a superb figure of a rider, tall, wide-shouldered, small-hipped and wiry, scarcely beyond his teens in years, yet exhibiting in his lean, lined face the sadness, the reckless hardness of maturity developed by life on the ranges.

"Wal, Manning, no man ever did so much for a stranger, an' for Wess Kintell, as what you did," the cowboy said with a slow and forceful earnestness. "I've shore been a hard nut, but to myself it always seemed every man's hand, an' every turn of luck was set against me. I wondered why you took it on yoreself to help me oot of the rottenest mess I was ever in. An' you've told me, yore trouble was so great thet you had to help some other fellar in trouble. Thet's a new idee, but I understand it. . . . An' heah's my hand, if you'll take it, for all thet's good in Wess Kintell."

Paul felt a significance in the steel-like grip of the cowboy's lean brown hand, and the gray eyes that met his piercingly. The moment and the place were not commonplace. Something deep and intangible vibrated from that viselike handclasp along Paul's nerves.

"Wess, I'm glad you are making a big issue of this moment," he replied. "I recognize it, though I may not be able yet to rise to it. . . . I've been down so long. This wild idea of mine—to fight it out here in this desert—may be futile."

"Wal, if the desert doesn't kill you it shore will cure," responded the Texan. "Yore bet is a good one. . . . May I ask, jest what yore trouble was? I've seen some drunks in my day, but thet last one of yore's beat them all hollow. I shore was curious aboot you, after you got me oot. I heahed you never was strong for likker until this time. You ain't a drinkin' man, I know. Jest one turrible drunk . . . ! What was to blame, Manning? Now, don't feel bad aboot comin' clean with it. Mebbe gettin' it oot will help. Anyway, then I'll understand an' never speak of it again."

Paul bent over to hide his face from the other's kind and searching gaze. To open that closed wound, to feel again the pang and the sting were not easy. But sooner or later he knew Kintell would want the truth.

"It was—a woman," he finally said awkwardly.

"Wal, I reckoned so. Someone you loved an' lost?"

"Yes."

"Ah-huh. Thet happened to me onct. It only comes onct, the real genuine article. Thet was what made me a rollin' stone. I shot the man. . . . Wal, never mind aboot thet. . . . Did yore girl die?"

"No. She was—faithless."

"Aw . . . ! Thet's even wuss. . . . An' 'pard, I'll bet she was thet gold-haired dame you used to be seen with last fall. It comes back to me now."

"Yes. She was the one."

"Wal, no wonder! Thet girl was the loveliest I ever seen. I'd jest come to Wagontongue aboot thet time, an' I shore recollect her. I seen her often. Not too tall an' real slim, but say what a shape! An' she had eyes thet could bore through a feller. Big brown eyes, wonderful bold an' bright. She was not afraid to look at anyone, thet girl."

"No doubt of the accuracy of your memory, Wess," replied Paul.

"An' she ran oot on you . . . !"

Kintell looked away across the desert. His lean brown jaw set hard. Paul divined that his admission had somehow pierced the cool, baffling armor of the Texan, and at that moment Paul could almost feel the intentness of the man, and something else that seemed imponderable, hard, even ruthless about him. The cowboy would not have taken such an episode lying down.

There was such a thing as revenge. Kintell had answered to that. The thought sent a hot gust, like a wave of fire, over Paul. . . . There had been a rival. All the time there had been a lover. But as swiftly as it had come the heat in his veins cooled.

The Texan spread a slow hand toward Black Mesa and

the wide desert beyond—somehow reminiscent of the eloquent gesture of an Indian.

"An' you reckon all this heah will ease you?" he queried.

Paul nodded. Ease him! He gazed down into the shallow gulch with its banks scarred by avalanches, its jumble of huge boulders, at the green-bordered pool shining yet strangely dark under the sun, at the mossy cliff with its streaks of gray, at the dark-portaled trading post among the cedars on the knoll, at the frowning black front of the mesa, wild in its magnificence of ruin, with its bleak rim reaching skyward. Then his eyes swept farther out to the gray desert, and once again he felt the strange, vague kinship with this desolation that had prompted his rash and inexplicable step.

"*Quién sabe?*" muttered the Texan, simply, as if he were alone. "Bitter water, hard as the hinges on the gates of hell. Stunted cedar an' sage. Rocks forever an' thet wasteland oot there. A black mountain with the face of the devil. A tradin' post over the reservation line. A wretched lot of Indians, stuck for life in this ghastly hole. Haw, haw . . . ! Thet's the ticket, an' my friend wants to live heah!"

It seemed beyond the Texan's comprehension. "Manning," he went on, "I've rode this country. The human bein's who live oot heah don't count. Nature rules heah. This desert will be locked in snow an' ice in winter, the coldest, dreariest, hardest place on earth. In spring when the thaw comes you'll wade in 'dobe mud for weeks. Then the dust an' sandstorms, shore the bane of a cowboy's life. A yellow wall of flyin' sand, thick as a curtain, swoops down on you, an' you pile off yore hoss an' cover yore face, an' suffocate. Then comes the blastin' hot summer with its turrible lightnin' an' thunder. Why, Texas hasn't got anythin' on this country for thet. An' altogether, it's jest one hell-bent range, fit only for rattlesnakes an' coyotes."

"Wess, you're way off if you are trying to discourage me. All that you say only strengthens my desire to come."

"Wal, by Gawd!" ejaculated Kintell, with a snatch at a cedar branch close by. "I get you now. Yore lookin' to help some more pore devils, red or white, jest as you helped me."

"No! I hadn't thought of that," replied Paul hastily.

"Shore, it's in the back of yore mind," declared the cowboy, as he arose to his lean height. "Wal, I reckon you're gonna need me powerful bad. . . . Let's go down an' look the place over."

"You go. Talk to the trader. You're a cattleman. Find out all you think I should know. Then come back and we'll decide how best to carry out my plan."

"Good idee, boss. I reckon I'll heah a hell of a lot an' see more."

Paul watched the lithe rider stride down the rock-strewn slope. "That cowboy will be good for me, if anyone could be," he said with a nod of his head. "He gave me a hunch. 'Looking to help some more poor devils . . . !' It sounds good. But I'm not out of the woods myself, so why should I bother my head about helping anyone else? Misery loves company, they say. Not mine. But are loneliness, solitude, desolation all I want? For God's sake, what *do* I want? What *do* I imagine I see here?"

Again he turned his gaze toward the desert, first the section near at hand and then to the gray horizon line. He failed to see what Kintell had pointed out. The early spring sunshine, pale and without heat, shone steelily down upon the little valley of the seeping spring. The place appeared abandoned. Red and gray boulders, slopes of weathered earth, scrubby brush and dwarfed cedars spread tortured, naked branches, like arms, to the sky. A forlorn garden patch with a broken fence of poles, a bare plot of sand which soon swallowed up the stream of water from the gleaming pool, the stained bluff glistening with its wet seepings and white residue, the long, low mud-roofed cabin with its gaping door, and above it all the stupendous slope of splintered cliff and jumble of rock and massed tangle of cedars, up and up in wild and ragged ruin to the black unscalable wall—all these passed in slow review before Paul's absorbed gaze, and instead of revulsion he felt only a strange sense of attraction, as if these evidences of nature's havoc had formed their counterpart in the abyss of his soul.

Black Mesa sheered up abruptly to the east behind the post; and far away, high on the rolling slope to the north, appeared the lofty lines of green poplar trees and the white walls and red roofs which marked the site of the government school and station, Walibu. Paul reflected that this nearest outpost of civilization encroached but little upon Bitter Seeps.

Farther northward the broken mesa wall loomed in lonely magnificence, until seventy miles away its battlements ended in a black crown against the blue sky. Below it and to the west spread the desert, so vast as to be staggering to the senses of man. Streaked by the black and suggestive lines of canyon, it reached to the dim, upflung plateau, topped by bands of purple and white.

This expanse held Paul Manning's gaze until at last it began to mean something for him. Somehow this melancholy waste had begun to give him the first illusive sense of peace. It rested him. The littleness of man, his futile despair, his brief span of life—what were they to this indefinite breadth of sage, broad as the dome of sky above it? For millions of years live creatures of some kind had eked out their short existences out on that lonely waste, and their bones had gone to nourish the roots of the sage.

In the foreground, just beyond the red knoll on which

stood the trader's cabin, a band of goats dotted the sage, shepherded by an Indian boy mounted on a burro. The lonely figure of the boy lent the only visible sign of life to the scene and somehow made it real. Beyond waved the gray sea of bleached grass and seared sage. Red rocks, like sentinels, stood up at intervals but they were blended into the universal grayness. This sameness extended for leagues on leagues, the long rolling swell of the desert. But keen sight and long study discovered real or miraged changes out there in the lonely gray sea. Ghosts of ruined walls and fallen castles showed dimly through the curtain of haze. Areas of flood-worn rock checkered the long levels that verged on the blue canyons. Farther on pale specters of mesas, domes, bluffs rose through the sweeping gray, until they appeared to end in blank space, beyond which the plateau, like a mirage in the sky, hung foundationless and unreal.

This dead sea of melancholy gray and its myriad manifestations of ruin possessed for Paul Manning a growing absorption. Under the brow of the ridge he would build a cabin with a little porch facing this scene and there he would gaze until the strength of the wasteland had entered into him, or until his restless spirit was quieted forever.

The dark figure of a ragged mustang and a wild rider suddenly appeared silhouetted against the skyline above the knoll. Paul heard the strains of a weird chant carried on the solemn air. The Indian slowed his horse's easy lope to head down toward the trading post. And presently Paul espied Kintell emerging from the post with a burly white man, no doubt the trader. The man was making forceful gestures and appeared reluctant to let the cowboy leave. The Indian rider dismounted before them to untie a pelt of some kind from his saddle. He went into the post, followed by the trader. Kintell headed for the ridge where Paul awaited him. When he had ascended to within speaking distance, he shouted: "No laigs—will ever take—place of a hawse with Wess Kintell." He found a seat, and removing his sombrero, he mopped his brow with a soiled scarf. "Wal, boss, you don't 'pear powerful curious."

"No. And that worries me. I can't stick to an idea any more than I seem to be able to stay in one place," replied Paul.

"Ah-huh. Thet last is a damn good habit—so far as Bitter Seeps is concerned. . . . Trader's name is Belmont. Guy I didn't like on sight. He fell for my line pronto an' I seen through him aboot as quick. Says he hails from Utah. I seen a sour-faced woman an' a slip of a girl, sorta bigeyed an' sad. An' I heahed a kid cryin'. . . . Belmont bought out the Reed brothers heah two years ago. He's runnin' a bunch of cattle oot on the range. Tradin' with the Indians, of course. An' last, but not least, he's sellin' rotgut whisky."

"How do you know that last?" queried Manning.

Kintell produced a bottle of liquor which he uncorked and smelled.

"Take a whiff of thet," he said with a grimace. Then as Manning drew back, Kintell tossed the bottle among the rocks, where it popped. "Never, no more for me—if I have to drink pizen like thet."

"Belmont didn't strike you favorably?" queried Paul thoughtfully.

"Not so I'd notice it," drawled the Texan.

"Well, that's no matter. I could buy him out."

"I reckon you couldn't. He's got a good thing heah, an' he ain't sellin'. Doesn't want no pardner in the tradin' post, neither. But I took it he'd grab most any cattle deal. Didn't pump him too hard. He's off the reservation an' has the only water for miles, except Walibu, which he says is all took up with nary a drop to spare."

"Lord of Bitter Seeps, eh?"

"I reckon. An' if you want to play with him, it'll cost you plenty."

"You advise against it?"

"Shore do."

"But, Wess, it's this place I want."

"Wal, you'll shore hev to take Belmont with it. An' *he* won't make for peace, believe me. But if you're set on a deal thet'll give you work an' a place heah, I'd say take an interest in Belmont's cattle. It won't be easy for him to stick you with me in charge an' you won't be oot a lot when you get sick of it."

"Okay. We'll go down," replied Manning soberly, conscious that he was no longer eager. "Suppose we look at the spring and have a drink of it before we see Belmont."

A short time later they were standing under the looming wet cliff that was mirrored in the deep, dark pool beneath. A hundred little threads of water trickled down with soft silky sounds, like the seep of blowing sand in the sage. The pool resembled a huge repellent eye, clear and dark and hard. In the shadow of the cliff it looked deep. At one side, an iron pipe ran from a barrel set in a niche of the cliff, and from this spilled a clear stream of water, splashing on a flagstone. For the rest, the pool was open to wild animals and to the stock of the range. Paul bent down to drink from the end of the pipe. The water was cold and bitter.

Color, sound, the shadow of the cliff, the white band of alkali, like crusted salt, the absence of frogs and water insects, and the rank green sedge—all gave the scene a compelling aspect, as if to force its undeniable power upon the spectator.

Trails led from it in three directions, the largest and most trodden of which struck off to the west, between the knoll and the base of the great slope of the mesa. Down this wide strip of sand and sage Manning espied the mound-like hogans, earth-covered frames, that furnished homes for the nomad Indians. Lean, ugly canines barked and slunk out of sight. Columns of blue smoke rose from the holes in the roofs of the hogans. A black disheveled head peeped from behind a blanketed doorway.

Paul slowly followed Kintell toward the trading post. It stood almost on the top of the knoll, which from this angle appeared to be low. Gray-barked cedars, with naked, twisted branches standing out from the scant green foliage, covered the knoll back of the cabin. It was a big house, irregular in shape, rough and crude, built of logs and clapboards, and roofed with red earth, in which weeds grew luxuriously. Evidently section after section had been added to this rambling jumble of cabins, each with a window but minus doors opening to the outside.

The ragged mustang stood haltered by a leather riata to the hitching rail. The little beast had a mean eye, a humped nose, and a broom-tail. A red blanket lay pressed in the saddle. Several Indians lounged on the porch. Manning was used to seeing Indians at Wagontongue, and had long ceased to look for a picturesque one. These appeared swarthy, beady-eyed, sullen savages. A squaw ambled out of the door of the post. She had a huge, round, pleasant face. She wore a dirty gingham dress and high-heeled shoes that had once been patent leather.

Paul sat down on the edge of the porch. "Ask Belmont to come out," he said to Kintell. Just after the cowboy had entered, an Indian girl emerged. She was young, and the dark face, with its great, dusky eyes, and the small bird-like head, with its tangled raven tresses, had a singular wild attractiveness. She wore a dark ragged skirt, silver-ornamented moccasins, and a purple velveteen blouse that revealed her full breasts.

Then, with heavy tread that shook the porch, a rugged white man in the prime of life strode out. With coarse and familiar gesture he gave the Indian girl a resounding slap on the backside. "Get the hell out of here, Natasha," he said, with a voice as hearty as his action. The squaw giggled, but the girl gave him a magnificent, blazing look of hate. At that instant the trader accosted Manning.

"Howdy, Mr. Manning. I'm glad to make your acquaintance." He had a big voice, a big frame, a big hand. His boldly cut features were not unhandsome, but gave an impression other than pleasant. For a desert man he had a pale complexion. His eyes were a shade between green and hazel. Evidently he was a hard drinker.

Paul shook hands with him, making a commonplace greeting. His instincts were always keen, and instantly he sensed something strong and inhibitive in this meeting.

"Won't you come in?" asked Belmont. "I can offer you a drink."

"Thanks, presently. I'd like to sit out here for a while," returned Paul. "I want to make you a proposition, Belmont."

"So your cowboy friend said. Glad to hear it."

Paul called to Kintell, who was trying to flirt with the Indian girl. She was shaking her dusky head and twisting her brown hands in the folds of her dress. She appeared to be a wild and shy creature.

As Belmont plumped himself down expectantly and Kintell joined them to squat after the fashion of outdoor men, Manning continued, "I don't know, though, just what kind of a proposition I want to make you."

"Cattle," interposed Kintell shortly.

"Strikes me fine," replied the trader, enthusiastically rubbing his big hands. "I'm runnin' only a thousand head or so. Can't attend much to range work. An' the Indians are lazy. But we could run ten thousand head between this post an' the river. There's a big basin out here, long easy slope, southern exposure an' good grass, where the snow melts quick."

"Reckon Mr. Manning doesn't aim to throw in any cattle at present," said Kintell. "He'd buy an interest. Then if the deal panned out he would go in deeper."

"I see," rejoined Belmont, plainly disappointed. "Well, I'd consider sellin' a half interest an' furnish the water. My partner to run the stock."

"That sounds reasonable and fair to me," spoke up Manning.

"Shore, so far as it goes," drawled the Texan. "How much a head?"

"Forty dollars."

"Too high. Cattle sellin' at Wagontongue for thirty."

"We won't haggle over that," returned Belmont impatiently.

"Any hawses?"

"Plenty of mustangs. You're welcome to your pick."

Kintell turned to Paul, spreading his expressive hands. "Reckon it's up to you now, boss."

"Then it's a deal," replied Paul, glad to get the wearisome details settled. He had a feeling that if he considered the matter further he would lose his interest altogether. And he must have some place to stay, some work to do.

"Wal, Belmont, you an' me will make the count of cattle. Then we'll all ride into Wagontongue, fix up papers, payments an' such. . . . After which I'll teach Manning to be a cowpuncher."

"Right-o," acceded the trader, beaming.

"Wess, I don't want to go back to town," said Paul

thoughtfully. "You won't need me. I'll give you a blank check. Get a lawyer to draw up the contract. . . . Go to my room and fetch all my clothes, everything. Buy me a saddle, bridle, blanket, spurs—all a rider needs—"

"You can buy all that right here," interrupted Belmont, with gusto.

"Wal, if Belmont wants to rustle with me we can make thet count today an' get off for Wagontongue tonight."

"Rustle is my middle name, cowboy," returned the trader heartily.

"Rustle or—rustler?" drawled Kintell, with a geniality that robbed the query of all save subtlety.

"Yes, I've been that last, too, in my younger days," boomed Belmont, with a loud laugh. "Suppose you come in, Manning. This post ain't no hotel, but I can put you up tolerable. An' Sister can't be beat as a cook."

Despite Paul's year of residence in Wagontongue, where he had gone from college at Lawrence, Kansas, to take up a career of writing, he had never been inside a trading post. The great, poorly lighted, barnlike place smelled of sheep wool, tobacco, hides and other odorous things Paul could not identify. A high counter ran the length of the room on one side and a low one on the other. Both were piled with colorful merchandise. Behind the low counter stretched rows of shelves packed with a miscellaneous assortment of objects, most prominent of which were saddles, blankets, bridles, harnesses, boots and sombreros, and a bewildering array of utensils for camp use. A rack of farming tools and one for guns, and shelves full of dry goods, mostly cheap gaudy ginghams and various colored velveteens, attested further to the trader's surprising stock of merchandise.

A wide door opened into a stone-floored storeroom containing barrels, tins, bins of carded wool and huge burlap sacks, stuffed full, and piles of stinking goat hides.

Belmont led Manning down a long corridor with an uneven earthen floor, covered by coarse blankets, and white-washed adobe walls thickly hung with blankets and scarfs. Doors opened into rooms on the right side, and windows on the left let in the light from a patio.

The trader entered the last room. Being at the end of that section of the house it had a window, as well as a door, and consequently was well lighted. It contained a narrow bed covered by a red blanket woven with Indian designs, a washstand, a bureau with a spotted mirror, and a shelf in the corner from which hung a curtain. The floor, like that of the corridor, was of uneven, bare earth covered by thickly woven Indian blankets. The walls and ceiling were adobe, pale brown in hue, cracked in places and stained by water. A small open fireplace of crudely cemented stones and a chimney of like construction completed the interior of the small compartment.

"Here you are," said Belmont. "A table an' lamp, with some fixin' up, will make you comfortable. It'll be cool in summer an' warm in winter. An' that's luxury out here."

"It'll be good enough for me," replied Manning.

The trader made an excuse for the fact that summer storms flooded the corridor at times, a defect he would remedy, and that when the dust storms raged in the spring it was necessary to keep door and window closed.

Kintell followed them with Paul's coat and belongings from the wagon.

"Let's rustle, Belmont," said the cowboy. "When I count cattle I shore count 'em."

"Right-o. It's a big range, but if you're not too damned good a counter we can finish before sunset. . . . Manning, make yourself at home. Loaf in the post an' learn Indian ways. My woman will call you when supper is ready."

Paul lay down on the bed with a sudden realization that

the impulse under which he had taken this serious step had evaporated. Like all of his late, restless, unhappy impulses! He had become a rudderless craft.

A faint pungent smell, not unpleasant, assailed his nostrils. It was not the mingled odor of blankets, wool, pelts and other Indian essentials of the desert so thickly charging the atmosphere of the trading post. It entered the open door from outside and permeated his room. Wood smoke, that was it. At the same time he heard the faint wails of a baby and a soft crooning song, somehow poignant and sad; then sounds came from a cabin just beyond the corridor. Paul could see a portion of a peeled log wall and a slanting roof covered with red adobe mud.

There was a mother in that cabin and Paul, keenly susceptible to grief, had caught the note in her voice. No doubt she was the woman Belmont had called Sister, probably a sobriquet for his wife. It seemed to be a young voice, however, sweet and slightly contralto; and it arrested Paul's wandering interest.

After a while silence prevailed and Paul fell prey to the dark mood he had feared, and against which this decisive step had been directed. He had to bow to what he could not break.

The four dismal walls of the adobe room appeared to press down upon him. They were stained and cracked, somber and inscrutable, like the walls of life which had fallen in upon him. They suited this uncanny place. For a long while he gazed around and upward, discovering much that he had not seen upon first glance. The nests of mason bees and wasps, a black spider spinning his web across a corner, faint Indian marks near the door, and a motionless praying mantis on the windowpane. He could see through those walls to the outside world, with its strife and beauty and passion, or through the ceiling to the blue sky and white clouds. Or he could make out of those blank spaces storied walls of his own conceiving. Did he not intend to go on with his long struggle to write? It all lay in the mind.

"Ah!" he mused bitterly. "That's it. . . . All in the mind! Happiness or hell, life or death, all in the mind. It is what you think."

And so the old, familiar, yet somehow inexplicable battle began all over again. He had won it before and he could do so again. And yet, why was it still so difficult to throw off the despair he felt? But to what end? He had struggled up out of the abyss; he had progressed; the beautiful and wonderful thing he had felt was dead; love was dead, hate was dead, vivid and torturing memories were dying. And he believed that he was ready to face the future, with courage and intelligence if not with hope.

Of the hundred and one plans that he had considered since his recovery from his futile debauch of oblivion, nothing had developed. They were futile as well. Still the days had passed. Something had been gained from merely living on.

This desert place of bitter water, this lonely upflung world of rock and earth and sage, this barren wasteland keeping its secret—was this the place that could save him? No! Those four blank walls had told him that. No place could give him back what he had lost. He need go no farther to seek, to search, to find what must be in his own soul, or else unattainable.

Therefore, this last and deliberate move to isolate himself on a forbidding and inhospitable desert was only another hopeless gesture. He would give it up. When Belmont and Kintell returned he would recompense them for their labors and abandon the cattle project. It would be far better to interest himself in lumbering, south of Wagontongue. The altitude was lower, the country one of forested plateaus and canyons, the water pure, the wild game abundant. Why had he not considered that? How infinitely preferable the fragrant, sun-flocked pine forests and the amber brooks to this rock-ribbed region from the bowels of which poured only bitterness! He had been mad to imagine that toil on a bleak, hard range might constitute his salvation.

Nevertheless Paul divined that wherever he went the same problem would present itself, the same shadow would keep step on his trail, the same naked shingle of sorrow would be his beat. Unless he could find something—not a place, nor any labor, nor an anchor to hold to, but some new meaning that would make life worth living!

"I am getting somewhere," he muttered aloud. "That cowboy—did he hit upon it?"

To alleviate his own trouble by taking up the burden of others! What a splendid prospect! But it was beyond Paul Manning. He was not good enough nor Christian enough to accept such a role. Never again would he pass by a fellow man in distress without lending a kindly hand, but to devote his whole future to benevolence—that was beyond him. What had he wanted before this blow had struck him? To travel, to experience, to know adventure, to achieve, to write the old dreams, to live and to love.

To live and to love! But it had been love which had desolated him. The strangeness of his nature loomed out at that moment; the recollection of more than one direct ancestor who had been ruined by an unrequited passion; the memory of his adoration for his mother; the fact that he recognized a strong feminine strain of tenderness in himself. But perhaps he had made too much of his infatuation for Amy. He was still young and healthy—at least in body, if not in spirit. He would forget in time. And then the old bitterness and despair swept over him. How could any kind of love ever be possible for him again? That was the insupportable truth.

So profound was Paul's absorption in his self-analysis that he paid no heed to a thumping sound at his door until he was sharply disrupted by a vociferous baby voice: "Da!"

Suddenly he became aware of the fact that the baby he had heard crying a short time ago had entered his door and was crawling over the floor toward the bed.

"Well! Say, youngster, where you going?" burst out Paul, at once amused and concerned.

The baby kept on with a singleness of purpose. He might have been a year or more old, and he was most decidedly pretty, though not robust. Reaching the bed he caught Paul's leg and elevated himself to a standing position and then, with the manifest delight of conquest, he crowed lustily.

Paul lifted him up to his knee, feeling a queer little thrill at the tight grip of tiny hands. "You're lost, doggone you. And what am I to do about it?"

Soft footfalls outside were accompanied by an anxious voice: "Tommy . . . Tommy, where are you?"

Paul did not reply as promptly as might have been required of him, and in another moment the quick muffled footsteps entered the corridor. A young girl peered in through the doorway and seeing Paul with his charge, she uttered a little cry of relief and surprise. Then she entered.

"Oh! The little rascal! I hope he didn't disturb you," she exclaimed, and the contralto voice was the one that Paul had heard crooning to the baby.

"Very pleasantly so," replied Paul with a smile. "I don't remember being so popular before."

"It was kind of you to take him up," she said, and coming forward she bent to lift the baby from Paul's lap. The baby had other ideas about that. He clung to his refuge, and a slight struggle ensued before the girl could lift the child into the hollow of her elbow. A vivid blush directed Paul's closer attention to her face.

"I—I did not know anyone was here—in this room, or I should not have let him out," she said.

"My name is Paul Manning," he replied. "I am going to be a partner of Belmont's in the cattle business."

"Partner?" she echoed.

"Yes. And live here."

"Live—here!" she ejaculated incredulously.

By this time Paul had discerned that she was more than pretty, though it took an effort to remove his gaze from her eyes. They were large, and either their dark topaz hue or their expression gave them a singular, haunting beauty. For the rest she had a pale oval face, sweet lips youthful in color and curve but old in wistful sadness, a broad low forehead crowned by rippling bronze hair with glints of gold in it.

"Yes, I'm going to live here for a while, until I can build a shack," replied Paul. "I'm a quiet fellow and won't be in the way."

"Oh! I—I didn't mean. . . . You're welcome indeed. I was just surprised."

"You are Belmont's daughter?" asked Paul.

"No."

"A relative, then—or maybe working here?" went on Paul kindly, wanting her to introduce herself.

"Working, yes. But I'm neither relative nor servant."

That low reply, tinged with bitterness, effectually checked Paul's curiosity. But he could scarcely restrain his gaze. And suddenly he became aware of a change in the girl, as well as of the fact that he had not really observed her closely.

"I am Louise—this baby's mother—and Belmont's wife," she added, a curious dullness about her tone.

"My God! Mother? Why, you can't be more than a child," Paul blurted out, shocked out of his composure.

"I am seventeen years old," she said, and if one were to judge from the solemnity of her tone she might have been fifty.

"Seventeen!" echoed Paul, and became suddenly silent, aware of an expression of intolerable pain in her eyes. It was the look of a hunted fugitive—of a creature fettered, tortured. It called to the depths of Paul, in a message that fired his pity and understanding. Through his own suffering he comprehended her trouble. She was literally a child, already forced into motherhood. If she had told him in so many words that her life was despair and misery—that she hated the father of this baby—the fact could not have been any clearer. And he had raved about his own loss, his own grief! What did he know of either?

Paul stared up at her, conscious of the significance of the moment, released and delivered from the past, flooded by the appalling reality of life; while she stared down at him, wide-eyed and wondering, somehow transfixed by what she had suddenly felt in this stranger but could not understand.

2.

PAUL SAT upon the porch of the trading post awaiting the arrival of Kintell and Belmont, who were expected that morning.

The noonday hour in the sun was pleasantly warm. Paul

had discovered a penchant for getting out of the bleak desert wind into the lee of a wall. A new direction of thought made all his hours increasingly acceptable. Everything pertaining to this trading post and to the cattle project he had entered was now a matter of interest. He tried in vain to dismiss the disquieting suspicion as to why he had changed his mind about building a little cabin up on the ridge. The lame reasons he gave himself would not down. And the dismaying moment came when he confessed that the girl Louise presented the most tragic, baffling and fascinating study he had ever known.

A farmer up from one of the scattered homesteads to the south came out of the post loaded with purchases. "Makin' hay cause the sun's goin' to shine," he remarked. "We're in for the spring thaw an' then damn few wheels will turn on these 'dobe roads until she dries up."

"How will we get around?" inquired Paul.

"Shanks' mare and 'dobe pancakes," the old fellow replied enigmatically, and left Paul to ponder that cryptic remark.

Paul enjoyed watching the Indians ride in on their ragged mustangs, hang around the porch and inside the post for hours before trading, and then ride away. He had at last seen some picturesque braves and squaws. But Natasha, despite her unkempt garb, was, so far, the one nearest approaching beauty. She lived back in one of the hogans behind the knoll and spent a good part of her time idling at the post.

It was surprising how many Indians came and went during the hours of midday. Paul seldom failed to see one or two dark riders on the horizon line. And there were a dozen or more ponies haltered at the rail or standing bridles down. Sheep and goat pelts, coyote hides, bags of wool and blankets were the principal articles of barter. The fact that very often a squaw brought in something to trade and went away without leaving it had strengthened Paul's conviction that the trader drove close bargains. Paul did not like the woman Belmont called Sister and had not been able to define her status there to his complete satisfaction. She appeared to be cook, housekeeper, saleswoman, and was never idle. She was a large woman, under forty, dark-eyed and hard-featured, and seemed to be a silent, watchful, repressed person of strong passions.

Paul had watched the woman wait upon half a dozen Indians, and though he could not understand a word of the language spoken, he deduced much from her look, her tone, her deliberation and care in weighing sugar or cutting goods, and from the sloe-black, sullen eyes of her customers. These Indians had become dependent upon the whites and they were a driven race. Right at the outset, Paul divined that which stirred his pity and augmented his antagonism.

While Paul sat there, thinking of these things, and using his eyes, the girl Natasha came out, sucking a red-and-white stick of candy.

How wonderfully dark was her hair—a soft dead black! Her eyes matched it. Her skin was dark too, the color of bronze. It had a suggestion of red. She wore a band of colored beads round her head and her hair was tied up behind in a short braid wound with white cord. Paul made a guess at her age—about sixteen. These Indian girls matured early and Natasha appeared to be developing voluptuously out of the girlhood stage.

It increased Paul's interest in her to become aware that, shy and wild as she was, she was covertly observing him. And when he was sure that her dusky, fleeting glances returned again and again to him he felt bound to admit that Natasha possessed at least one of the same rather disconcerting tendencies of the young female of the white race.

Kintell's arrival with Belmont in a much overloaded wagon put an end to Paul's mild flirtation. It also, he was quick to notice, put an end to Natasha's mood. As Belmont leaped out she flounced away with a whirl of skirts that showed her bare, shapely brown legs above her moccasins. Paul wondered why her expression had changed so suddenly, and why she had vanished at the mere sight of the trader.

"Hyar you are, Manning," called Belmont boisterously, handing Paul some documents. "All fixed up, money got an' receipted. When you sign on the dotted line we're set to make a million."

"Thanks. If they need only my signature we'll be on our way in a jiffy," replied Paul with a laugh.

"Babbit's runnin' eighty thousand head of cattle, Miller brothers most as many, Cartwright cattle outfit fifty thousand—all on range no better'n ours. Kintell had it wrong about the price of cattle. Thirty-eight dollars a head for two-year-olds! Manning, there's millions in it!"

"Wal, boss, heah's mail from Kansas City," drawled Kintell, with his lazy smile. "Letters, papers, magazines—shore a lot of truck that I opine will make you ferget you're a cowboy on the lone prairee."

"Maybe it will," declared Paul, eying with interest two fat envelopes addressed in his sister Anne's neat handwriting. Besides there was a formidable array of letters, from his parents, lawyers, bankers, and employees. Paul had quite forgotten that he owned a thousand-acre farm, huge wheat elevators, a store, an apartment house and other property.

"Wess, can you compose business letters, pound a typewriter, add columns of figures, and perform other secretarial duties?" queried Paul calmly.

"My Gawd, boss, I swear I cain't hardly write my

name. An' as for figgers, say, I could add up a column one hundred times an' come out with one hundred different answers."

"How on earth will you be my right-hand man, then?" protested Paul, for the fun of seeing Wess's confusion.

"Wal, I can fork a hawse, sling a diamond hitch, rope an' hawg-tie a steer—an' throw a gun," declared the cowboy somberly. "Reckon thet's aboot all you'll need round heah."

"I was kidding you, Wess. . . . Did you buy the books?"

"Say, thet bookman near dropped daid. Said he had only a few on yore list, but would send for the others."

"Okay. Let's rustle my bags and see if I can turn around in my room afterward."

It required four trips for each of them to unload the wagon, and on the last one, when Paul staggered into the long corridor behind the overburdened cowboy, he saw Louise Belmont standing in the doorway at the other end. She smiled at Wess. And after he had stumbled into Paul's room she smiled at Paul too, and said: "Looks as if you were going to stay awhile."

"This load does—indeed," panted Paul, halting at his door to set down three heavy bags.

"I am—glad," she added hesitantly.

"Thanks. The same goes for me—too," replied Paul constrainedly. It was impossible not to meet her eyes. And this time he met them fully and penetratingly, with a freedom he had not before permitted himself. He was to see the gladness she had confessed—a shining lovely light—dispel that dark and haunting shadow which had seemed so apparent a moment ago. Paul sustained a distinct shock, not so much at the loveliness of the eyes, but at the subtle intimation that his presence there for an indefinite period could cause such a transformation.

"It's so terrible here. . . . I hate . . ." She checked her

speech. Instantly Paul realized that she was not a child, that she was not afraid or shy but passionately candid. But his surprise, his pause, his piercing gaze, which no doubt forced her to think of him as a young man, a stranger, different, sympathetically and impellingly drawn to her, brought a flush to her pale face.

Paul wanted to say that perhaps he could make it a little less lonely and hateful for her there—that he had books, magazines, music. But something inhibited him. This moment did not seem one for kindly courtesy. He did not know what it called for, but he knew it was not the time.

Her lips parted, her gaze drooped, and she turned away with the red receding from her cheeks.

Paul must have worn a strange expression on his face when he entered his room, for Wess, after one gray glance at it, threw up his hands.

"Say, cowboy, I didn't tell you to stick 'em up," declared Paul testily.

"Not in so many words, pard," drawled Kintell, and sat down amidst the baggage.

"All right. How'd I strike you?"

"Wal, pard, can I talk oot straight?"

"Kintell, you need never be afraid to tell me what you think. You can bet your life that if I don't like it, I'll say so," said Paul, shutting the door.

"Don't get sore, then, Paul," returned the cowboy earnestly. "We're bucked into somethin' oot heah an' it'll take us both to beat it. . . . I seen the little lady look at you with them strange eyes an' I seen their effect on you when you come in jest now."

"Okay. They *are* strange, and they sure nailed me. . . . But I don't know how," returned Paul with a laugh.

Kintell made a significant gesture with his brown hand toward the cabin outside the window.

"Peach?" he drawled.

"Who? The little lady that looked at me . . . ? Yes, come to think of it, she is."

"Pard, I reckon you an' me are a couple of doomed *hombres*," went on Kintell, lowering his voice, and wagging his hawklike head.

"Doomed!" echoed Paul. "I don't get you, Wess." But he did understand only too well.

"I shore was stumped when I seen thet girl," rejoined the cowboy, ignoring the meaning of his employer's statement. "She come up to me the other day with a list of things she wanted me to fetch from Wagontongue. An' while she was aboot it she hinted thet I should block the cattle deal, but not to give her away to Belmont. I was plumb stumped."

"Well!" exclaimed Paul, astounded. "But just now she said she was glad it looked as if I meant to stay awhile."

"Correct. I heahed her. Wal, so long as I didn't block the deal she could be glad you'd come, couldn't she?"

Paul nodded thoughtfully. No doubt Kintell's reaction to this place and situation was much like his own.

"Paul, I never looked into such strange eyes in all my life. Beautiful, shore! But it wasn't thet so much. They hurt me like hell."

"They hurt me too," returned Paul.

"Thet girl is sufferin' wuss than heartbreak. Jest a kid, for all her full-breastedness. But thet's the baby. I feel so damn sorry for her thet I'm sore at myself. What am I so sorry aboot? Becawse she's a kid, married to thet big-haided ham . . . ? Nope, it's becawse of them eyes . . . ! Queer situation, this, an' don't you overlook it, Manning. This Belmont is deep, slick, hard as nails, crooked as a rail fence. I saw him chuck the Indian girl—the pretty one—under the chin. She hissed like a viper. I cain't figger oot who this 'Sister' dame is. Not his real sister, believe me. An' *she* hates the girl like pizen. I got thet pronto."

"Wess, what I got is that the girl hates Belmont worse than poison," whispered Paul.

"Why wouldn't she? Natural. She's shore not his class, nor the 'Sister' dame's either. . . . An' this is yore deal, boss! What have we rode into?"

"I don't know. But I'm glad," returned Paul with strong feeling. "If that poor kid is glad—then so am I."

"Yeah?" drawled Wess, with an eloquent glance. "Pard, you shore had a sweet time with the last female you got mixed up with—an' she wasn't even married."

"That's not what I mean—and you know it!" flashed Paul angrily. "Do you want to lie down on me and run out of Bitter Seeps?"

"Say, bozo, you don't savvy yore man," declared the cowboy scornfully.

"All right. Let's lay off the heavy stuff awhile. . . . Where are you going to hang that six-gallon bonnet?"

"I've a tent ootside in the cedars. It has a board floor. Okay till fall."

"Get busy here, then. . . . Let me see. It'll take some job to make this room habitable. Wess, your boss is going to be a luxurious cuss."

"Like hell he is! Did you happen to observe, pard, thet yore room is sometimes under water?"

"Belmont said a little water ran in during summer floods. But he'd remedy that."

"Ah-huh. We won't risk it. I'll make some low stands to keep yore bags off the floor. . . . You'll want a long box to store firewood in. These nights will be cold clear into July. An' what else?"

"Shelves to go here. A table to set here under the window."

"So you can see oot, huh?" drawled Wess dryly.

"No. So I can see to write, you blockhead," retorted Paul. "I must get a lamp with a good shade—probably we'll have to send in for that. Borrow or buy some new blankets for the floor. I want a mirror I can see myself in. Look at yourself once in this glass."

"Holy mavericks! Once is plenty. No girl would leave home for a mug like thet."

"Haven't you got girls on the brain?"

"Shore. It's a swell way to be. . . . A few looks in this glass, though, would rid me of all my vanity. Reminds me of them funny mirrors at Coney Island. I was East onct, traveling with the Hundred an' One Ranch ootfit. Some trip."

Paul scarcely heard the loquacious cowboy. At the moment he was fingering the red tags on two new, heavy suitcases. He had forgotten these. They had been packed in Kansas City nearly five months before and had never been opened. Paul lifted them carefully onto his bed.

"Shore I wondered what was in them two bags," observed Wess. "You handle them kinda funny. Eggs, china or dynamite?"

"Dynamite, pard," replied Paul fiercely.

"Quit yore kiddin'."

"Wess, I've forgotten *all* I put in those bags. But believe me, there's the damndest lot of truck to dazzle a woman's eyes! Cost far into four figures! Now what on earth will I do with it all?"

"Why, hell, pard," drawled Wess in his soft voice, "thet's easy. Keep 'em for another girl."

"Wess, you have the most wonderful philosophy. I've noticed it before in such regard. . . . Your theory, then, is that in case of death or loss—or say, treachery—the thing to do is to get another?"

"Cer-tin-lee an' pronto!" declared Wess vociferously.

Paul swore at the cowboy and drove him out to fetch lumber and tools. Kintell had touched rudely upon tender spots. Yet Paul found that he could laugh. The Texan was droll, unique, and altogether a remarkable character. Paul had just begun to appreciate him, and to realize that he was singularly helpful. Paul sat down on the bed and with a hesitating hand touched the red tag on the nearest of the two grips. A melancholy and detached pathos attended the memory of the passionate, boyish zeal and rapture that had been wasted in the loving selection and purchase of the gifts in that bag. He could think of them now, almost without bitterness. Yes, something had happened. The time might even come when he could look back at a searingly bitter experience of life with eyes of thoughtful tolerance.

Kintell turned out to be a first-rate carpenter and handy man. By midafternoon the racks were finished, the shelves were up, the long heavy woodbox with its lid was in place, and the room had been thoroughly swept and dusted. Paul had to buy new blankets. Belmont showed no eagerness to lend. But he furnished a table, a suitable lamp, a better mirror, and towels. Paul had decided not to whitewash the ceiling and walls, but made instead an onslaught upon Belmont's small stock of Indian baskets, scarfs, beaded ornaments, and other small articles that would lend color and attractiveness to a room.

Arguments, however, anent the most becoming positions for the last batch of things Paul had bought increased with every objection he raised.

"Lemme do this, pard. You haven't no taste atall," complained Kintell.

"Say, you big lummox, I've forgotten more taste than you ever had," retorted Paul. "But I suppose if I don't bar you from this room you will fuss about it. So go ahead, interior decorator. Spread yourself."

"Interior decorator? Haw! Haw! Thet's a good one, by gosh. I shore have painted my insides seventeen shades of red. . . . No more, though, pard. Thet last an' only drunk of yores queered me. I'm on the water wagon now, an' what's more, henceforth *you* air on the wagon, too. Savvy?"

"Water wagon, eh? That means Bitter Seeps."

"Wal, Bitter Seeps, then," declared Kintell, as if he had been dealt a body blow. "Hell! We cain't stay heah always. We'll live cheap, save our dough, an' when we got ten thousand haid, we'll sell an' pull fer a decent ranch. Find ourselves a couple of swell girls an' settle down for life. How aboot thet, pard?"

"Sounded great, up to the last," rejoined Paul with a dubious laugh. "I wish I could think so. . . . But look here, Wess." And Paul lifted from the bed a large photograph of a lovely face that had been responsible for their isolation at Bitter Seeps.

"My Gawd, pard! You ain't gonna leave thet oot?" entreated Kintell.

"Yes. Safest way, Wess. I'll put it on my bureau."

"Lemme see." The cowboy took the photograph and glared at it. He shook his lean head, and it was certain that resentment slowly was giving way to reluctant admiration. "Pard, if a man could hawg-tie a woman like her, an' *keep* her where he could always *have* her, why, I reckon he might be fairly happy."

"Wess, try and spring that idea on some of these females today."

"I'm not joshin'. I mean thet. . . . Lordy, but she's pretty to look at! An' men air such pore fish. . . . Paul, I reckon the good Lord never had nothin' to do with creatin' lovely women."

"Whatever are you doing?" called a soft voice from the corridor. "Such pounding and shouting . . . ! Oh, how nice and cozy!"

Louise stood framed in the doorway, graceful, big-eyed, strangely disturbing, at least to Paul.

"Come in," he said constrainedly, wondering if she had heard Wess's doubtful approbation concerning her sex.

"Howdy, lady," drawled Wess, as he tossed the photograph back on the bed, where it flopped to expose the face that had inspired the cowboy to his Homeric language.

"Oh, what a lovely girl!" she exclaimed as she entered. "Please may I see?"

Paul handed her the picture with conflicting emotions. There followed another moment of silence.

"Your sister?" she asked.

"No. I have one of Anne here somewhere."

"How beautiful! I never saw anyone so lovely. . . . Who then?" she asked directly, her strange eyes seeking Paul's face.

It was not often that Paul was at a loss for words. He felt a rush of blood to his cheeks. Kintell relieved the situation with a laugh, not altogether mirthful.

"Aw, thet's only an old flame of the boss's," he drawled. But his gray gaze held a singularly bold expression. Wess did not intend to allow any doubts to accumulate in her mind.

"Old flame is right," spoke up Paul suddenly, no longer tongue-tied. "I was engaged to this girl once, Mrs. Belmont."

"Please don't call me that," she begged. "I told your cowboy I didn't want to be called Mrs."

"Boss, she did at thet, but I forgot," admitted Wess.

"How shall I address you?" queried Paul.

"Louise—or Louie. I like Louie better," she announced simply.

"Oh, I see," replied Paul.

"So you were engaged to this beautiful girl once?" went on Louise, studying the photo. "I should think—for a man —once would be for good."

"She gave me the gate," said Paul frankly. He was glad that he could confess it.

"Jilted you!" exclaimed Louise incredulously.

"Rather hard to believe, isn't it?" went on Paul lightly. "Young, handsome fellow, college graduate, good family— and rich."

"Wal, Louise, she didn't know he was rich," interposed Wess.

"I don't savvy you men," returned the girl in confusion.

"Mrs. . . . Louise, I'm simple enough," said Paul hastily. "Wess there is a perfect devil. Especially with women, I fancy. But as far as I'm concerned, perhaps I didn't have the qualities to hold a woman, and so—" He broke off with a rather forced laugh.

"Oh, how could she?" cried Louise softly, and dropped the picture as if it burned her fingers. "So that was it."

"That was what?" asked Paul curiously, conscious that her reaction was somehow sweet to him.

"I felt it—saw it in your eyes."

"What?"

"That you had been hurt."

"Yes, I was pretty badly hurt," admitted Paul. "It was a bad case, I guess. But thanks to my cowboy pard here, I weathered it, a sadder, a wiser, and surely a better man. I must have been pretty much of a young fool, a conceited ass, and certainly no catch for a beautiful woman who loved society, travel, clothes, jewels."

"Probably you're very lucky to have escaped her," declared Louise solemnly. Then with a tinge of melancholy, "You and I should be good friends."

"Thank you. I'd be pleased, I'm sure. But just why—"

"Life has gone wrong for me too," she interrupted bitterly.

"Indeed. I'm sorry, Louise. I guess I had a suspicion of it. . . . You mean the same way as I?"

Her voice was low. "No, I've never really loved anyone except, of course, my baby—but that's different. . . . But when I . . ." Abruptly she paused, as if her thoughts were somehow beyond words.

"You mean—Belmont," Paul blurted out almost fiercely. "But why did you . . . ?"

They were suddenly interrupted by Kintell who stepped down from the box to confront them, cool with eyes of gray fire. "Don't talk so loud, you kids. . . . Louise, me an' Paul want to stay on heah. Want to turrible bad now we're acquainted with you an' see how—how lonely you air. . . . Do you want us as real friends?"

"Oh, I do. I do," she whispered, with a catch in her voice. "It's been different since you came. I don't know how. But—"

"Okay," interrupted the cowboy brightly. "You can trust us. An' I reckon there's no sense in yore waitin' to unburden yoreself, if you're ever gonna do thet."

"Louise, he is right," interrupted Paul, suddenly ashamed that he had blurted out his question to her.

"Oh, I can't tell you anything," whispered the girl nervously. Somehow she seemed to be a sensitive, young creature caught in a trap.

Paul took her hand. The instant he yielded to this kindly act he regretted it, yet was keenly affected as she responded with a glad pressure, with quick tears and warm soft flush, all vividly betraying what a stranger she had been to another's sympathy.

"I daren't tell you much," she replied fearfully. "I don't remember my parents. I lived with an aunt in Peoria, where I went to school. My aunt died. Then I had to work. Belmont came to visit the people I boarded with. They had a farm near town. They were queer people. Belmont had some hold on them. He took me to Utah with him—promised me work—a home—everything. I was only a child. That was two—nearly three years ago. We lived on a ranch outside of Lund, at a place way off across the big river lost in the canyon country. He kept me closely confined there with this woman he calls Sister to watch me—and married me just before he moved out here to Bitter Seeps."

"How could Belmont marry you without your consent?" asked Paul sternly.

"I was scared to death of him."

Kintell turned toward her with a tense face. "Did he make—force any religion on you?"

"No."

"What kind of people did you know?"

"We didn't meet many, but of course we saw people, and heard them. But we never got acquainted."

"Ah-huh. Has this dame Sister always been with him, since you came?"

"Yes."

"Is she his real sister?"

"He says so."

"How did Sister take yore comin' to the ranch, first off?"

"She hated me on sight. She was mean, cruel to me. . . . Beat me until Belmont caught her at it. They quarreled often. She has changed since we came here. Lets me alone."

"Lets you alone? Humph! I shore see her watchin' you. What you mean?" went on Kintell sharply.

"You ask so many questions. . . . I talk too much. For one thing, she used to make it impossible for any boys or men to get near me, in Belmont's absence. Now I have perfect freedom. I know *she* wants men to see me."

"But how aboot Belmont?"

"He pays little attention to me—in the daytime," went on the girl, somber-eyed. "He works early and late, as you have seen. He leaves me to myself, except . . ."

"But doesn't thet—thet *hombre* love you?" queried the cowboy.

"Love me!" she echoed scornfully. "He loves only money and drink."

Kintell turned to Paul with his characteristic sweeping spread of hands. "Pard, you heahed her. It's wuss than we feared. . . . An' if you're askin' me what pulled you to Bitter Seeps, I'm shore tellin' you."

Paul did not answer. Somehow he accepted the cowboy's implication. He felt a sense of shame too that Kintell must seem to Louise more deeply concerned over her than he. The cowboy, however, had been swayed wholly by primal emotions. The delicacy, the danger of the situation had not occurred to him. He did not think. Paul felt deeply for the girl, he had no idea how deeply, but his intelligence prompted him to proceed more slowly. Belmont was a dominating man who would hold on to whatever he possessed. Moreover, Paul sensed a peril in the Texan himself. He was an unknown quantity, a wild product of the ranges, whom no age or law could restrain.

"Your coming was an answer to my prayers," murmured Louise, looking up at Paul with eloquent, appealing eyes no man could have resisted. All at once he noticed that the shadow of havoc seemed to be gone. "I prayed for someone to come. . . . If it hadn't been for Tommy, I—don't know what I'd have done, even . . ."

"Hush!" cried Paul, clasping her hand. "What are you saying? We have come, if it means anything to you. We shall stay. . . . Promise me you will not think of such a thing again."

She shook her bronze head sadly. "I can't promise, but perhaps you can give me some hope. . . . Oh, you can!" She released her hand to offer it to the cowboy. "Thank you, Wess. You are wonderful to understand. And I don't feel forlorn and lost any more."

Then she slipped out, looking back, pale, but somehow radiant, and leaving Wess and Paul to stare impotently at each other.

"Holy mackali!" exploded the cowboy, and sat down limply on the box. "Did it happen to you, pard?"

"What?" asked Paul shortly.

"Did you fall fer her?"

"Don't be a fool!"

"Which is to say don't be a man. See heah, boss, your gray matter may be workin', but it's not aboot her, unless you fell like a ton of lead. This ain't no little deal. It's as big as this damned range. It's as Gawd-forsaken an' turrible as this heah hellhole. . . . Paul, think aboot this little woman an' her baby if you want me to stay pard of yores. I knowed there was somethin' deep an' crooked aboot this heah Belmont."

"I am, Wess. God knows, Belmont may be everything you say he is," rejoined Paul earnestly. "But we can't go off half cocked. Whether she hates him or not, she is his wife. We have no moral or legal right to interfere. . . . Besides, how do you know she's telling the truth?"

"Paul, don't you know truth when you see it in a woman's eyes?"

"Yes, I do. But . . ."

"An' didn't you see some of the hell fade oot of them eyes?"

"I—I really don't know . . ." said Paul helplessly.

"An' did you see what come? Somethin' like the first burst of sunrise? Light, hope, life? Did you see all thet, pard?"

Kintell was hopeless. The situation was hopeless. But yet there seemed to be a great and heaving lift to the unknown forces deep within Paul's breast.

"Wal, I reckon we can now put this heah frost of a woman in plain sight," drawled the cowboy, and taking the photograph of Paul's lost sweetheart he placed it conspicuously on the bureau. Then, as that position did not appear to suit him, he tacked it on the wall, close to the mirror.

"There! Every time you look at it you'll shore compare her to this real girl heah—who's gonna grow into a woman pronto—an' love you as turrible as she hates Belmont. . . ."

"Wess, you're a romantic damn fool, that's all," Paul burst out. "This whole idea would be wrong—even if it wasn't so crazy. . . . I'm sure nothing such as that will ever come to pass. . . ."

Kintell hesitated by the door. "Paul, you're a smart *hombre* aboot some things, but aboot some others you shore are dumb." With that blunt statement he went out.

3.

PAUL MANNING did not really grasp the raw and elemental quality of his new life until he straddled the log fence of a corral and watched the Indians with a bunch of ragged, wild-eyed, little mustangs.

"Wal, I've seen wuss dogies, at thet," remarked Kintell, who stood inside the corral, lasso in hand. "Boss, air you gonna pick a hawse oot fer yoreself, or leave it to me?"

"I'll make a stab at it once, anyway," replied Paul, and proceeded to choose the best-looking animal in the band.

"Okay. You're some picker, pard," said the cowboy, and it was a dubious compliment. He uncoiled the lasso and made a loop about three feet long. "Git oot of the road, redskins, an' give them some room."

The herd of mustangs, a dozen or more in number, bunched against the fence across the corral, and watched the cowboy with the whites of their eyes showing. Kintell approached leisurely. He did not whirl the rope, but presently gave the loop a gentle toss. It fell over the head of the roan Paul had selected, and instantly there was a stamping melee, out of which the roan plunged. Kintell came down hard with the lasso over his knee and dragged the mustang to a halt. Then hand over hand he worked his way closer, until he had the roan by the head. Leading him outside of the corral, Kintell put a bridle on him and then a saddle.

"Come on, boss, an' break in them new duds of yores,"

called the cowboy cheerily. "Let's see how much aboot hawses you know."

Paul was not sure about Wess. But as he was in for it, and really did not care what happened, he stepped down and got aboard. He was not exactly a novice and he was not afraid. The roan did not start off very auspiciously.

"Dig in with yore spurs an' hang on," yelled Wess, who for some reason appeared about to burst.

The roan did the digging in. He put his head down, and began to plunge over the soft red ground, sinking in above his fetlocks. Probably he would have unseated Paul the first buck but for the handicap of the mud. The second pitch sent Paul high and when the saddle came up to meet him with a terrific jolt, Paul flew off into the air, turned a half somersault and alighted on his head and back in the mud. The severe jolt did not hurt him. Paul got up, to find that the red adobe mud came up with him in generous sections, and his new boots lifted huge pancakes that increased in size and weight with every step. He was not surprised to see Kintell purple in the face.

"Wal, boss, you didn't stay up long but you shore lit nice," he said, as if strangling.

"I'm some picker, all right," returned Paul good-humoredly. "Catch that skyrocket for me and I'll ride him or die."

The Indians rounded up the roan and Paul got on him again, this time with some advice from the cowboy. And by dint of strenuous and desperate holding on he managed to ride him. Then Paul swore at Kintell and ordered him to choose a horse that was safe for a tenderfoot to ride. In due course they were both mounted and riding off behind the Indian guide. Once in the slope up the ridge the mustangs did not bog down in the mud.

"Pard, I was glad you got back on thet varmint after he piled you," said Kintell. "Belmont an' Sister were both watchin' you. An' I seen Louise peekin' from her window."

"Was she?" queried Paul quickly, and looked back. Her cabin was out of sight, however, from where he was.

"Louise is always lookin' fer you, pard," added the cowboy significantly.

"And if you're not always looking for her, then you're talking about her," declared Paul irritably.

"Shore. What else?" returned Kintell coolly. "I reckon you an' me don't understand each other yet."

Paul did not press the point. The fact was he felt that he was neither being honest with Wess nor with himself. He would not have cared to confess that the possibility of Louise Belmont's watching for him was something which gave him a secret, disturbing pleasure.

It was the middle of April, and in sunny places the frost had thawed out of the ground, leaving the red adobe earth like soft putty. Paul had made light of this spring defect of the desert, but his inexperienced conceit did not last long. He had elected to ride the range with Kintell despite his partner's protest. But Paul had an instinctive sense of what he needed. He meant to dare the desert and Black Mesa to do their worst. He meant to be outdoors in all kinds of weather, by day and night, to take what came, to endure the hard life of that upland country, to learn all it could teach a white man. Paul had fortified himself. In the face of every white man he saw reflected the profound character of this ghastly desert.

From the elevation they soon surmounted, the magnificent sweep of barren land struck Paul first with an exhilaration to which he had been a stranger. Free, wild, open range land! Somewhere in the past ages his forebears had looked out on such a desolate gray expanse. The instant grasp of it gave a leap to his blood. The next thing Paul was aware of was the raw penetrating wind that had no respect for his leather, fleece-lined coat. He began to shiver, and momentary dismay filled him at the thought of what this wind might be like in winter.

"The idee of this range ridin' may not strike you first off," Kintell was saying. "But in time it'll come to you. A foreman who knows his job will keep track of his cattle. This won't be any hard job fer us, though it'll take ridin' an' a right smart bit of discomfort. I reckon two or three Indian riders, which we can hire for next to nothin', will help us a lot. Belmont ain't no cattleman. I don't know what the hell he is, but I can gamble on a lot he ain't. . . . We want to know the lay of this range, especially the basin Belmont took me to. Most of the stock was down in there. A swell place for cattle, I'll say, but sorta tough on riders. There's lots of draws openin' into it an' some tolerable big canyons. One of these heads heah in the basin an' runs down into the breaks of the Little Colorado. I didn't see it. Belmont told me. An' from the rim of the pleateau it's four thousand feet down to the river. A swell place, pard, to lose yore cattle an' yoreself. You'll see pronto. . . . Did you fetch yore field glass? Good . . . ! Gosh, when I think of what a glass would have saved me years ago!"

They rode on, with the Indian a little in advance. It appeared that he could not walk his mustang. He loped ahead and to and fro, a squat, long-haired semisavage who fitted the scene and did not appear to be aware of the cold wind. Scant sage, gray in color, grew close at hand, and purple in the distance, vied with a bleached grass to cover the stony earth. Isolated rocks stood up here and there, and occasionally a crumbling ledge, and far off, scattered ruins of red crags, all of which led the gaze to the hazy lines of canyons, dim walls and distant plateaus.

After a while the chill wind blurred Paul's eyes so that

he lowered his head and sought to protect them. His feet were cold and he became aware of the inadequacy of his gloves.

"Wal, heah we air on the rim of the basin," announced the cowboy presently. "You'd never know the break, cawse it jest don't show in thet gray. . . . Take a look, boss. Some country, an' big as all outdoors. Belmont said it was a shallow basin. He was loco. It's a valley, an' I reckon at least thirty-odd miles by fifteen."

Thus prepared and admonished, Paul took the glasses Wess handed him. What he saw was so different from what he had expected that he exclaimed excitedly: "Oh, wonderful!"

"Shore—to look at," agreed Kintell, nevertheless pleased. "Now, boss, take a good long squint without yore glasses an' then with 'em. Then you'll know more."

To Paul the valley appeared shallow in depth and small in its dimensions though he had been assured that such an illusion would prove erroneous. What struck him first was the universal grayness, shading to purple in the distance. His untutored gaze registered an oval bowl set in the vast plateau, dotted with tiny spots and marked with irregular threads, all leading to a black gateway at the far end.

When Paul applied his binoculars to the scene his conception changed. The slope at his feet was long and it went far; the gray floor of the valley stretched endlessly; the tiny dots were grazing cattle, and the irregular lines gorges of varying depth; and the black gateway was far at the extreme end of the wide mouth of a canyon.

He handed the glasses to Kintell without a word. Something gripped him by the throat. Places were the most vital and compelling things in the world, next to human life. Perhaps they were more important, because they had evolved life and had sustained it through the course of the ges. Whatever happened to people—birth, growth, trouble, defeat or success, love, passion, joy, loss, death—all were vitally affected by the part of earth in which they took place. A new respect was born in Paul for the wide earth.

"Boss, you take the right-hand side," directed the cowboy, his keen eyes sweeping the gray slope. "Go down to the bottom an' then mosey along up the valley till you get tired. Then ride back. I'll take the left hand, an' send the Indian up the center."

"Fine. But what'll I do?" asked Paul.

"Wal, nothin', except see everythin'," replied Kintell with a laugh. "When we meet again we'll swap observations—an' I'll tell you what kind of an ootdoor gazabo you're gonna make."

Left to himself Paul rode along the rim until he found a suitable place to descend and then headed the mustang down. It was steeper than he had expected. There were places where he had to dismount, and finally he took to leading his pony altogether. When he reached a level and gazed back upward he was amazed at the height.

Then he mounted again, and keeping to the edge of the shelving slope he rode on. It did not take Paul long to realize that he liked this place. For one thing the wind did not get at him down here. Rocks, clumps of sage, the white grass took on an intimacy not noticeable above. He was insulated down here. The sun felt warm upon his back; there was a dry fragrance in the air even if the ground appeared moist; rabbits scurried ahead of the mustang; coyotes and foxes streaked over the rocky slope, suddenly to vanish; little gray birds flitted from bush to bush, uttering plaintive notes.

Paul forgot his companions. He rode on and on, until he came to the first draw on that side of the valley. It appeared to be a rough, narrow, stone-walled gully filled with brush, and he dismounted to explore it on foot. And soon he found himself lost in the loneliest and quietest place he had ever been in. The gully turned and twisted, but it was not long. It soon headed into a shallow ravine that shelved out to the plateau above. He retraced his steps, halting to rest in the deepest part of the gully.

He came upon a beautiful lizard, with bright spots and jeweled eyes, sunning itself on a rock, and when he touched the creature with a stick it made off sluggishly. It had just come out of its dormant winter state. He saw more rabbits, a tawny cat he decided was a wildcat, a swooping hawk the color of the stone, a mound of brush and debris where some animal had a home, a fireplace where, no doubt, Indians had camped, and a trio of wide-winged, grisly-necked buzzards that arose from a dead cow. This last Paul investigated. Buzzards could scarcely have cut out a hind quarter of the cow and made off with it. He found mustang tracks. Indians? Paul felt elated at his first personal touch with the work of beef thieves.

Riding on, he found himself among grazing cattle and then suddenly, like a youngster, he felt in his element, making believe he was a cowboy. Paul discovered that he could think as never before. He was alone; he had all the time he needed, and the environment, so lonely and tranquil, seemed profoundly provocative. He rode on for miles, sometimes absent-mindedly, but for the most part keenly aware of the scene.

The westering sun told him that the afternoon was far advanced and that he was hungry. Next time he would bring a lunch. Turning back, he tried to trail the pony tracks he had seen and was pleased to find that he could do it.

As he rode, Louise flashed into his mind more than ever until finally he gave way to the fascinating thought of her

It was not easy—no, it was not possible to be blind to the look in her eyes when she watched him. Nor could Paul be indifferent to it. Her situation affected him in conflicting ways. What could be done for her seemed beyond him. She was there at Bitter Seeps, a living symbol of its tragedy, a sweet-lipped, fair-faced girl with such wonderful eyes that they haunted him. He had these last few days conceived the hallucination Wess had inspired, that Louise's topaz eyes had lost their dark shade of unendurable pain. Sentimental romancer that he was, perhaps he had imagined this transformation; yet somehow he must make sure. Then he cursed himself for his thoughts.

"It'd be just like me," he muttered aloud, "to get the notion that poor girl is happy just because I have come. . . . I can't kid myself. But she said so . . . ! And if it's true—*why*, and what am I going to do about it?"

Paul could not bring himself to the point of analyzing the cause of such a possibility. He fell back to less poignant conjectures. Wess Kintell was falling in love with the young woman and that was a problem. That the cowboy had been a rogue among girls seemed to Paul fairly obvious; and if he got hard hit in the present instance, a serious situation might ensue. It occurred to Paul that the young, hungry-hearted girl might fall in love with Wess, but he found himself unreasonably scouting that belief as farfetched. He thought with an inward conflict which was both pleasurable and painful that Louise was much more likely to be drawn to him. But how bad that would be for her! Whatever had been her reasons for marrying Belmont, she was still his wife, the mother of his child. It seemed unfair of fate to heap more trouble, more frustration, more pain upon her young head.

Long before Paul reached the trail to the ascent he espied Kintell and the Indian silhouetted against the ruddy sky.

And when he had surmounted the slope to meet them on the rim, the sun had set in shades of dull, sinister red over the western ramparts of the desert. Paul became aware again of the piercing wind and the pains in his bones and muscles. The Indian galloped his mustang ahead. Kintell put his to a trot, and Paul had to follow at that gait despite an increasingly painful stitch in his side and sundry aches which were new to him and hard to bear.

When at last they arrived at the farther edge of the plateau it was none too soon for Paul Manning. Twilight had fallen upon the vale of Bitter Seeps. The pool gleamed pale and cold under the dark cliff, and above them the great jagged and tortured rise of the mesa loomed in towering majesty. The bold band of rim rock on the level crown of the mountain caught the last faint red of the sunset. The Indian guide sang a doleful chant on the way down. Dogs as wild as the coyotes answered him. The smell of cedar smoke greeted Paul, and this with the glimmering of a light gave him welcome assurance that he had never before adequately appreciated warmth and rest and food.

At the corral Paul crawled off his horse and awkwardly removed the saddle, blanket and bridle. Twilight had given way to dusk.

A broad bar of lamplight flared out of the window of Louise's cabin, and Paul saw her in the doorway, a slender white figure against the dark background.

"Oh, you are back," she said softly. "I had begun to worry. . . . How was your first ride on the range?"

"Wonderful," replied Paul with enthusiasm.

"But you were limping. And your voice is weak!"

"Well, I'm all in, of course, but it was great."

"Were you hurt this morning, when that mustang threw you?"

"Only my feelings. I lit in the mud."

"Your cowboy Wess is a cute one. He will play tricks on you."

"So I have observed. The son-of-a-gun . . . ! Is supper ready?"

"Just about. You must be hungry. I will fetch you some hot water."

"Don't trouble." But she was gone. Paul walked to the corner of the trading post and began to kick the heavy round cakes of mud from his feet. It was no easy task. The stuff adhered like glue. While he was still stamping his feet, Louise came out carrying a little pail.

"You sound like a mule," she said with a little laugh. "Mr. Manning, you must learn to be patient with 'dobe mud—and everything else out here."

"Yeah, and I've never been patient all my life," he replied.

She entered the corridor and then his room. Presently a light gleamed and flared. Paul thanked her as she was leaving the room. There was a tidy red fire burning in his fireplace. Who had built it? Paul did not need to inquire. Pulling off his boots he stood close to the fire. His hands were numb, his feet like blocks of ice. And as he stood there, grateful for the precious heat, he realized that never before in his life had he known the real value of fire. Standing there, cold and lame and weary, Paul experienced a sudden rush of feeling that made him forget his weariness.

The supper bell rang before he had completed his toilet. When he presented himself in the long, stone-floored kitchen of the post, Kintell was regaling Belmont with a recital of Paul's first range ride, while Louise, wide-eyed and eager, sat listening. Paul had only to hear the end of the story to realize that Wess had made a good yarn of it. This exaggerated narrative had no doubt been concocted for Louise's benefit.

"No wonder he could scarcely drag himself along!" she exclaimed.

"Manning, I got to hand it to you," said Belmont with his bluff laugh. "But if you're not used to tough weather and hard riding you should break yourself in easy."

"What's that cowboy been giving you?" queried Paul coolly. "I had a fine ride. Sure fell for the open spaces. Celebrated my initiation as a cowboy by finding a dead steer that had been shot. Left hind quarter gone! I was tickled pink."

Belmost swore lustily. "Well, partner, it doesn't tickle me. That steer would have fetched forty dollars next fall."

"Indian work?" queried Kintell, much interested.

"I don't believe so. Rustlers from across the river."

"Rustlers. Say, this will be like old times," drawled the Texan. "Belmont, I can track a grasshopper over bare rock."

"That so? You must be a cowboy from way back. But lay off tracking rustlers without orders," replied the trader gruffly.

While this conversation had been going on the little Indian woman, Gersha, placed the supper upon the table. The woman Belmont called Sister did not take her meals with them. She hovered over her stove or table, at the far end of the long room, a somber figure, watchful and silent. Paul never forgot the fact of her presence.

The meal began, and for him it was no different from those that had gone before, except that he was hungrier. Belmont's boast about his housekeeper's cooking had not been an idle one. Paul had not let any constraint or sense of something out of the ordinary interfere with his appetite. This night he addressed himself to the hot and tasty food with something more than hunger, and that was the pleasant virtuous sense of having earned it. It was impossible, however, not to feel strange in that environment, in the shadow of something that seemed impending. Belmont apparently had no sense of it. He probably was a two-faced man, but here he seemed sincere and satisfied. The girl presented the tragedy of the situation, and the woman the riddle. If Belmont was conscious of either he certainly did not betray it. Paul reflected that the trader was too bold, too hard a man to concern himself with the feelings of women. They were useful, perhaps necessary to him and his establishment, but Paul had yet to see the slightest evidence of sentiment in him.

Louise was the first to leave the table, which she did without excuse. Next Belmont stamped out with heavy tread, going into the trading post. And at length Kintell shoved back his plate.

"Wal, pard, there's one way I haven't got you trimmed, an' thet's shore stowin' away the provender," he drawled admiringly. "Where do you put it all? Why, man, you'll bust!"

"Wess, I never was so hungry and I never tasted food so good," he explained, and he spoke in a loud enough voice for Sister to hear.

After dinner, Paul quickly realized that he was dead tired, and was only too content to excuse himself and go to bed.

The next morning he awoke stiff and sore. When he hobbled into the kitchen he greeted everyone at the table with a smile and a cheerful good morning. He laid his khaki knapsack beside Louise and said: "Will you be good enough to fix up a lunch for me? I don't propose to famish today."

"Indeed I will," replied Louise, and she appeared pleased at his request.

Belmont seemed disposed to follow Kintell's lead in poking fun at Paul's lameness.

"Have yourselves a good time, boys," Paul returned good-naturedly. "I've got a job that's going to be good for my soul. What it does to my poor flesh and bones won't count."

Paul meant this literally and sincerely, but it must have had a particular significance for Louise, whose telltale eyes dropped. The observing cowboy drawled, "Wal, there's no tellin' what range ridin' will do fer a feller."

"It'll make a man of you," declared the trader gruffly.

Paul was getting into his fleece-lined coat when Louise came in with his knapsack.

"Thanks. Lordy, what a lunch!" he exclaimed gratefully. "Was Sister annoyed?"

"She was actually nice—for her," replied Louise.

"Look out for that mysterious dame, Louise. . . . Well, I'm off. Wish me luck."

"Good luck," she said with only a hint of a smile.

Paul divined that it would take much to bring the roses to those pale cheeks. The thought made him singularly depressed.

He plodded on over the flagstones outside. The spring morning was bright, steely, raw, with dampness in the chilly air. When he stepped off the stone walk, it was to plunge his feet into the red mire. And by the time he reached the corral he was sweating, and his legs seemed stretched out of joint. But the pains had gone. Kintell and two Indians were wading around in the corral amidst a bunch of muddy mustangs.

Presently, from his seat in the saddle, Paul glanced back toward the post to see Louise waving at him through her cabin window, and at the same time holding up the baby to point to him and wave the tiny arm at him. It gave him a particularly strange feeling about the mystery of the situation here at Bitter Seeps. Occasionally, from his room, Paul had heard the baby cry, but Louise seldom, if ever, brought him to the post. Whether or not Belmont had any interest in his son was as much a mystery as the many others that seemed to pervade Bitter Seeps. Eventually, with the thought that he would ask Louise more about the baby, Paul addressed himself to the task at hand.

Thus the day began for Paul, with the tedious climb in the mud, and then the grim prospect of facing the raw wind. Kintell was less loquacious this morning. And soon he took to the left rim of the basin with the Indians. Paul went down, and in the still, gray solitude below felt the mood of yesterday steal upon him.

He headed up the middle of the valley and soon found that, despite its appearance from the ridge, it was not level. Little threads and lines viewed from above proved to be dry arroyos and willow-bordered gullies, the main one of which contained running water. Paul followed this for miles, until he appeared lost in an immensity of gray desert. The surrounding slopes were remote. At noon he came to a slow rise of ground, an elevation around which the stream swerved. It appeared to be neither hill nor knoll nor mound, but just a terraced elevation of land and rock in the middle of the valley. The summit was grassy, with great, bare, flat slabs of rock and scattered trees of low height and of a kind unknown to him. He got out of his saddle to ease his cramped limbs and walked about, conscious of a lonely pleasure in the isolated spot. From the summit he could see cattle everywhere and counted until he could not discern which dots were steers and which rocks or bushes. Most of the stock ranged west of this elevation, in a league-long swale that could not have been observed as well from the rim above, even with field glasses. Paul found a dry seat in a sunny spot overlooking the westward sweep of the valley, and here he ate his lunch. It was a strangely peaceful hour. Paul wondered how much of this sort of resting and looking filled a range rider's life. At least he would be alone for hours on end and the thought was comforting.

Paul named the elevation Solitude Hill and, leaving it reluctantly, he knew that he would return again and again. There was something out here for him vastly greater than the objective which he had come to fulfill. What? He could not readily define a thing that he only vaguely felt. But on the long way back this day, until he grew weary again, and aware of increasing pangs, the gray, enclosed waste of grass and sage and rock gave him a nameless pleasure. At length, long before he had reached the foot of the slope, he was forced to get off and walk for a while. Then he mounted again and rode on until once more the pains became unendurable. Thus riding and walking, hunched over his pommel and hobbling along, he got back to the ascent, which he essayed on foot. Then he was indeed to learn what a laboring heart meant, and numb legs of lead, and bursting lungs. Hot and wet he surmounted the rim and rode alone across the plateau and down to Bitter Seeps.

Hours later the sight of the red hole, shining like a ghastly quagmire in the waning afternoon light, roused in Paul a gloomy revulsion. At last he reached the flagstone walk, not any too soon, and scraped the mud off his boots with a stick. As Paul went by Louise's cabin, she suddenly opened her door to come out with a steaming pail.

Paul managed a smile and a husky word.

"You poor man! Why, your face is gray!"

Even if Paul had been able to respond, he would not have ventured to confess just how her solicitude pierced his misery. But he looked at her and it was certain that she extended a hand, only to withdraw it.

"Can I do anything—for you?" she asked hesitatingly.

"No—thanks," he whispered, shaking his head, to enter the corridor and his room. Her soft, almost eager, glance had stirred him. While getting out of his heavy coat and boots he noted how clean and cozy his room looked, the white lawn curtain at his window, the neat arrangement of some of his wall ornaments and pictures, the cheery little fire of hardwood fagots—all betraying the thought and hand of a woman. He lay down on his bed, pulling a blanket over him. And he surrendered to the sensations of his burning, aching body. Sleep would have claimed him shortly, but Paul suddenly felt in need of dinner first. He got up, put on easy shoes, and shaved. The hot water stung his face. He found again that the hard water of Bitter Seeps refused to soften soap.

In the big room of the post, Sister was haggling over a trade with an Indian brave whose lean visage and scant garb, especially his worn-out moccasins, betokened poverty. Belmont was weighing wool with the obvious care and strict precision which Paul had learned to doubt.

That day customers had tracked in much mud. It covered the stone floor and filled up the cracks. Paul went out on the porch. More than a dozen squaws and braves were there, standing around on the mud-encrusted floor, talking in their low tones, waiting for nothing. It was the sunset hour and the red flat looked like a ploughed field of wet mud. The road leading from it, winding out into the desert, appeared to be the only solid ground visible. He had learned that those smooth, apparently substantial areas of red adobe were a delusion and a snare. They made life miserable for both man and beast.

He observed an Indian squaw plodding up from the

spring, burdened with a huge earthen olla full of water. She sank to her ankles and every dragging step she lifted a pancake of adobe eighteen inches in diameter. She turned off under the knoll toward the hogans. Paul watched the Indians departing from the post. Wind must be a part of their desert lives. They seemed slow, phlegmatic, indifferent, stoic. A small flock of sheep waded by, dribbling down from the ridge above on the way to the spring. Some were heavy with lambs. They wallowed along, bleating piteously, with barking shepherd dogs behind. The little shepherd boy had more difficulty stemming the mire than his fleecy charges. Life ground on at Bitter Seeps. Snow, ice, thaw, mud—they were all the same.

Next morning Paul had to drive himself to get up and dress. His cheerfulness at breakfast deceived neither Louise nor Wess, both of whom advised him to rest this day.

"I won't be licked by a mangy little mustang and a world of mud," he retorted.

The day was cold and dark, with lowering clouds and a fine sharp sleet and a still rawer wind from the north. Yet it had not been cold enough to freeze the mud. Paul found that the piercing sleet penetrated like little blades of ice. He wondered gloomily why everything on the desert was fiercer than elsewhere. Wess hovered near him until Paul gave vent to his irritation. Then he disappeared.

Down in the basin Paul remained on the edge of the slope. Without the sun this gray obscurity was something from which to shrink. He rode miles farther along the northern slope than before. The cattle were not in evidence. Paul rode until he fell off. A rocky wall, broken into sections, invited shelter. He tied the mustang in the lee of a cliff and set himself the task of starting a fire. It seemed impossible. Repeatedly he tried. Sticks, leaves, grass were too wet, and his hands so numb that he could scarcely strike a match. But he kept on trying until his state became so serious that he realized a fire was imperative. It was conceivable that, if he grew so cold he could not ride, he might perish there before Wess found him. At last he found a nest of straw and twigs, which a pack rat had built under a shelving rock. Down to almost his last match, panting and shivering, with hands like frozen clods, he finally succeeded in starting a blaze. Sight of a flame seemed to be a revelation, but that was nothing compared to the feeling of warmth on his body. A man had to get out in the open to be confronted by these elemental sensations. Paul's lesson that day included discovery of the beauty, the glory, the blood-warming importance of fire.

He spent hours in that spot, which had at first appeared dismal and bleak, but which gradually changed until he felt that there was an intimacy in the rocks, a meaning in the husbanding of fuel. He ate his lunch there and was loath to leave. The return ride was cruel and it was late in the day when he reached Bitter Seeps, physically and mentally spent.

Next day the battle was on in earnest. Paul had pitted himself—his untrained flesh and an unquenchable spirit—against the infernal mud, the stinging wind, the endless miles, the hard seat of a saddle. And it took all he had. Grim and steeped in gloom he rode out in his effort to conquer the desert.

The sunset came when he seemed to feel that the ache in his bones, the soreness of his muscles had eased. Realizing this he felt a moment of exultation. The cattle business was nothing; his old vacillation was something else again. And as the days passed, the sun grew higher, the wind warmer, and the mud with reluctance let go its hold. Its dominance for that year was over.

"Pard, it's shore been a drill," drawled Kintell. "An' if you ain't game then I don't know my callin'."

"Wess, I showed yellow many a time," admitted Paul dubiously.

"Hell! It's what you tackle an' the way you stick that counts with me."

Belmont had his word for it. "Manning, I can't see what there was in it for you—to fight those raw, muddy weeks of spring as you did. But nobody can call you tenderfoot now!"

But it was the look in Louise's eyes that brought home to him most vividly his victory and the change it had wrought. And yet he belabored himself with the thought that there was nothing in her gaze that intimated more. At the same time he was not too sure he was pleased with this assurance, either. But he drove himself to think that there was no more between them than what had been called forth by her misery and despair, and the omnipresent aura of desolation and tragedy that hovered over Bitter Seeps.

One evening, later that month, an unusually large number of Indians were on hand, evidently taking advantage of the slackening of the cold and rainy days.

By night the huge barnlike room, inadequately lighted, and weird with its shadows and the soft-voiced bartering Indians, always presented to Paul a fascinating place. He sat down on a counter and began to pick up words of the Indian language and decided to jot them down in his notebook. Wess walked up and down the stone-flagged floor, smoking a cigarette, and apparently oblivious to his surroundings. That part of the post had been built years before. And Paul tried to imagine the stories which had been enacted there. Presently Natasha came in with her fat mother, and while the latter made purchases the girl lolled around, dusky eyes alight. She liked white men; there seemed to be no doubt about that, except in Belmont's case. Wess, who had vainly been trying to flirt with her several times before, had bought her a bag of candy and tried to get her to talk to him again. But a giggle and a "No, *señor*" were about all he could achieve.

"Say, my redskin beauty, don't talk Mexican to me," he said in disgust.

"Wess, you don't go about it right," declared Paul.

"About what?"

"Why, shining up to the pretty little lady."

"Wal, what's wrong with my shinin'?"

"It's too obvious. You should be more subtle."

"Wal, let's see how you'd go about it."

Paul had only been teasing. He had no idea Natasha would talk to him any more than to the cowboy, but he believed in a deferential and friendly address to anybody feminine, as opposed to the bold and obvious. Leaving the counter he approached the Indian girl, who sat beside the stove munching her candy. The big lamp, almost overhead, shed a yellow circle of light all around her.

"Natasha, I want to learn to talk your Indian language," he said with the most winning smile and voice he could muster. "Did you go to the government school?"

"Yes," she replied shyly.

"How long?"

"Ten years."

"So long? Well!" ejaculated Paul, pleased with his unexpected success and amazed at the girl. "You ought to speak English well. Can you read and write?"

"I can read. But writing—not so good," she returned with a giggle.

"Did you like to go to school?"

"Yes, until I grew up," she replied archly.

Lifting a box nearer the girl, Paul sat down close to her, to look at her with undisguised attention that could easily have been misunderstood.

"Tell me about it, Natasha," he said earnestly.

Paul found himself staring into the dark impassive face and dusky smoldering eyes of an Indian girl whose education apparently was on a par with that of a white girl of her age.

"Natasha, how old are you?"

"Sixteen."

"And you went to school for ten years?"

"Almost."

"Well, go on. Tell me all about it."

"*Sí, señor,*" she replied.

He went on, with a smile, "As you probably know, I'm a partner of Belmont in the cattle business. But I'm going to be a writer and write books about the desert, the Indians, the white folk who live here. I'll pay you well if you'll tell me all about yourself, and the school, your people, everything! Will you?"

"Yes, *señor,* only I'll not take money from you."

At this juncture Paul's absorption was rudely broken by a sharp hand on his shoulder, and a familiar voice. Paul looked up to find Wess at his side, and to see, in the full flare of the lamplight, Louise standing there with dark, blazing eyes.

"I was jest tellin' Louise heah thet you'd won our bet when you made Natasha talk English," said the Texan, without his usual drawl.

Paul arose, outwardly cool and collected, to include Louise in his reply. "Yes, I have won. It wasn't so difficult, though very amazing. I had the surprise of my life."

Louise inclined her head, as if to accept his explanation of his keen interest in an Indian girl, but her eyes belied her action. Without speaking she turned and disappeared into the weird shadows of the post.

"All right for you, Indian girl," said Wess banteringly, and led Paul away.

"Didn't you see her comin', you sap haid?" he demanded in a fierce whisper. "I fell all over myself tryin' to tip you off."

"Tip me off! What for?" ejaculated Paul, quite bewildered.

"To Louise's ridin' in on you an' ketchin' you sweet on Natasha. Did you see her eyes when you got up with yore slick little speech? Aw, no, them eyes didn't say much atall!"

"Wess, I wasn't sweet on Natasha," protested Paul.

"Say, don't try to kid me. Thet little redskin has got real class, an' you fell same as I did."

"You're crazy," declared Paul shortly.

"Wal, I was wonderin' if this Bitter Seeps had got into me, too," drawled the cowboy pessimistically. "You shore air dotty, though I cain't say what aboot. Belmont's crazy with greed to get rich quick an' beat it somewhere. Sister is crazy to murder Louise or lay her open to Belmont's rage. An' Louise is crazy about *you*."

"Wess, I've a mind to bust you one on your gabby jaw," threatened Paul, his patience gone.

"Bust away, boss. But it won't change the little fact thet I've got things figgered oot correct."

"Am I a moron?"

"What's thet?"

"A moron is someone with the mentality of a child—whose mind has never developed."

"Wal, so far as women air concerned you're a moron, then. You shore air, Paul."

"Why? Because one woman made a fool out of me?"

"No. It's because you air so dense. Lord, I like you the better fer it, pard. An' thet's the reason women fall fer you. It's the plaintive look in yore eye. You air a little lost boy, Paul."

"Am I? Well, maybe," replied Paul, laughing despite his irritation. "But that would hardly explain Natasha's falling for me, as you call it."

"Hardly. Take it from me, if you ever meet her oot in the dark or on a lonely trail—good night!"

"Very well, my wise and irreproachable guardian, I am forewarned and forearmed. Now as to Louise. Why am I a moron in regard to her?"

"Cain't you tell a jealous woman when you see one?"

"Wess, I saw that look in her eyes. But how can you be so sure? After all, she knows little enough about me—"

"Wal, she is," said the cowboy doggedly. "I'd stake my life on it. When she seen you with Natasha she jest stopped daid still in her surprise. Then her eyes began to light up. An' when she flounced aboot with her haid up like an outraged queen, I seen her face turn as red as a beet."

Somehow, the cowboy's words made Paul's sense of guilt increase, not unmingled with a secret tinge of pleasure.

"Wess, she might have been feeling only ashamed of me," he said hopefully.

"I'll say. But of herself more. Take it from me, pard. This kid never met any man of yore kind, not since she growed up, anyway. She was jest like a powder magazine waitin' fer a spark. She jest up an' fell in love with you. When a woman hates one man for wrongin' her, she's more liable to love another, especially if he's fine an' upstandin'. An' back of it heah, Paul, is this lonely soul-killin' hole. . . . Go oot an' kick yoreself around the block an' see if you can get the thing into yore haid."

Paul surrendered to the spirit of the cowboy's caustic advice and went out upon the front porch of the post. The mystic black night, full of bitter wailing wind, appeared to stretch vaguely to the bold ridge tops. Out there coyotes barked their wild, staccato notes. Down toward the spring all was impenetrable gloom and silence. The mesa lifted its dark crown to the stars. Paul grasped the strength, the inevitableness of these things of the desert, but they did not enter his soul. He felt only troubled. After a moment he went back into the post, down the long corridor, to his lighted room. There, her back to his fire, which evidently she had just replenished, stood a slender white-faced girl whose blazing eyes drew him like a magnet. It was Louise.

Paul advanced slowly. "Many thanks, Louise, you're spoiling me," he said.

Louise did not reply. She seemed considerably agitated. He tried to find casual words.

"You disappointed me . . . this afternoon. I thought you were above such things," she said in a low voice, less full of reproach than of pathos.

"I'm sorry. How could I—disappoint you?" returned Paul haltingly. Her eyes were great starry gulfs that seemed to behold all of man's iniquity.

"You were making love to that Indian hussy."

The scornful tone in which she accused him sent the blood into his cheeks. If it was not anger that swept over him, it was indignation mingled with guilt.

"Don't you think you're jumping at conclusions, Mrs. Belmont?" he replied sharply. "And even if it were true— if I wanted to make love to Natasha, why shouldn't I?"

At his brutal answer she seemed to wither.

"No reason. I'm just being a fool, I guess," she said helplessly. Looking beyond him she started to turn away. Paul could not endure her tragic look. He hesitated, torn between pity and indignation, knowing that he should let her go, but pulled irresistibly the other way. He caught her hand.

"Louise, you did not answer my question. Why shouldn't *I* make love to Natasha?"

"Because your cowboy means to . . . because Belmont does," she whispered passionately, and her eyes blazed with such fire that only the revelation behind her words could have made him think of anything but their beauty.

"Because I believed *you* were above such—such—" she broke out bitterly. "Your coming gave me the only happiness I've had since I came to this horrible country. . . . You seemed unlike him. You seemed a man to respect. . . ."

"Louise, your insinuation was unfair," Paul interrupted quickly. "How could I have understood your meaning? Wess bet me I couldn't get her to talk English. I did. In a flash she caught my interest. But not because she's a pretty little savage. It was what she said about school. . . . And I told her I was a writer—that I would pay her to tell me her story."

She turned to him, relief suddenly evident in the glow of her eyes. "Paul—please forgive me," she said tremulously. "It was so hard for me not to think—I know I was unreasonable, but I just couldn't help it—after the hopes your coming here gave me. . . ."

What he had seen in her expression dragged from Paul a rash promise.

"Louise, I *will* help you if I can," he burst out.

"Oh! If only you could!" she cried, the havoc in her face suddenly dramatically gone.

"Go now," he whispered, as she faltered, not from lack of courage but from the failure of her voice. She left then, and Paul sank into the chair before his fire. She had proclaimed a feeling for him, openly, bravely, without any sense of guilt or hesitation. She seemed all soul, one of those strange natures that must love or die. This time Paul had truly felt in her a great need. She did not seem to importune a return of what she felt, though that wish perhaps lay at the depths of her heart.

Paul sat there for a long time, until the fire burned down to ruddy embers, forgetting his weariness in the revelation that Louise had made to him.

All during that night he sat there, torturing his mind with thoughts of what he could have done to prevent the girl's present plight. He had come. And it had happened. Whatever the issue, he must see it through. But he must protect Louise as well as help her. He was at a loss to know how to keep from compromising her without failing in what he now realized she seemed to want—to be with him. Nevertheless, this had to be done. Morning found Paul fixed in mind on all except his doubtful status in this unprecedented affair. He tried to persuade himself, however, that only his pity, his manhood, his sense of chivalry were involved.

When the first red glow of dawn shone through his window, he had found little sleep and no more resolution of his problem.

4.

"For my part I prefer the mud," said Belmont, his big bold eyes staring out over the desert.

Paul pondered that cryptic remark. To him the early morning promised a sunny beautiful day, suggesting that the belated spring had really come. The sun had not yet topped Black Mesa, but far out on the desert a gold-red flush brightened the cold gray of bluffs and walls. The great white peaks that dominated the region could be seen clearly this morning, the first time since Paul's arrival. Far across the Painted Desert and the vast valley of the Little Colorado began the heave and rise and bulge of the dark wasteland which terminated in the dim bulk of the mountain of Twin Peaks, with their snowy cones piercing the blue sky.

"Wal, I'm from Texas, which shore ain't no Gawd-forsaken country like this," drawled Kintell, which was his answer to Belmont's puzzling preference.

"What say you, Doetin?" asked the trader of the old Indian who stood with them on the porch. His bronze visage resembled a mask of wrinkled parchment. He was lean and gray, yet upright, and he had the look of a falcon in his piercing gaze. He was the first Indian Paul had observed with light eyes instead of dark; they were of a nameless hue, perhaps somewhat like flint. The desert was the place for marvelous eyes in man and beast and bird. Doetin swept his gaze around, and with a stately gesture replied: "Wind."

"Ha!" ejaculated Belmont disgustedly. "Come in, old-timer." And he led the Indian into the store.

"Funny jokes," declared Paul with a laugh. "Belmont prefers the mud. . . . Wess, they must make something of wind around this place. I had all I wanted last month."

"Pard, it ain't blowed yet," drawled Wess reflectively, as he lit his cigarette.

"Oh, excuse me."

"Every range rider knows wind," went on the cowboy. "An' he hates it. I've faced it on the Staked Plains of Texas an' in the Pan Handle, an' on the Nebraskie prairie in winter where it shore *does* blow. But I reckon I never seen no wind."

"How come? You'll give me the willies."

"Pard, wind itself ain't so bad. It's what it carries. Cold, sleet, snow, dust, sand. An' of them all, Lord deliver me from sand!"

"Sand. You mean blowing sand?"

"I do thet," replied Kintell emphatically. "Crowther, the government farmer up heah, was tellin' me this neck of woods was the hell-bentenest place for wind. He's been heah twenty years. Reckon the wind don't blow no harder'n a Kansas cyclone. But it packs a load. There's a hundred miles an' more of sand, clay, gravel where nothin' grows, not even greasewood, an' when the wind gets to hummin' across thet flat, believe me, it must be tough. Wust of all, Bitter Seeps gets the brunt of a sandstorm."

"All in the day's work, Wess," replied Paul, mimicking one of his cowboy's favorite expressions.

"Yeah? Wal, let's stay home an' flirt with the girls."

"Girls?" echoed Paul dubiously.

"Shore, you flirt with Louise an' I'll have another go at Natasha. Paul, sometimes I jest wonder if yore mother knows you're oot," drawled the cowboy.

"Oh, hell, Wess!" ejaculated Paul impatiently. "I admit I'm not very bright. And I'm certainly not evil-minded."

Kintell changed subtly. "I reckon I was only kiddin', Paul. You're shore hot-haided. An' I talk too much. Bitter Seeps has got on my nerves. . . . I'll rustle oot an' saddle the hawses."

Paul went back to his room. Soon he heard Louise's footsteps in the corridor. When she appeared at the door with his lunch this time, a far sterner battle than that of the bitter elements was suddenly renewed for Paul. Looking up at her he saw with surprise that these last weeks, so trying to him, had benefited her. The cheeks once strained and hollow had rounded out into beauty; the impression of frailty had vanished; the topaz eyes shone with lovely lights and shades; and in the smile she gave him, almost a ghost of a gayer spirit was breaking forth.

"Well, this is even better service than one might get in the best hotels in Chicago and New York," he said gallantly.

"Really? I heard that all the best hotels have room service," she said innocently.

"Ah, yes, but not with such a charming waitress."

"You're teasing me," she retorted blushingly. Somehow she seemed so much a wistful child, even with her visibly full-breasted figure and long rippling hair. The fact of her having been forced into marriage and motherhood made this immaturity seem all the more tragic to Paul.

"I see you're not much accustomed to flattery from men," he went on, still with an effort at lightness.

She turned on him passionately, at once all woman. "What would you expect in a place like *this* . . . with men like Belmont and his cronies?" Her voice was scornful. "What is there to expect but hate and boredom and men who always *want* something when they talk to you. . . ."

"Please forgive me—I didn't mean to tease you . . . and I really meant what I said," replied Paul contritely.

As abruptly, her mood changed again. "It is I who should be sorry, Paul—really . . . but it's not easy to keep from being hateful and suspicious—even of you."

"I do understand," he said gently. Then an idea struck him. "You said you were bored with life here. . . ."

"I suppose I should be ashamed . . . but there's really so little to do here. Of course there's Tommy—but he doesn't take much care, and Gersha helps me look after him. And Sister won't let me do anything at the post except fix your meals and look after your room. . . ."

"Well, what I had in mind was I'm planning to start writ-

ing soon. I hate to use a pen, and lead-pencil writing fades.
. . . It must be typed. Could you learn to use a machine?
I have one."

"I don't need to learn," she replied eagerly. "I used to
type for my aunt. All I need is a little practice. Oh, I'd be
so glad."

"Of course I'd pay you."

"You would not!"

"Why?"

"Because I couldn't take pay from you. To work for you
would be enough!"

"Nonsense. If you will not let me pay you—well,
I won't—"

"Please!"

So magnetic and passionate an entreaty over such a triv-
ial matter made Paul smile.

"Would Belmont object?" he queried dubiously.

"I wouldn't care if he did," she said with sudden spirit.
"But I cannot see Belmont refusing money for anything."

"You mean he would take what you earned?"

"He would."

"Well, that settles that."

"But, Paul, it doesn't. I'd love to work for you. . . . Go
ask him—and make my wages very small."

Although, all at once, he was a little uneasy at what he
had done, Paul repaired to the store, and approaching Belmont, who was behind the counter talking to Sister, he
broached the subject: "Belmont, I must begin my writing
or I'll get so far behind I'll never catch up. It will have to be
typed. What do you think of the idea of Louise working
for me?"

"I think well of it, Manning," Belmont replied. "She has
little enough to do. Sister won't have her in the kitchen an'
I don't want her in the store. She moons at the window too

much. The kid is sleeping his life away. She has plenty of time. Yes, it's a good idea. . . . What will you pay?"

"Well, not very much."

"Ten dollars a week?"

"Yes, I can afford that."

"All right. Put her to work."

Louise awaited Paul at the end of the corridor, all eyes.

"You are frowning," she said when he came up.

"Am I? But it's not about your job. You have that."

"I knew before you left. . . . What is it?"

"He said the baby was sleeping his life away."

Her face suddenly set again in that haunting mask which so wrenched Paul's heart that he had to resist wanting to take her in his arms. "As if *he* cared . . ." she said bitterly. "All the time Tommy was so sick *he* hardly ever came near us. It was Sister who suggested that it might be the water, and to get milk from the Indians. . . ." Then she brightened somewhat. "But Tommy is much better now, thank heaven."

"I was wondering about him. You hardly ever take him out of your cabin, and I seldom hear him cry."

"I've kept him in during the cold weather—he's still so frail, and Belmont, for some reason or other, doesn't want him around the post . . . but Tommy's so good. He hardly ever cries or makes a fuss." There was a glow in her eyes that somehow seemed to lift the weariness and hate from them.

"I am glad," replied Paul in relief. "Louise, do you sit mooning at your window?"

"Belmont said that too?"

"Yes."

"I have spent hours at my window," she went on, suddenly lifting her eyes, the flash and depth of which startled Paul. "But I'd hardly call it mooning."

"What were you doing, then?"

"Watching for you."

"Have you nothing else to do?" he demanded, startled by her guilelessness.

"Nothing that eases this so," she replied and she pressed her hand on her breast.

"Louise! Do you realize what you are saying?" he whispered hoarsely.

"Perfectly. It is such a relief to tell you."

"You child—"

"Ah, Paul—no child any more," she interrupted.

"But have you no feeling that it is wrong to—to talk . . . ?"

"Talk," she repeated, as he faltered in his speech. "No. I acknowledge no ties that bind me to Belmont. . . . Can't you understand? You were kind, good, and there was something in you. . . . Oh, be patient with me!"

"I should scold you," he replied, and it was easy to see that he was trembling. "But I can't. Louise, if it is possible for a thick-skulled man to understand you—I do. Only I don't know what you want."

"Just to be with you—see you a little now and then." Suddenly clutching his coat she put her cheek against his shoulder for a moment. Then she broke away and fled.

It was long before Paul felt released from the strong emotion that had overcome him. Twilight had stolen down. The room had grown chilly. He built a fire on the hearth and watched it blaze and flame. Presently he lighted his lamp. The sheep were bleating down by the hogans; from out on the desert came the wailing note of coyotes. The wind moaned about the silent house. He felt Bitter Seeps and the shadow of Black Mesa settling down upon him with their intangible and fatal hold.

5.

THE WARM SUN, the blue sky, the feeling of real spring in the air, the gamboling of lambs around the corral and the whistling of the mustangs—these might have been responsible for an exhilaration new to Paul, but he had a secret dismaying suspicion that there was something more.

It was most satisfying to walk on dry ground, to climb into the saddle without excruciating pangs, and to face a long day's range riding without dread. Paul was pretty well broken to horseback by now and had begun to believe he would revel in it someday.

Paul also noticed that Louise had made a small wooden enclosure on her front porch in which the baby played on warm mornings. He seemed thin and not too strong, but prattled and talked to himself at a great rate, while Louise hovered solicitously near. As far as Paul could see Belmont seldom went near the child.

One day Kintell espied straggling cattle coming down into Bitter Seeps. "Ha, look at thet. Doggone! Our waterholes have dried up."

"Didn't we expect that?"

"Shore. But not so soon. It'll cause the stock to work this way an' hang close. Grass not so good at this end of the basin. . . . I've an idee, boss. Let's build a dam oot there in a likely place, an' hold some water. If Belmont had been any kind of a cattleman he'd have done thet."

"Okay. When shall we do it?"

"Wal, let's see. Accordin' to dope we're gonna have hell with sand ontil along in June, then we'll get roastin' sun thet fries lizards on the rocks, an' in August turrible thunder an' lightnin' storms—an' floods. Why, if you can believe these gazabos, the canyons run full an' you don't want to be in one when a flood comes down."

"Cheerful, comfortable place—this desert!"

"Ain't it hell, though? Paul, you got me skinned to death as a game guy. An' thet worries me powerful much."

"Wess, I'm only a bluff."

"Wal, a bluff goes a hell of a ways, if you stick. An' I'm saying' yore name is Paul Stick Manning."

"My name is mud."

"Aw, wal, of course, when it comes to wimmen," drawled the cowboy shrewdly. "Same with every man."

When they rode up on the plateau Wess made the observation that the white peaks so clear and bold just after sunrise were now obscured in haze.

"What color is thet, boss? Too gray fer smoke."

"Looks like cloud."

"Ump-umm. I'll tell you what it is. Dust, by thunder! Dust way across the Painted Desert."

"I see. The old redskin knew his wind, didn't he? Well, cowpuncher, you go back home and make up to Natasha, or loaf around waiting for your pie."

"An' what'll you do?"

"Me? I'll ride the range as usual, and report upon my return."

"Yes you will, like the little old lady who kept tavern oot west. An' thet was like hell . . . ! I'm ridin' with you today, boss, an' it's a good bet I'll be leadin' you back pronto."

"Not on your life!" ejaculated Paul vehemently. "Wess, the fact is I'd like getting caught out in any kind of a storm."

"Wal, thet's natural, even fer a man. But not in a sand-storm."

"I'm in for everything."

"Say, boy, you air feelin' yore oats. I'm glad, 'cause you shore were a sick tenderfoot fer a coupla weeks. But boss, you gotta show some sense."

They halted their mounts as usual upon the rim of the plateau. The scene this day appeared indescribably different to Paul. No wind was blowing there, which was a marked contrast in itself. The still air was balmy. The great basin shone almost white under the bright sun; the rims all around stood out clear-cut and rugged; the grand wall of the canyon far to the north stood up with its broad gold band and black-fringed crown; Kishlipi in the east showed its notched and cedared slopes as never before; and to the west the magnificent wandering line of Echo Cliffs ranged away leagues beyond Black Mesa.

"Oh, wonderful!" burst out Paul.

"Pard, I'm bound to admit it's pretty nifty this mawnin'," drawled the cowboy. "But we're miles up an' away from Bitter Seeps. Thet's why, an' allowin' fer a sunny day."

"So long," replied Paul, and started his mustang down. He waited awhile before Wess broke out.

"Bull-haid tenderfoot! If I was yore boss, I'd fire you," yelled Wess, red in the face, and he spurred his horse after Paul's.

"I am, at that," muttered Paul ruefully. "But I'm aching to have things happen. And Wess always wants to spare me."

Nothing happened for hours and miles on end. The rolling floor of the basin presented a familiar yet more interesting aspect. It seemed to breathe of spring. Paul encountered straggling cattle working leisurely away from the swale around Solitude. They were heading toward water. Kintell, riding far to the left, always kept Paul in sight.

Paul's first intimation of a change in the perfect conditions was when he missed his shadow on the ground. Then he was surprised to find the sun had paled so considerably that all the brightness was gone, and it appeared a round queer orb through thin clouds. A second look above acquainted Paul with the fact that these clouds were low and gray, and coming swiftly from the south. He reined his horse and surveyed the valley for a sign of Kintell. Presently he located the cowboy on top of a knoll, motionless, eyes evidently intent upon the sky. Paul headed back to join him.

"Wal, boss, what you want to do?" inquired Kintell. "Hang around heah in the valley or make tracks fer home?"

"I think we'd better go. I'm sorry about my bullheadedness," replied Paul soberly.

"Flyin' high an' comin' in gusts," said the cowboy. "I reckon we can beat it."

With that he set off at a brisk trot and Paul fell in behind. He calculated they were six or eight miles from the rim, and as many more across the plateau to Bitter Seeps. His mustang was sure-footed, which allowed Paul to watch the darkening sky.

Down here in the valley, there was not the slightest wind. The silence seemed ominous and oppressive. Warmth still prevailed, but evidently was a reflection from the ground. A tendency to cough and an itching in his nostrils acquainted Paul with the fact that he was inhaling invisible dust. Then he smelled it. All the blue canopy overhead gradually became overcast by a gray scudding smoky mass, through which the sun showed faintly red. The dust clouds had begun to take on a tinge of yellow. As if by magic the beautiful valley was transformed into the old, gray, dreary place, with some indefinable aspect added. The cattle banded, and bunched in herds, uneasy and restless.

Reaching more level ground the cowboy urged his horse to a lope. Paul followed suit, and at that gait they covered ground rapidly.

"Walk an' save yore hawse climbin' oot," advised Kintell, at the foot of the slope. "We may hev to ride to beat hell."

Paul was reveling too keenly in the singular atmospheric effects to feel any concern. Still a growing excitement attended this absorption. Every time he halted to catch his breath he gazed back into the basin, and then at the strange mushrooming clouds sweeping across the sky, and at the weird sun. Its color was deepening. All the hues were deepening. Another zigzag climb left Paul only one more steep slant to surmount. It seemed that a very few moments added much to the spectacle.

"We ain't seen—nothin' yet," panted Wess. "Wait till we get on top—an' then you'll hev yore teeth jarred oot."

They ascended the last lap. Paul, bathed in hot sweat and out of breath, turned to gaze southward. And what he saw stunned him with awe and fear. Far across the desert a yellow, sky-high wall appeared to be advancing toward them. It thinned toward the west, and thickened the other way.

"Boss, it's shore a sight," exclaimed the cowboy. "Colored sand! Like a painted curtain . . . ! Look! It's swooped down into the far end of our basin. Golly! Whoever talked aboot prairie fires . . . ! Storm? I'll tell the world. Look at thet queer sun . . . ! Paul, it's some sight, but we ought to rustle."

"Oh, no! It's great!"

"We got six miles an' more to ride over rough country.

An' if thet wind ain't doin' ninety miles an hour I'll eat it."

"But Wess, look! How strange, magnificent! This is worth all it cost to get here."

Paul experienced only the ecstasy of the artist who had waited years for a sublime phenomenon of nature. He strained his eyes. He swept their gaze from the far sunny rim of Black Mesa, and the clear desert beneath, back to the colossal yellow wall, and then up at the darkening canopy through which the sun burned magenta, and down into the basin, filling the far end with rolling swirls and scrolls of dust, yellow and red and purple. The storm moved over that area like the down-dropping clouds of a tornado, in a few moments obliterating the far half of the valley. Kishlipi had been swallowed up. The march of the wall overcame buttes and mesas, the ragged rent of the canyon, the clay dunes, to encroach upon the sage waste. Its most sinister and stupendous effect appeared aloft where the top of the wall met a fiercer gale which curved it in grand, sheeted and coalescing clouds far out over the desert.

"Listen, pard! Holy mackali!" cried the cowboy.

Paul's ears filled with a low roar that swelled while he listened. It was warning enough. Yet he felt reluctant to leave. Every second the spectacle changed. The marvel was that he stood in the midst of a still, thick air, which as he gazed began to lift and puff, and then to move. In another moment he saw a league-wide billow of yellow, faintly tinged with red, gray and white, pour over the distant rim into the valley, to roll and descend and spread like smoke from a volcano. And the vast oncoming wall, broken by the void at its foundation, changed its front into a terrific tempest of dust-laden currents of wind, wildly broken, streaked and striated, its lightened ramparts leaping across the purple-veiled sun. And the low roar swelled into a rolling thunder.

"Fork him an' ride!" screeched Kintell. "It'll ketch us shore'n hell!"

Paul leaped astride and spurred after the cowboy. The mustang was light-footed and swift. Spur and roar united to make him fly across the plateau. On a dead run the two horses held their own with the pursuing storm. Paul looked back, thrilled to his soul. The yellow wall, sky-high and solid and straight of front as a wall of stone, was scarcely a mile behind, and sweeping on with majestic and fearful momentum. It was a race between the elements and man-driven beasts. But directly ahead lay the rough belt of the plateau, rocks and shale, washes and ridges, ground over which it would be perilous to run a horse. Kintell rode into it at full speed and Paul fell in behind him. They lost only because they had to swerve aside from a straight course. And the pursuing thunder bellowed at their heels. Paul felt the patter of flying pebbles against his back, a pressure that bowed him forward in his saddle. His sombrero flew off and, sailing like a swallow, never came down in his sight. Kintell kept looking back, his lean jaw set. Fear at last edged into the tumult of Paul's emotions. Why didn't Wess halt to seek shelter under one of the rock ledges? They were caught. The slender junipers bent over flat, the tumbleweeds careened madly ahead, the sheets of gravel flew along the ground.

Paul, fearing for his eyes, did not look back. Abruptly the wall was upon him, pushing his mustang ahead. He raced for a moment with the advance, half buried in the whirling dust devils before the solid pall. His strongest sensation of all then was the smell of dust that clogged his nostrils, and next the seething, bursting roar.

Paul's horse fell, throwing him far forward. He alighted with a scintillating, blinding shock, and all went black.

Movement, pain, vague senses preceded a voice that

cleared Paul's consciousness. It was Louise's cry, close to him, yet seemingly muffled. He felt her take hold of him. His feet knocked against something hard. The din in his ears lessened. A door slammed. Then he was lying upon a bed.

"Now, Louie, don't look like thet. He ain't daid," came in Kintell's panting voice.

"Oh, that bloody gash!" came her poignant cry. "He's the color of death!"

"Feel—for his heart."

A little hand slipped inside Paul's shirt. It shook upon his bare breast—over his heart—and clutched there a second, and then pressed quiveringly.

"It beats. . . . He's alive!"

"I reckoned so. He had a hell of a spill—behind me. But I don't think he's even bad hurt. I packed him behind a rock till the wust of the storm blowed by. Had my finger in thet cut. It ain't deep. Feared his neck or back was broke. But they're okay. . . . Wipe the blood off him while I fetch some whisky."

Kintell went out, and then Paul was about to open his eyes to assure Louise he was conscious and not in great pain. But she leaned upon him, breathing with a love and tenderness that Paul had never known. "Darling—darling . . . ! If you were dead . . ." she cried, kissing his cheek, his mouth, and pressing her face convulsively upon his breast. Then she arose. Paul heard the sound of water splashing into his basin. Next moment she was gently washing his face. Swift, heavy footfalls sounded in the corridor. The door burst open.

"Has he come to?" boomed Belmont.

"Not yet," replied Louise.

"Let me see." Belmont put a rude finger above the wound in Paul's temple. It made Paul wince and decided

him to recover promptly. "Bad place, but not a deep cut.
. . . Kintell, is this all?"

"I reckon so. Jest knocked him oot. . . . Hold up his
haid, so I can pour some likker into him."

Paul opened his eyes. "Nix for me, Wess," he said weakly.
"I don't need it."

"Wal, doggone . . . ! I'm shore glad you come around,
boss."

"Are you all right?" asked Louise, bending over him.
"Can you lift your head, so I can put this pillow under it?"

"Manning, I'm damn glad," sang out Belmont, in hearty
relief. "Kintell thought you might be bad hurt."

"Nothing, I guess, but a knock on the noggin," replied
Paul, sitting up dizzily. "Louise, please hand me my little
mirror."

"Boss, it's high up, an' won't hurt yore handsome mug
much."

"Wess, I'm not so scared of that as of having my gray
matter scrambled. . . . Well, I was lucky, as usual. . . .
Louise, please bandage it for me. You'll find everything,
there in that leather case."

Belmont made for the door. "I left a customer. You're
not hurt, Manning. You'll get used to being piled up."

"Is it a sandstorm?"

"What? This little dust-blow?"

"Oh, Lord!" ejaculated Paul helplessly.

"Belmont, it was nasty to be oot in," declared Kintell
stoutly.

"Marvelous to look at, too, before it reached us," added
Paul. "But, kidding aside, isn't this the real thing?"

"Yes, of course, in the way of a dust storm," admitted
the trader with a laugh. "But when the wind comes on to
blow and pick up the sand—then you want to duck for
cover."

"Believe me, I'll duck," declared Paul, as Belmont went out.

Louise did not show a dexterity that matched her gentleness in the dressing of Paul's wound; nevertheless it proceeded to his satisfaction. Louise's touch was a caress. She lingered over the operation until the cowboy drawled: "Louie, what you gonna do if I fetch him home someday all shot up, or with a laig busted?"

"Oh, dear!" wailed Louise. "Don't ever . . . ! But I never was so—so squeamish and clumsy before."

"Shore, I savvy. Fer a woman it all depends on who the man is she's workin' over. Now, I'll bet, if Paul had packed *me* in gored by a bull, or somethin' like, why you'd never batted—"

"Get out, you cowboy devil!" she cried frantically.

"Aw, Louie, I didn't mean nothin'," he drawled. "I was only kiddin'. But I'll beat it oot, anyway."

"Paul, isn't he dreadful?" she asked, almost in tears.

"Wess is pretty trying at times," admitted Paul.

"There, I think that will stay," she said presently. "Lie back and rest. Does your head hurt?"

"I'll say," replied Paul, as he let her make him comfortable. "Louise, my conscience hurts, too."

"Your conscience? Really, I didn't know you had such an inconvenient thing. What have you done now?"

"I wasn't unconscious when Wess packed me in here and laid me on the bed."

"No? You certainly looked it."

"Well, I wasn't. When Wess went after the whisky I was about to open my eyes . . . only I didn't."

"Oh! You—you devil. Were you making believe you were dead—just to see—?"

"Louie, I couldn't because of you."

"Mercy! What did I do?"

"Don't you remember?"

"I haven't the slightest idea," she replied, but though her eyes met his frankly a slow blush crimsoned her face.

"Then I shall not tell you."

"Paul, I was quite beside myself. But whatever it was—I am not ashamed."

6.

PAUL AWAKENED late in the night. His head throbbed with a dull pain and he could not go to sleep again. Then the wind with its burden was not conducive to slumber.

It seemed that above and away from the post sounded a steady, low roar, scarcely discernible. Round Paul's corner of the post, however, and the cabin and court, the wind blew intermittently, and with a quality of force and sound new to him. A gust would come swooping hollowly down to carry sand and pebbles rustling and pattering against the walls. It would lull a while, to return softly with a whine, and a swish as of silk lashing the windowpane, and then a low seeping sound. There was menace in it, and the whisper of the desert, hard and inevitable.

Then the clatter of horses' hoofs and wagon wheels distracted Paul from his melancholy absorption. It came from the direction of the river and ceased somewhere outside. Paul heard faint footfalls, apparently from the front of the post, and once a distinct jar, as if a heavy object had been deposited somewhere. After a while he caught the sound of the wagon going back in the direction from which it had come. It was then that Paul thought there was something unusual going on. Travelers seldom or never passed through late at night. Someone perhaps from the canyon and the Utah line had called on Belmont at two o'clock in the morning. Somehow, the occurrence intrigued Paul and added another angle to the complexity of Bitter Seeps.

It lingered in his mind and was uppermost when he went in to breakfast next morning.

"How are you?" asked Louise, after greeting him, and Belmont, in his bluff way, made the same inquiry.

"Not much worse for the wear and tear of range riding," replied Paul.

"Better lay off today," advised the trader, in a tone that was an order rather than a suggestion.

"Why so?" queried Paul curiously.

"Dust blowing. You couldn't see much."

"My idee, too, boss," chimed in Kintell.

"Okay. I feel punk at that. I'll spend a day catching up with my work."

"I like what I've read very much," interposed Louise shyly.

Presently Paul voiced the question in his mind, and though he put it casually he looked straight at Belmont.

"Who was your visitor last night?"

"What?" queried the trader, with an almost imperceptible start.

Paul repeated his inquiry and added: "I heard a wagon come and go."

"Didn't hear it. Somebody going through, likely," replied Belmont briefly.

Thereafter Paul addressed himself to his plate during the remainder of the meal. He had caught the trader in a lie. It did not make any particular difference to Paul, yet somehow it stuck in his memory. Later when he went to his room with Wess, he asked him if he had heard the wagon.

"I shore did. An' thet ain't the first time," rejoined the cowboy with a snort. "Believe me, boss, this heah is a queer joint. You see my tent is only the toss of a stone from the road. Next time I get waked up in the wee small hours I'm gonna sneak oot in my socks an' have a look."

"Do by all means. What do you think he's up to?"

"I dunno—but mebbe it's no business of ours at thet," returned Kintell ponderingly. "But this *hombre* has got my goat, boss. For instance, I know he's sellin' whisky to the Indians."

"I thought that was only illegal on the reservation," returned Paul.

"Naw, it's against the law anywhere. I jest seen a couple of Indians yesterday goin' off with paper sacks that looked powerful like they had bottles in them."

"Can't we do anything about it?" queried Paul.

"Not unless we can prove he was doin' it—an' besides, what would thet do to Louise? So I guess we cain't get oot of stayin' on heah, an' the way I look at it, as much fer Louie's sake as fer our cattle. Do you figger thet way, boss?"

"Yes. We're here to stay," rejoined Paul strongly.

"An' believe me, we're in deep. I jest love thet girl, Paul, an' not in the way I'm used to fallin' fer dames. I been tryin' to pump her aboot Belmont's doin's. But she's mum. An' she's scared at what she has already said. She's fond of me, pard, but Lord, not in the way she is of you. She has asked me a thousand questions aboot you. An' I've told her all I know. . . . Wal, she's changed. Thet turrible look has gone from her eyes. Gone!"

"It has, thank the Lord," agreed Paul fervently.

"Excuse me, boss, fer bein' serious. Do you know Louie is in love with you?"

"I'm afraid so," replied Paul reluctantly.

"If it was jest an ordinary case, you know, it needn't jar us. But Louie has got it bad, pard. Turrible bad! Shore the first love she has had an' too big fer her ever to hev another. What air you gonna do aboot it?"

"God only knows!"

"Thet was how I figgered. All the same I can feel somethin' workin' heah, somethin' comin' to a haid."

"Wess, can you explain that?"

"No, doggone it, I cain't. But every time I take a drink of this alkali water or look into Bitter Seeps I have a queer hunch thet thet's what is wrong. Anywhere, a man is what he eats an' drinks. . . . Did you know that Belmont never drinks thet water?"

"I did not."

"Wal, it's a cinch he doesn't. Belmont drinks pop, ginger ale, and hard likker. . . . Thet's only another of the funny things aboot this gazabo. . . ."

"Hey, cowboys," called Louise, from outside. "Belmont wants to see you in the store."

"Okay, we're on our way," replied Paul.

"I'll tidy up your room," she added.

They found the trader in his office, a little cubbyhole back of the counter.

"Manning, I've got a chance to pick up two hundred-odd cattle. Mixed herd. Twenty dollars a head. Is it worth ten dollars a head to you to throw in with me in the deal? Otherwise, it'll be sort of confusing and make a lot of work for you. I'd run this bunch into the basin with ours. And you'd have a lot of branding to do. What say?"

"Very attractive proposition at that low price. What do you think, Wess?"

"How come you can get them so cheap?" queried the cowboy.

"My friend across the Colorado needs money bad and

quick. If he drives north to the railroad, it'll cost him most as much in time and loss."

"Ah-huh. Looks okay to me."

"Is it a deal, Manning?" asked the trader.

"Yes."

"Fine. You're a most satisfactory partner. I'll start an Indian rider over today to clinch the buy. No hurry about payments. I won't need money until I go to Wagontongue."

"How aboot a count, Belmont?" asked the cowboy. "Heah or there?"

"Both. I'll ask for his. And you can make your count here. The cattle will have to come to Bitter Seeps for water. It's a long drive from the river, an' only a couple of water holes."

"Where will they cross?"

"I don't know. Probably at the Fathers' Crossin'. Why?"

"Wouldn't the lower crossin' at Lee's Ferry be better?"

"Easier, to be sure. But several days out of the way," replied the trader brusquely. Evidently now that the deal had been consummated, he wanted to terminate the interview.

"Wal, I don't savvy," returned Kintell coolly. "Shore, I haven't rode thet canyon country. But I got the lay of it from our government farmer. You cain't drop cattle down over thet Paria Plateau. They'd have to come by House Rock Valley anyhow. An' what'd be the idee of drivin' 'em up to the Crossin' of the Fathers when you could swim 'em across a good many miles this side?"

"Kintell, there's no one on this side who knows the canyon trails. But at that I'm not positive which way they'd cross. Besides there's no telling how the river will be at this time of the year. It's no skin off us, so long as we get the stock in good shape."

"Shore not. Reckon, though, if you don't mind, I'll go along with yore Injun rider an' help on the drive."

"That wouldn't do at all," declared Belmont impatiently.

"I see. How come this feller's so friendly with you thet he'll sell at half the market price?"

"Kintell, you're most damned inquisitive, not to say more," declared Belmont, his face reddening.

"Shore. I'm Manning's foreman, an' if he's makin' deals, it's my duty to be thet."

"Certainly, in reason. But your hint is offensive to me. . . . My advice to you is to stick to range riding, if you want to keep your job."

"Aw, I see. Thanks, Belmont," replied the cowboy dryly, with a queer little crisp ring in his voice. "I'm shore I meant no offense."

Paul thoughtfully followed the cowboy out of the store, down the long corridor. Louise was dusting Paul's room. Kintell passed on out, and Paul joined him.

"What do you know aboot thet?" queried the cowboy, and his tawny-gray eyes appeared to shine with piercing sparks which oscillated like a compass needle.

"Belmont buffaloes me, whatever you mean by buffalo," returned Paul dubiously. "He makes me feel like a sore thumb."

"Boss, I'd kicked on thet deal if it hadn't been fer jest one thing. It never would do fer us to let Belmont throw a bunch of his own stock in among what you an' he own together. I've seen thet tried. An' it's confusin' even if both pardners air honest. An' I ain't so damn shore this trader is honest, even in a plain cattle deal. Air you?"

"Belmont doesn't inspire me with confidence. But I had an inkling that if I didn't accept his proposition, it'd be worse for me somehow."

"Two hundred-odd haid. More'n two thousand bucks fer you to cough up! Don't like it, Paul. An' I'll be jiggered if I'll let him skin us. I'm gonna get mean an' sneaky, believe me."

The dust blew sometimes, in red, yellow and gray sheets, most uncomfortable to face. A haze hung over the plateau. Down the wide valley between it and the mesa clear areas varied with swirling clouds of dust. The wind appeared lessening in volume.

Paul left Wess and went back to his room which, thanks to Louise, was the most comfortable place in the post. He had not obtained a peep into her cabin, but he would have wagered that it was cozy and tidy and clean, despite the dust and sand.

He sat down to his writing. This was the first day since he began range riding that he had stayed at home. It did not take long for him to observe that this fact reacted singularly upon Louise. He did not count how many times she slipped in, but she came continually, and finally he said with a disarming smile: "Louise, can't you think of some more excuses to come in?"

"Oh! You heard me? I—I hope I didn't disturb you," she replied confusedly.

"Would you like to sit on the arm of my chair and watch me write?"

"You are fooling."

"Or on my lap. That would be inspiring."

"I think you're horrid," she flashed, reddening. "But I would. So there!" She flounced out, and Paul, to his regret, was not disturbed again that day.

On the following day Paul and Wess braved the still-blowing dust. For some reason their several Indian riders, engaged and instructed by Belmont, had not showed up lately. Kintell put that down against the trader. Paul thought the red men were just lazy and averse to coming out of their hogans into the dust-laden wind.

"Nice day at thet, down in there," said Wess, as they halted on the rim.

"Wess, suppose we hang together from now on," suggested Paul, ponderingly. "That spill of mine wouldn't have been so fortunate if I'd been alone."

"Pard, sometimes you show some little sign of human intelligence. I was fer tellin' you pronto thet we didn't ride separate no more. We don't know what the hell we're gonna run into heah."

Paul led the cowboy to the elevation that he had named Solitude. It brought forth pleased exclamations from Wess.

"Swell place to loaf an' watch," he concluded. They rested, ate their lunch, talked and studied this more rugged and complex half of the valley. Wess expressed surprise more than once to find it so unexpectedly different, and a better range for cattle, but harder going for riders.

"Strikes me now I think of it," observed Paul, "that there were twice as many cattle in sight on my last trip here than there are now."

"Hell you say," exclaimed Wess.

"Grazing back nearer Bitter Seeps, I suppose. But where are they?"

"Search me! I reckon we seen close to five hundred haid between heah an' home."

"Yes. And half that many in sight from this point on. Where are the other two or three hundred?"

"Haw! Haw! Haw!" laughed the cowboy idiotically.

"What ails you, you darn fool, that you give me the laugh at a sensible question?"

"Nothin'. I'm perfeckly wal. Jest had a funny idee."

"All right. But whenever you can make *me* laugh, too, get busy, will you?" rejoined Paul testily.

Paul had acquired a habit of studying distant points with his naked eye, and then applying the field glasses to them to train his eyes. In this way he sighted a column of smoke arising from one side of the rocky notch which led down into the canyon. He studied it for some time before handing the glasses over to Wess.

"Smoke. Way down at the end, where the canyon opens. What do you make of it?"

"Wal, I'll be doggoned! So 'tis. . . . Aboot fifteen mile, I reckon. Now, ain't thet jest the most interestin' sight we've seen around heah?"

"Why? Logically, it is an Indian camp fire."

"Shore—logically. But tell me, will you, if there's been a single logical fact aboot this whole deal? Reckon thet's an Indian fire. But mebbe it ain't. I've been among redskins a lot. Ordinarily they don't build a big fire. They don't waste wood like white men. Thet's no location fer a signal fire. Doggone me, I'm jest as curious as an old woman."

"You interest me, cowboy. Let's ride around to see what it is."

"Cain't be did. Not from heah. Besides it's too far. . . . Boss, I'm shore thinkin'. What excuse could we give fer layin' oot all night?"

"Tonight?"

"No. We haven't any grub or blankets—nothin' to drink. But some other night, when we'd planned fer it."

"Excuse? Do we need one? Let's just come, that's all."

"I'll bet you my gun thet if you spring it on Belmont tonight he'll be strong agin' it."

"You'll bet Belmont would oppose our camping out?" queried Paul incredulously.

"I'm backin' thet idee."

"But it seems so absurd."

"Wal, mebbe. I get queer idees. Suppose fer sake of argument thet tonight, at supper, you make some spiel to Louise aboot how you'd get a big kick oot of a one night's camp."

"I'll do it, Wess," declared Paul, and suddenly became thoughtful.

That afternoon the wind dropped, and when the riders topped the plateau there was no dust to face. The sunset, however, showed the effect of dust-laden air, for the whole west from horizon to zenith was one dark purple veil, centered by a dull red orb. They were to find that Belmont had ridden off to the north and had not returned. His absence was doubly manifest in the covert vigilance of Sister and the marked gaiety of Louise.

At breakfast next morning, however, Paul had his opportunity to test out the trader's attitude toward their staying away overnight from Bitter Seeps. Directing his remark to Louise, he said: "I've found the grandest place way down in the basin. It's a kind of low hill rising from the floor. Trees, rocks, grass and sage on it—it's really a beautiful spot. But it's so far that we can only stay an hour or two before it's time to start back. I think I'd like to pack some grub and blankets, and camp out there one night."

"That would be fun. You'd like it," replied Louise. But immediately she grasped that such an adventure would keep Paul away from the post, and her smile vanished.

Wess kicked Paul under the table.

"What's that about camping out?" queried Belmont, with more than his usual gruffness.

Paul told him, less fluently, for he saw that the trader had heard every word.

"No. That's silly," he replied. "Another tenderfoot stunt."

"Belmont, how air we gonna ride thet far range withoot

stayin' away one night anyhow?" asked Kintell, as if seeking information.

"The Indians will work that end. By the way, you can lay off today. I'm expecting the new cattle before sundown. Kintell will want to make his count before they drift over the hill."

In Paul's room, later, the cowboy expressed himself: "I told you, pard. Thet *hombre* has some reason fer not lettin' us lay oot overnight. An' I'll gamble it has to do with the smoke we seen."

Paul had no time to reply before Louise came in wide-eyed and pale.

"Wess, I heard you," she interrupted in a low, tense voice.

"Ah-huh. You would . . . ! Wal, never mind, Louie. It's nothin' to fuss you."

"Wess, by 'thet *hombre*' you meant Belmont, didn't you?"

"I reckon so."

"And you implied some very strong, underhand motive for his opposing your camping out, didn't you?"

"Louie, I'm not shore aboot his reason, but what he said come right oot from the shoulder. He wouldn't stand fer our goin'."

"Louise, it looked queer to me," interposed Paul.

"Oh, I know. You boys misunderstand me. I came in to say that I think it was mean of him, if not worse. And if I were you, I'd go anyhow."

"Preciselee what we will do," rejoined Kintell. "Louie, you're shore a square-shootin' kid. But you wanta be careful not to let Belmont know you'd go agin' him like thet."

"I don't care any more what he finds out."

"Louie, you're nervy as wal as square. . . . How long air you goin' to stay heah?"

"Until someone takes me away!" she replied with a sudden burst of passion, and turned to go.

Paul leaped up, feeling his face blanch. But the girl had left the room. Kintell cursed under his breath.

With a gesture expressing futility, Paul sank down in his chair again.

"I've been shore of thet fer some time," Kintell said. "An' I think she'd leave him pronto if she had any place to go, an' if it weren't fer the kid. I shore respect her fer it—an' wal, if *you* don't take her away, I will."

"For me to run off with another man's wife . . . ! My God! It's unthinkable."

"Wife—aw, hell! But there it stands. Circumstances alter cases, pard, an' when this case is all in—wal, it'll be altered all right!"

Paul found writing extremely hard that day. Louise's frank admission haunted him, and Wess's declaration had further upset his equilibrium. It put the situation in a more desperate light. He should have realized that Louise could not endure this degrading position at Bitter Seeps forever. She would be driven to take steps that could result only in tragedy for her. Belmont would not divorce her and he was the kind of man who would be brutal and violent. And there was the baby, who was as much a part of this tragedy as was Louise. At length Paul found work impossible. And when he gave it up for the time being he found that a brooding, inexplicable mood had settled upon his mind.

As his store of firewood was nearly exhausted, Paul went out to the pile of cedar he had hauled in, and set to work with the bucksaw. It was the most backbreaking labor he had ever undertaken, and he worked himself into a rage.

Louise found him there.

"Paul Manning, what *are* you doing?" she cried.

"I'm sawing wood—and saying nothing."

"I mean, are you trying to kill yourself?"

"Not that I know—or care," muttered Paul, resting upon the bucksaw.

"Didn't you hear the dinner bell?"

"No. But I don't want any dinner."

"Oh, Paul! What is the matter with you lately?"

"I don't know. I guess that knock on the head made me loco."

"Nonsense. You weren't hurt. But you are cross. Strange . . . Are you angry with me?"

"I certainly am," replied Paul, trying to glare at her, but without much success. Even if Louise had not been so lovely to look at, her undisguised concern about him and longing for his favor would have defeated any show of severity.

"But, why? What have I done now?"

"You told Wess and me you would stay at Bitter Seeps until someone took you away."

"If I *could* go with anyone—it would be you." Her voice was low and suddenly filled with bitterness, and another haunting emotion that Paul, for the moment, could not fathom.

"You don't look like it's killing you here," he replied, trying to hide a leaping agitation. "You are gaining . . . Really, Louie, you are beautiful."

"Paul, I know you are kidding me," she said somberly.

Paul shook his head, "It's true, and it doesn't help matters any. I wish you were—ugly," he replied ungallantly.

"How sweet of you, Paul!" she said musingly. "But why?"

"Belmont wouldn't want you then."

She reddened to the roots of her lovely hair. "He doesn't want me so much . . . as he did." Her low voice broke a little.

Louise's mood abruptly brightened.

"Do you want to know what I'd love above all else?" she asked with a golden flash in her eyes.

"I'm afraid to hear you say it."

"You must. I saw a picture in one of your magazines of a lovely gown! I'd love to wear it—and have you take me to a dance."

"There! I told you you were a child . . . ! Louie, can you dance?"

"I could. I haven't danced since I went to school. Oh! so long ago. But I could . . . I'd have feet like wings!"

"Do you realize that you are deliberately, shamelessly making love to me?"

"I am doing nothing of the kind," she retorted hotly.

"Very well, if you don't know it—keep right on. But I won't answer for the consequences."

"You! Why, Paul Manning, you avoid me like the plague. . . . Oh, look! There come the new cattle. Paul, I don't feel happy about this new deal of yours with Belmont."

"Neither do I—or Wess either," replied Paul ruefully, as he gazed at the long string of cattle approaching the post. "But I haven't paid him yet."

"You will have, by this time tomorrow," said Louise. "I heard him tell Sister he'd get your check and ride into Wagontongue with it."

"Wagontongue? That'll give Wess and me a chance to stay away for a night. Look! There's Wess climbing the corral fence. I'll join him and take a look at my latest folly."

Before Paul reached the cowboy a line of cattle two and three abreast impeded his progress, and he could not cross to the corral. Perched upon a boulder he attempted to make the count of the cattle himself. But when they crowded thick he missed some and gave counting up as a bad job. Owing to a slowing up of the animals in the lead it required the best part of an hour for them to pass on down to the pool. Three horsemen followed along in the rear, the last of whom, a swarthy, thick-set man, grimy with dust, halted at the cowboy's call. At this juncture Paul strode across the lane to join them. Evidently they had exchanged the greetings of one cowman to another.

"Calkins, this is my pard, Montana Slim," announced Wess, laconically indicating Paul as he came up. "We been knockin' aboot heah fer a week."

"Hod do," returned the other, casting sweeping hard eyes on Paul. "Where's Belmont?"

"I reckon he's oot in front."

"Is Belmont's pardner hyar now?"

"Yep, he's heah. . . . How fur you drive today, Calkins? Stock looks gaunted up a bit."

"Been comin' steady since yestiddy," rejoined the cowman.

"Gee whiz!" ejaculated the loquacious Wess. "How'd you cross the river?"

"Swum her," answered Calkins briefly, and rode on.

"Lose many haid?" called Kintell after him.

"No, we didn't lose none," replied the other without turning.

Paul gazed up inquiringly at Kintell, to be struck forcibly by that individual's fierce expression. And in another moment the cowboy burst into an explosion of profanity that outclassed anything of the kind Paul had ever heard. It ended from sheer lack of breath on Wess's part. Then the red left his face and he became silent.

"Was that for my edification?" asked Paul.

"Shore, if you mean education," replied Wess, and after lighting a cigarette he looked down with his fiery eyes now steady. "Climb up heah, boss."

"How many cattle in the bunch, Wess?"

"Two sixty-nine haid, by my count. I'm pretty accurate, boss. . . . Two thousand six hundred an' ninety pesos, simoleons, bucks, dollars, otherwise good old American coin."

"That's what I owe Belmont?" asked Paul.

"Accordin' to yore deal on the face of it, yes. . . . Pard, did thet bunch of cattle strike you funny?"

"Why, no. I didn't see anything to laugh at."

"Did they strike you queer?"

"No."

"Wal, then, did they strike you familiar?"

"I guess so. Looked like our own herd. But all cattle would look alike to me."

"I should smile they did look like our own herd. . . . Listen, bozo, an' get this into yore handsome haid. The bunch of cattle I jest counted come from our own herd."

"What!" ejaculated Paul, thunderstruck.

"They've been rustled from our herd," continued Kintell tensely. "Stole, an' drove around heah by that scurvy-lookin' ootfit of Belmont's. An' you're bound to a deal to buy yore own stock."

"Cowboy, are you drunk or crazy?" queried Paul gravely.

"I'm clear-haided, boss. You can gamble on me, now I've got over my mad . . . Listen. I had a hunch aboot this deal. I didn't fall for Belmont's easy, off-hand proposition. An' after you showed me thet blue smoke oot in the basin, I shore begun to figger hard. An' when Belmont put the kibosh on our campin' oot, then I figgered harder. All right. The cattle come in as you seen. I made my count. An' as I was doin' it I reckoned I'd seen some of them steers. The brands meant nothin', 'cause we supposed Belmont was buyin' from the same cattleman whose brand was on some of the stock we had. However, I never made shore until I seen thet big bald-faced red steer with a left club horn. I recognized him. I *knew* him. An' then, believe me, I coppered the deal. Thet's why I pretended to be what you thought loco when I was talkin' to Calkins. I wanted to make him lie, an' he shore did. . . . Swum the river, my eye! Boss, them cattle haven't wet a flank for months, if they ever did. The amazin' wonder to me is thet Belmont an' his ootfit should be so brazen aboot it. Half a cowman could figger them. I reckon he hasn't sized me up as the real thing. He thinks you a tenderfoot sucker, an' fer the rest, he doesn't give a damn."

Paul had never been strong on profanity, but at the end of a considerable tirade, he judged by Wess's response that he had not done so badly.

"Fine! Oot of sight! Atta boy!" ejaculated the cowboy, rubbing his hands fiendishly. "Of all the low-down, skunky, crooked deals I ever heahed of this is shore the wust! I'm so mad I'm seein' red. Fer two bits I'd waltz back there an' shoot the belly off Belmont an' thet lyin' Calkins."

"Easy, cowboy. It's a good thing you have an old head like me with you now," replied Paul with a cold, little laugh. "We're skinned. And if I ever was as mad before, I don't remember it. . . . The thing is what to do now."

"Doggone! I'll be jiggered if I know."

"We've always got to think of Louise. I won't leave her here alone with this black-hearted devil."

"Take her away!" flashed Kintell.

At the cowboy's words, the sudden bitterness, and what had seemed almost terror that had leaped into Louise's eyes when he had brought up this very same subject, swept over Paul.

"No, Wess . . . that would only disgrace her, if it did not lead to worse," he rejoined strongly. "Besides, in spite of what she said, I'm sure she wouldn't really leave so quickly, just because of a statement made on the spur of the moment. . . . After all, there's still the baby—Belmont's child. I have a feeling there's something more to this situation here—something she still hasn't told us. And remember, pard, I came out here to solve my *own* problems."

"Haw! Haw! You're doin' it, I don't think," the cowboy replied scornfully.

"Wess, if you don't think deeper than that I'll be disappointed in you. What is a crooked cattle deal to me? What is this job to us? This Bitter Seeps, though, this flinty poisonous place, means a tremendous lot to me. I'd never have lasted this long but for Louise. Something about that girl gives me strength. I start to slide to the depths. Then I remember her and I pull out. . . . Wess, it's hard to explain. But I have what you call a hunch. All I went through last winter—that miserable time—and what led up to it, and my finding Bitter Seeps, my desperate resolve to change myself through its powerful influence, and then this big-eyed girl, there's no sense in denying it at this moment—all of it, Wess, the whole strange mess, seems to me to have been intended. It was made for me. And I'm going to see it through the right way or die trying."

"Paul, I'm sorry I went off half cocked," replied Kintell contritely, and his lean face paled perceptibly. "But if you're gonna get deep I'll go you one deeper. You don't reckon much on the way you pulled me oot. But I do. I know I'd be in jail now if you hadn't come along. Jail is no place fer a bird like me. Onct more would have done fer me. Wal, thet's thet. . . . I'm glad you spoke oot so serious. I respect you now more'n I ever did. Jest why you wanted to toil an' suffer in this windy hellhole sort of flabbergasted me. But I see now. An' I admire you fer it. I think you're pretty much of a man. . . . This girl Louie complicates it turrible. She's sweet to me. She makes a brother of me. An' she worships you, even though she's takin' her life in her hands doin' it. Jest thet, an' nothin' else. An' thet's shore all right with me, seein' how you're goin' to love her. It couldn't be helped. . . . An' last, heah's my cyards face up. I'm not only goin' to see you through this awful desert drill, an' Louie through her ordeal, but some way or another, I'm shore we're all goin' to get oot of it."

7.

A STERN and brooding hour alone out on the desert definitely and finally committed Paul Manning to the course of action he had in his excitement outlined to Kintell. And the cowboy's Homeric declaration of his unalterable resolve to stand by him and Louise had confirmed him in the course he planned to take.

Added to Paul's contempt for the trader, there had developed a cold hatred, no doubt engendered by his feeling for Louise. But now a hot rage possessed him at the cheap crookedness of the man. Paul had cautioned Kintell to play the part of a loquacious, dull-witted cowboy with a propensity for conceited jokes and tricks, but meanwhile to be a cunning and bold spy looking into every detail of Belmont's questionable business and domestic life.

"Wal, boss, we shore can get the goods on this *hombre*," Kintell had said, "but I doubt if we could prove it in court. So make up yore mind we're in fer a loss."

Paul did not voice his sentiments on that score. His problem was to work out some plan to release Louise from her bondage. Paul had arrived at a point where he meant to free the girl at any cost. His feeling for Louise was so deep that he had not even tried to analyze it, yet he still seemed to deny to his questioning conscience that he loved her. But why? The thought of her—and she was always in his mind—was to restore her happiness and to set her free, but what lay further he somehow felt unwilling to face just yet. Why he still held himself back he could not understand—and it was one of the strange things that somehow seemed a part of the inscrutably somber atmosphere that pervaded Bitter Seeps.

The day was warm, bright, beautiful. The desert sparkled on all sides. Far north the red spires rose. Black Mesa stood boldly in the foreground, the sand and clay dunes to the south blazed like a colored mosaic. But Paul got no joy or peace out of them.

Upon his return, Louise hailed him from her cabin door. She wore an enveloping coat and was in the act of tying a scarf over her head. Her face was grave.

"Hello! Hope you're not going to Wagontongue," said Paul blankly.

"No. Belmont is going to drop me off up at the government school. Tommy is not at all well again. He hardly will eat and though he seems cheerful . . . I'm so worried about him."

"I'm very sorry. I hope it . . . is there a doctor at Walibu?"

"Yes. If he is only at home!"

"Can I do anything? How will you get back?"

"On one of the Indian wagons—I guess. . . . Paul, I called you to tell you this will be a good chance to take your camping trip."

"We'll grab it. How long will Belmont be gone?"

"He never says. But something is up. You watch. I've a hunch he'll go back from Walibu and then across the river into Utah before returning to Wagontongue."

"Thanks, Louie. That means several days, at least. . . . But you'll be back in a day or two, surely?"

"Unless Tommy grows worse or the sand blows. It's bad sometimes up Walibu way."

"Well, good-by and good luck."

"Oh, Paul!" Her voice broke poignantly. She started to say more, but instead turned back into the cabin. Paul strode into the corridor toward the store. There were a dozen Indians present, and more out on the porch, among whom Kintell stood out conspicuously. Belmont was in close conference with Calkins and another man, evidently one of his riders. And the omnipresent Sister stood behind the counter, somewhat less taciturn and aloof than usual.

"Here's Manning now," boomed Belmont, as Paul came up. "Pardner, shake hands with my Utah friend, Dave Calkins."

The Utah cattleman evinced a surprise he made no effort to conceal. "Hod do, Mr. Manning. Glad to know you." Then he turned to Belmont. "What was your cowboy up to, stringin' me out there?"

"How so?" asked Belmont with interest.

Paul allowed the cattleman to explain the incident of his meeting with Kintell, and it was easy to see that the trader did not take it without offense and curiosity verging on anger.

"Queer stunt for that cowboy. Manning, I'm afraid you'll have to fire him."

"Oh, Wess is just a damn fool," replied Paul with an easy laugh. "You don't savvy him, Belmont. He never means anything. He's a kind of a smart aleck of the range. Always joshing and trying to fool people. I get out of patience with him sometimes. Don't pay any attention to him."

Belmont looked appeased, but the Utah cattleman struck Paul as being a less impressionable character.

"Wal, damn fool or no, he had the count correct to a steer. Two hundred sixty-nine. An' they was pilin' by pretty thick."

"Manning, will you accommodate me with a check for your share?" asked Belmont.

"Not all of it," replied Paul, who was prepared for this demand. "How will half the amount do, and balance when I get remittances from Kansas City?"

"I need it all," rejoined Belmont bluntly.

"Sorry, I'm afraid I can't manage it. May I remind you that I did not propose the deal? As a matter of fact, I was not even keen about it."

"You seemed eager enough. . . . Has Kintell or anybody been talking to you?"

"Certainly not. I'm willing enough to go through with the deal. But give me a little time, will you? Cash payments are not the rule in cattle deals out here."

"They are with me."

"Very well. Take it or leave it. I don't care one way or another," replied Paul coolly, and went out to stand just outside the door. He distinctly heard Belmont curse and Calkins say: "Take what you can get. I tell you this cowboy Kintell is no fool. He made one out of me."

At that moment Sister intervened to say something which Paul could not hear. In another moment the trader came out.

"All right, Manning, I'll agree to your proposition," he said suavely. "I was put out, as I have some big bills to meet. Would you mind letting me have the check now?"

"Not at all," rejoined Paul.

"Good! You can give me a note for the balance. Louise is taking the baby to Walibu and we're in a hurry."

Paul lost no time acceding to the trader's demand. Then Belmont concluded: "You and Kintell better saddle up right away. Drive this bunch of cattle off the plateau before they spread all over. And watch them close. They might drift back toward the river."

Kintell's opinion of this dubious suggestion was withheld until he and Paul mounted the plateau slope to see the scattered herd grazing toward the basin. "Hell! They know the way as wal as we do."

"Wess, let's get off among the stones here and play mumblety-peg till it's safe for us to go down and get our grub and blankets."

"Okay, but what'n'll is mumblety-peg?"

"I'll show you."

Paul selected a shady spot under the lee of a rock, one that permitted a view of Bitter Seeps and the three roads leading to and out of it. However, Paul forgot all about the game in his attention to the winding white road wandering up over the red desert toward Walibu. He did not have long to wait. Belmont's wagon, with the horses in a fast trot, clattered away from the post and could be heard up the ridge.

"He's shore bawlin' the jack," muttered the cowboy. "Wonder what's his big hurry. Certainly cain't be his love fer thet kid—pore little duffer—he looks all eyes and skin."

"Louie told me she had a hunch Belmont'd come back and drive over Mexican Hatway into Utah before going to Wagontongue."

"Ah-huh, the —— of a pot-bellied thief," muttered Wess. "Wal, teach me your mumblety-peg an' after I get the hang of it I'll go you two bits a game."

Paul proceeded to illustrate, and when he offered the

knife to Wess for a little practice, the cowboy waved it aside. "Aw, I don't need any practice fer that kind of a deal." And it developed that he did not, for he gave Paul a beating which absolutely proclaimed him a master at the game.

"Son-of-a-gun, you! Old hand at it, eh? I'd hate to play poker with you," protested Paul.

"Aw, I'd hate to take yore money, pard. All games except love air easy fer me."

They played and watched for several hours until at last Kintell's sharp eyes spied a crawling line of dust on the Walibu road. Belmont returned faster than he had gone. He did not tarry long at the post, and presently several horsemen rode off from the porch to the north. Paul put the glass he was carrying on them.

"Belmont and three men," Paul said laconically, handing the glass to Wess. The cowboy made no comment, but there was a wicked look in his eye.

"Pard, you hang up heah while I ride down after a couple of blankets an' some grub."

"Hadn't I better help you?"

"Nope. I can manage. I've got the canteens filled in my tent. An' I'll grab my two blankets. All thet's fussin' me is to slip one over on Belmont's beady-eyed Sister."

He rode rapidly down the slope and disappeared into the court at the back of the post. Paul settled down for a wait. The prospect of an adventure and of getting conclusive proof of Belmont's guilt gave zest to the project. And Paul needed it. A dark mood had crept like a lichen over his mind. He lay back against the stone and found a dreamy pleasure as well as a melancholy sorrow in thinking of Louise. A clattering of hoofs on rock brought Paul upright, and he was amazed to see Kintell returning so quickly.

"Okay. Thet kid is a peach," he said, dismounting. "I found yore knapsack an' a bag on yore bed, all packed full of grub."

"Louie!"

"I'll say. . . . rustle yore hawse while I untie these blankets. You can pack them an' one canteen."

With brisk action at hand, Paul cast off his morbid abstraction and trotted back to fetch his mustang. In another few moments they were headed across the plateau. Driving the cattle delayed them somewhat, but before midafternoon they were down in the basin, and sunset caught them far along the north slope, at a point about even with Solitude. The place where Kintell elected to camp was a sheltered grassy plot in the mouth of a side canyon.

"Pile off, you," he said. "Unpack an' hobble yore hawse. . . . Cottontail rabbit won't go so pore fer supper, huh? Wal, you start a fire while I go kill a couple."

Paul attended to his tasks with a slow methodical enjoyment. It was dry, lonely, silent, wild there under the yellow rock ruin; the sun had gone down red and gold in the west; the rugged valley had a ruddy cast; the smoke from his campfire smelled like burning leaves in autumn.

He heard a shot, and after a while another. When twilight began to steal up from the basin Kintell returned carrying two rabbits.

"Only two shots?" queried Paul, smiling.

"How many do you s'pose I'd need?" was the cowboy's drawling retort.

"I never saw you shoot, Wess."

"Neither did them cattle thieves. . . . I jest cain't get them off my chest. . . . Wal, we'll have broiled rabbit in a jiffy, an' if thet ain't good I don't know nothin'. Spread oot the packs an' see what Louie stole fer us."

Paul opened his knapsack and the first thing he spied

was a white envelope. With a start he snatched it up to see his name in a small, neat handwriting. It was unfamiliar, but of course could be no one's else but Louise's.

"Well!" he ejaculated.

"What's thet?"

"Must be a note from Louie."

"Love letter! Jest like a woman to pick oot a time when you couldn't grab her."

"Wess, you sure are a dishonorable cuss," replied Paul, musingly.

"Dishonorable nothin'," snorted the cowboy, always testy on that point. "Louie is as good as gold. An' you air sort of a halfway decent guy, if a slowpoke about wimmen. Swell chance of you an' Louie hookin' up right now, I don't think. Not till she's free, anyhow, an' I hope we can make thet soon."

"Make it? Wess, how *can* we ever do that?"

"I don't know yet. But there's ways. Elopement, divorce, sudden death, an' all them things operate fer lovers."

"Sudden death for Louie or me wouldn't be a solution. Not a very happy one!"

"Nope, not atall. We gotta pray for sudden death to come to Belmont. . . . Paul, thet *hombre* doesn't *love* Louie. He spends most of his spare time with Sister. I'm beginnin' to suspect Louise won't let him spend it with her. I'll have the dope on him pronto soon as these nights get warm. My idee is you could buy Louie from him."

"*Buy* her?" exclaimed Paul, shocked.

"Hell, yes. Thet's an idee, believe me. They still do it up in these parts, you know."

"It certainly is," replied Paul soberly, as he put Louise's letter, unopened, in his pocket.

"Heah, help me skin the cat with these cottontails."

Darkness had settled down by the time Wess had the

rabbits broiled. He had spitted each upon a sharp stick and held it over the hot coals, turning it round and round.

"I reckon thet's done brown," said he, handing one to Paul. "Salt an' pepper plenty now, pard. An' with a biscuit mebbe it won't go good!"

"Smells delicious. . . . Wess, there are a dozen biscuits, with cold meat, cake and pie in my knapsack. I didn't open the bag."

"Pie! Apple pie? Aw, thet kid! Go slow on the biscuits an' meat, pard. But we'll clean up the soft stuff. . . . Now, pard, ain't this grand? Somethin' different oot on the trail. I'd of been daid or in a madhouse, or mebbe I should say prison long ago but fer this heah sort of life. . . . We could almost ferget Louie's trouble an' our thievin' pardner, an' thet Bitter Seeps hole."

After a hearty and most delectable supper, Paul threw some brush and wood upon the fire, and bending to the blaze he eagerly opened Louise's letter:

DEAR PAUL:

You were out when I had a chance to tell you and now I see you climbing the slope, in that way of yours when you are troubled.

Tommy is ill. I am taking him to the doctor at the Indian school. He has never been strong or well, as you know. He just seems to fade. It tears my heart out. Bitter Seeps is no place for a child—any child for that matter.

I wanted to tell you that it is probably Belmont's cronies who stole your cattle for him to get more money out of you. Don't pay him a dollar. Whatever deal you have made, don't keep it. There is some deviltry afoot, some plot to cheat you. Belmont is going to Utah thinking I do not know.

He would kill me if he knew that I told you. But I can't hide it any longer. I love you, Paul. I will not see you cheated further. You will never regain what you put into that cattle deal. I wish I had the courage to persuade you to leave me here—you will never be happy with this situation as it is. But I haven't. Your voice, your step, to see you—that is all I have to keep me up. If it weren't for you, darling, and Tommy, nothing could keep me from drowning myself in Bitter Seeps—that cold spring which has called me ever since the day I saw it first.

You have suffered, Paul. It was in your eyes when you came here. And this terrible place has worn upon you as upon me. But don't be unhappy because I can't help loving you. Long years ago when I read stories and dreamed dreams, there was someone like you. And it is nothing to worry you. I ask nothing. Yet if somehow we could be free of Belmont, I'd be your slave—forever.

                                        LOUISE

Paul reread the note, and then dropped his head in a passion of fury and sorrow.

"Wal, what ails you?" queried Wess roughly. "Reckon I was wrong aboot Louie's letter."

"Read it," replied Paul.

The cowboy knelt on one knee and spread the paper to the dying blaze. When Paul looked up again, it was to see Wess looming dark and silent above him. Silence seemed a fitting thing for both of them. Presently Kintell strode away into the blackness, and the lonely night surrounded Paul. The fire burned down to a bed of ruddy coals, in the heart of which he saw two great topaz eyes, so sad, so eloquent, so yearning that he had to hide them under more fuel. Then the fire crackled again and sprang up to brighten the lonely circle. At length Paul spread his saddle blankets on the grass, and composed himself to rest if not to sleep. When slumber did at last overtake him, Kintell had not yet returned.

Sunrise found Paul riding behind the cowboy far along the northern slope, gradually working up out of the rough and broken basin. Cattle were scattered all over the gray-green bowl, but not so thickly as Paul remembered upon the occasion of his first sight of this end of the valley. Kintell worked up to the rim, where on the comparative level they rode at a brisk trot.

The magnitude of the scene quite precluded Paul's thinking of the object of their thirty-mile jaunt. They were approaching the environs of the great canyon. In front of them and all across the deep basin there was a wild and rough terrain which narrowed to a gap beyond which was the desert. The gateway was of weathered rock that led down between walls of yellow and red and black. Across the basin to the left an irregular break in the desert led back beyond the Painted Desert and marked the canyon rim; and to the right the rolling plain swept away to the base of the huge, gray-walled, black-fringed, snow-patched mountain that was the north wall of the great canyon. Paul guessed that the Colorado spread its wide and yawning gulf beyond that rolling plain. There was an immensity and sweep to the desert, a manifestation of age in its eternal gray, which was accentuated only by the rims and crags. As he turned his eyes to the south, Kishlipi appeared a weird purple shadow against the black lava cones which glittered in the sun and contrasted with cones of clay in shades of violet, mauve, heliotrope, blue. Beyond lay variegated patches of sand, colorful as a quilt, and still farther beyond the infinitude of the desert hazed in the full tide of the sun.

Kintell's objective was the last level of the basin, under the red gate, where Paul previously had seen the column of smoke. To the surprise of both men they rode into a broad, freshly trodden cattle track.

The cowboy whooped. "Heah we air, boss, plain as the nose on yore face." And halting his horse he traced the track with his eyes over the rim and down to the plain. The sight made Paul burn with rage. Belmont's perfidy stood as bare as the cattle trail beneath his gaze.

"So far so good," Wess was saying. "We don't need to go down. We'll jest foller these tracks an' see where they go."

All afternoon that track led straight northeast, gradually working down into the vast depression of the plain, until only the tip of Black Mesa could be seen. The trailers came upon the ashes of a fire, where the drivers had made camp, and here Kintell decided they had best hole up for the night. Grass and sagebrush grew profusely in this swale, in contrast to the barrenness of the higher parts of the plain.

Paul Manning had his taste of a cold, windy, desert night, lying out unprotected, and ringed about by wailing coyotes. Next morning Wess had to walk miles to catch the drifting mustangs.

"Looks like bad weather," he announced. "An' if the wind blows oot heah we'll be in a tough spot."

"Bet you two to one the cattle track will soon head for Bitter Seeps."

"Ump-umm!" returned the cowboy.

The sun did not come up as it normally did. Thin wisps of cloud, mare's tails as Kintell called them, showed against the pale cast of the sky.

In less than two hours the cattle track swerved abruptly, making a right-angled turn toward the middle of Black Mesa. The drivers responsible for the herd had left the bridge and the ford behind them.

"I knowed it, but jest had to make shore," declared Kintell. "They're haidin' to go off the plain, down to the road, north of Bitter Seeps."

"Then we might as well make tracks for the post," replied Paul, thinking of Louise.

"Wal, it ain't much farther stickin' to the cattle trail. Two days' ride either way. An' more shelter under the mesa, in case we get ketched oot."

The wind began to blow from the south, steadily increasing in intensity. Kintell stuck to a brisk trot. He kept looking to the southward, and at the slowly changing sky. Paul added half again the number of miles he judged the distance to be to Black Mesa. Perhaps ten miles ahead, the level plain roughened with an outcropping of rock, ledges and ruined walls, until it became a plateau with isolated low buttes and straggling crags that resembled lost cattle from a herd. All the while the riders were climbing gradually. Sheets of dust blew softly along the ground; whirling yellow columns rose high above bare spots on the plateau. All the landmarks to the south were lost in dark obscurity.

"Wess, if we can't get back to the post tonight, it's okay with me," said Paul to the worried cowboy. "I'm getting a kick out of this ride."

"Say, pard, if we lost our way on this plateau an' a sandstorm should pile down over us, you might get yore last kick. An' thet's no kiddin'."

"We can't lose our direction so long as we can see. Bitter Seeps is over there, under the low end of the mesa."

"Shore. But s'pose we cain't see no more?"

"Wouldn't these mustangs take us in?"

"Thet's somethin' we don't know. Most hawses will find the way home. But these Indian nags might go some other way. . . . Say, it's thickenin' up down there. Doggone our luck!"

An hour later thrilling excitement had become a grim ordeal. Out of the vague, opaque obscurity in the south suddenly stood out a wall like red stone. The gray haze had been dust. But this was sand. One had mobility and thinness, if not transparency; the red wall appeared stationary and solid. It spread from west to east and looked like the desert standing on end. It was moving, of course, but the movement could not be perceived.

"Let's beat it fer the rocks," yelled Wess, and spurred his horse into a gallop. Paul caught up with him. Then the cowboy increased his gait to a run. Soon it became a race. The mustangs were fleet and they scented danger. Paul had not recovered from his fear of another spill as the ground slid under him and the dusty wind stung his face. That five miles was an anxious run, but it brought the riders to the rocks.

"Look fer a shelvin' rock to hole up under," shouted Wess. They rode here and there on the lee side in search of shelter. Kintell turned away from one place after another that Paul thought might do. There had come a singeing from the wind.

"Gosh! We gotta hole up pronto an' there ain't any holes," complained Kintell, gazing anxiously at the red wall, now well up on the plateau. Half of Black Mesa had been swallowed up. "Heah's some stones thet slant a little. Tie yore hawse good. An' when the sand hits us put yore scarf over yore face an' yore coat over yore haid."

Paul's rock stood far higher than his head, but though it would break the force of the wind it afforded little protection overhead. A heavy stone provided means to halter his horse. This done, Paul took off his coat and stepped out to watch the oncoming storm.

It appeared totally unlike the dust storm. Neither beauty nor magnificence marked its sweeping approach. It was terrifying. It seemed to swallow up the earth, rather than to pass over it. Only when Paul attempted to gauge its speed by marking rocks and sagebrush in the foreground could he get any perception of its terrific velocity.

As the storm bore down upon him its aspect grew awful. Seen at close range the wall of sand was streaked red and yellow and black and lifted great columns aloft. The roar accompanying it transcended any sound Paul had ever heard. Dust and gravel pelted into his face. Quickly he sought his shelter, covered his face and sat down to wait.

An engulfing roar, a sweeping tremendous commotion of air, and a dreadful blackness settled down upon him. Paul waited curiously, fearfully for something to happen. Nothing transpired right away except a seeping of sand down over the rock. It soon made the coat sag down with slowly increasing weight. Paul felt the sand run in little streams from the coat, down upon his legs and around his back. He felt the space between his back and the stone fill with sand. The time came when he had to slant the coat, and shake it to relieve himself of a burden tiresome to uphold. He found the pockets had to be emptied. Finally when he had exhausted the air under his scarf he was forced to lift it.

What little light remained filtered through a yellow medium. Above and all around the fiends of the air were unleashed and shrieking. In a twinkling Paul's eyes and lungs took in flying sand. Making haste to pull the scarf down he was hard put to it to wipe the sand out of his eyes. At length the tears flowed copiously, washing it away. Meanwhile he had coughed and sneezed, and otherwise labored with the weighted air. His breast heaved. He could not inhale sufficient oxygen.

Realization came to Paul then, and cold sweat poured out of his pores. The danger of becoming smothered seemed great at the moment. Though he nearly strangled breathing through the silk scarf, he managed to get enough air to live on. The dry musty odor of earth clogged his nostrils until he could no longer smell. He became aware of stinging eyes and smarting lips from the particles of alkali with which the air was impregnated.

All these sensations were augmented by the shrieking wind until Paul felt them insupportable. In what seemed a very short while the sand piled so high about him that he would soon have been buried alive. He kept scraping it away with his hands.

This state wore on until Paul suffered horribly. Several times he was on the verge of collapse. But he fought with all his will and instinct to hold on to his consciousness. When he seemed utterly spent there came a slackening in the storm.

He could not tell whether night had fallen or whether the opaque blackness came from the flying sand. The roar had rolled away to leave an intermittent moan. He threw off the coat and scarf. It was all he could do to get to his feet, so cramped were his muscles. Against the weird gloom, the rock and his horse stood out black.

"Hey, Paul, where air you?" came Kintell's call from the shadow.

Paul answered, and presently the cowboy staggered up to him.

"Hell, wasn't it, pard? I darn near sloped to kingdom come once, believe me. . . . Must be night."

"My God! It was awful, Wess," replied Paul huskily. "What'll we do now?"

"Hang right heah. If we'd got ketched oot in the open it'd been curtains fer little Paul an' Wess."

"Will it come back on us?"

"Shore. But not so turrible till sunrise. I've fetched over some water an' grub. Wash yore eyes oot, pard, an' take a drink. Then eat a bit. I'll untie the blankets. Mebbe you can sleep some. I'll watch the hawses."

"I'll take my turn," said Paul.

To relieve his eyes of the acrid irritation helped Paul not a little. There was no relief, however, for the oppression and burning of his lungs. Then he ate and drank. Meanwhile the storm continued to abate, except for intervals of whooping gusts, at which time Paul had to cover his head again and gaspingly stick it through. Kintell built a little fire of sagebrush and greasewood. How spectral the shrouded rocks looked in the red flare! There was nothing real. The fine particles of sand sifted down like a red mist; now and then a gale shrieked by with a demoniac mocking of the helpless human beings caught in its embrace. Paul slept and took his turn on guard, and slept again, while the hideous night wore on.

Dawn was the strangest thing that Paul Manning could have imagined in his most morbid moments.

There was no gray, no sky, no horizon. Yet a light came diffused as through saffron and strongest in the east. With this, which seemed to Paul to be sunrise on some other world, the wind arose. Kintell insisted that they eat the remainder of their food before it became impregnated with sand, and be chary of their water. He still had the largest canteen full and there was a pint remaining in one of the others. The cowboy asserted they would not need food, but drink was imperative. He stretched the blankets tight from a corner of Paul's rock to the ground, and anchored them with stones. Within this improvised tent they retreated, and sealed it as hermetically as possible.

It served to protect them until the furious gale, sweeping round the rock, half solid with its leaden weight, flung the blankets aside. Then they were forced to cower under their coats and breathe through their scarfs. Black and yellow intervals, which were differing degrees of storm, attended them that day, whether of hours' or moments' duration, Paul could not tell. It seemed that strangulation clutched him by the throat many times: that the infernal seeping of sand would build a grave for him. But always in his extremity there came a lull, and he would recover. He fought sleep as if it were a beast. To give up and cease to gasp for breath would have been ecstasy. Hunched under his black hood he roused at last to Kintell's voice.

"She's lettin' up. I seen the sun flare like a prairie fire. An' there's a break in the clouds. But we cain't trust it'll clear shore in the mawnin'. We gotta get off this plateau tonight."

Paul threw his coverings off. All about him appeared an opaque dusk. The moan of wind was like a knell. Staggering up he eased his cramped muscles.

"Hawses a-rarin' to go—an' we got to get them to water, or use up our own," shouted Wess. "I cinched up yore saddle. One of them blankets blowed away. . . . Come on, pard. Stick close to me. Once off the plateau we cain't get lost."

"How do you know which is the right direction?" queried Paul, getting into his coat.

"Face straight from the rocks. We cain't miss thet long draw between Black Mesa an' the plateau. An' if it blows hard tomorrow we can find better protection under the Mesa."

When Paul rode behind Kintell from the lee of the rock, he faced a stiff wind laden with grains of sand that cut like tiny blades. The horses needed no urging. They had to be held to a trot. Paul bent his head so that the brim of his wide sombrero shielded his eyes. He could see the dull gray earth, the pale rocks, and the black object that was Wess's horse. Kintell yelled back for Paul to keep the wind square against his right cheek.

They rode on, trusting to the horses. It would have been impossible for a man to see a hole or the brink of a precipice. Rocks, however, gleamed gray out of the gloom in time to be avoided. If anything, the wind lessened, and at length Paul was sure of this because it ceased to carry sand. Dust, however, was still hard to contend with. Some two hours passed by before the mustangs broke their gait.

"Goin' down," yelled Wess. "Feel yore way. We may be goin' to hell, but I hope we're gettin' off the plateau."

"Go slow. I have to walk," replied Paul, laboriously dismounting.

"Okay. I'm with you."

Leading their horses they slowly worked down a slope, gradual in some places, steeper in others. Its conformation of soft earth, with occasional loose shale, struck Paul as being identical with that of the slope above Bitter Seeps. Still they were surely thirty, possibly forty, miles north of the post. The gloom grew thicker. Every step appeared to be down into a void. But they kept on and on, gaining more confidence as nothing untoward happened.

"Pard, she's easin' oot," whooped the cowboy.

"What—is?" panted Paul.

"Why, the slope, you dumbhaid! Cain't you feel it?"

In a few more minutes the hoofs of Kintell's horse rang on hard ground.

"Ho! Ho! The road, by gosh! Paul, come on. It's the

road. We've struck straight off the plateau. Aw, I don't know! Pretty fair! Cheer up, pard. We're okay!"

Paul's spirit lifted so vitally that he forgot his pangs. Dread of getting lost in the sandstorm had dragged at hope and courage. They were on the road. Something like the effect of a horrible nightmare faded from Paul's mind. He mounted.

"Blowin' stiffer'n hell down heah," growled the cowboy. "I'm nigh on to stone blind."

Paul opened his lips to reply when a fierce gust of dust-laden wind filled his mouth. He spat angrily. What a devilish persistent thing, this desert wind!

"Shet yore eyes," called Wess. "It'd take a cyclone to put these hawses off the road."

It was noticeable to Paul that against a strong gust of wind his mustang would slow down to a walk; then when it passed by he would take to a trot again. He was tiring. Paul's exultation failed at length. The fiendish gusts swayed him in his saddle. At last when some huge rocks loomed up in the gloom Paul called faintly: "Wess, it's rest—or fall off."

"Yeah? Wal, I reckon you think I'm ridin' high, wide an' handsome. Gosh, how I been waitin' fer you to squawk."

They found a leaning rock with a roof like a porch. Paul stretched out on the hard ground with a sense that never before had he known the sweetness of inaction and rest. While Wess was voicing their good luck, Paul fell asleep.

When he was aroused he saw daylight for the first time in many hours. Morning had come again, not bright, but still far removed from that hellish continuous film of yellow and red sweeping by. He saw a slope of huge sections of cliff and patches of green cedars.

"How air you?" asked Wess, giving him another shake.

"Dead. How're you?" replied Paul weakly.

"Also daid. But we gotta come to life, pard."

"I'll be okay, soon as I limber up. . . . Oh-h . . . ! I couldn't begin to tell—all that's wrong with me."

"It ain't over, by a long shot," declared Kintell, haggard and drawn. His face was caked with dust, and sand ran out of his hair. "If you're able to ride, we'd better rustle."

Paul hobbled about until he was able to stand erect, then wiping his eyes with a wet scarf, he announced: "I'm the ridin' kid from Bitter Seeps."

But for once the cowboy was neither loquacious nor prone to humor. They set out on jaded horses. Northward the road appeared unclouded for miles, except for circling dust devils. What might have been blue sky showed above the far end of the mesa; in the other direction, however, a tattered shroud of dust obscured the road. Black Mesa itself was hidden in gray.

A steady current of air appeared to be sucked northward through this deep pass between mesa and plateau. At frequent intervals a down-sweeping blast of wind came on with a yellow pall of sand. It swooped over the riders and went on with a howl. Then a gray sheet of dust raced along the road, headed with tumbleweeds and scattering gravel. It rustled by. Billowing, rolling, clouds came driving up the pass, to twist and whirl, to puff aloft and go on. Between these onslaughts the riders caught their breath and prepared for the next. The hours and the miles dragged on.

It sustained Paul to realize that he could make the grade. His will fixed on that. Those weeks of range riding had developed him to this endurance. He hated the fierceness of this wind; he hated the leagues of road, the dust, the sand, the pebbles, the grim slope of Black Mesa; yet he felt a birth in him of something that was not hate. He recognized the force and matter of nature pitted against the spirit and strength of man. Somehow he divined that man had evolved from these forces and would be victor in the end. Inanimate things, driven physical things could not kill spirit.

As the hours dragged by interminably the blasts of gale came less frequently, which permitted the air to clear. Conditions therefore favored the riders. But it turned out at length that when the gusts did come it was with great violence, and carrying streams and sheets and clouds of sand. But they were endurable because they passed swiftly.

"Pard," sang out Wess after a long silence, "I got a glimpse of the post. We're most there."

Then it was that Paul's glad eyes recognized the environs of Bitter Seeps. The forbidding black rim of rock, the long austere slant of the plateau, the ghastly pass with its tortuous road, all appeared to merge in the end of the world. For from over the red ridge and the bold dark cliff hung a sinister cloud of somber hue, from which trailed long curling tails and streamers of sand, solid and mobile in the gray shroud of dust they carried along. They would lick at the post like tongues of fire, flatten the cedars, tear up the ground into furious whirlpools, and swirl down the pass, enveloping the riders with hollow roar and yellow pall, to sweep onward.

When Paul limped into the protected court of the trading post, where the flying sand ceased its merciless onslaught, he understood the primitive cave man, the cliff dweller in his cell like a wasp's nest high on a wall, the Indian in his hogan. For since man came down out of the trees to stand erect he had to have a home. Black Mesa, for all its nameless repellent features, shut out the wind, the sand, the heat, the cold.

8.

Again a hard bright steely day succeeded the sandstorm. In sheltered sunny places, as outside the corridor wall on Paul's end of the post, where the bleak desert with its gleaming rocks and yellow dust devils could not be seen, it was possible to be comfortable. Paul could not stand erect, let alone mount a horse. Kintell did not ride out, and advised his comrade to rest for several days. Louise had not returned from Walibu, and Paul surmised the storm had delayed her.

Early morning of the fifth day, Wess's rude but reluctant word aroused Paul from deep slumber.

"Ow-w!" groaned Paul. "Now I know how easy murder is."

"Mebbe I don't," retorted Wess with a dark glance. "It's late.

"Belmont and Louise got back late last night. The kid was with her—an'— Oh, but that's not the worst thing."

"Yes?" queried Paul, suddenly occupied with a queer burning along his veins. "What's up?"

"I got up when I heahed a wagon an' wanted to make shore. Belmont drove in from the north, his hawse hitched on behind. An' at breakfast he said he'd come from Wagontongue. Talked a lot. All het up like he gets when there's somethin' in the wind fer him. I didn't let on what a —— liar I knowed him to be."

"He never went to Wagontongue at all," asserted Paul. "What was the sense of his lying about it? Maybe he changed his mind on account of the sandstorm."

"Pard, the only way we can figger thet *hombre* is to figger him crooked. Believe me, his interests are north of the river."

"I had that hunch long ago. And Louie strengthened it. . . . Wess, did he—"

Paul fell victim to swift deadly pangs that checked his query as effectually as if he had been choked.

"Did he what?" asked Wess.

Slowly Paul turned his shamed face away.

"Did Belmont what?" repeated the cowboy gruffly.

After a moment Paul replied: "Did he go to Louise's cabin?"

"No. He drove round in front. I heahed him in the store. Reckon he was alone then. I hung aboot under the trees. After a while I heahed voices. They come from Sister's room. You know thet opens off this hall, but on the other side, an' it ain't connected with this wing. Wal, Belmont went in there, an' he stayed."

Paul wheeled on the bed as if his bare flesh had been touched by a burning brand. "My God! Then Sister is his wife, too?"

"I had thet figgered all along. This still happens round here you know, law or no law. . . ."

"But doesn't it stand to reason that Louie must know?"

"Thet is the way it looks to me. But you cain't tell aboot her. We know she's concealin' a lot more'n thet. Belmont would do anythin'. He's no spring chicken. I'll bet he's fifty-five. An' Sister is huggin' forty, believe me. . . . Wal, the plot thickens. But somehow it strengthens our case."

"We must face Belmont with his guilt," declared Paul fiercely.

"Yeah? But we still got to prove it. . . . Cheese it, heah comes Louie."

The girl entered carrying a tray. She was smiling, but

Paul could see the dark circles of weariness about her eyes as a result of the strain of the past few days. "Good morning," she said brightly. "I've fetched breakfast for my rider," and she laid the tray upon Paul's knees. "Fruit, cereal, toast, a lamb chop, and cocoa. How's that for Bitter Seeps? I got the grapefruit up at the school."

"Louise, how is Tommy?" inquired Paul.

"He's much better," she replied, relief evident in her dark eyes. "I was terribly worried that first day, during that long ride to Walibu, but the doctor was there. He said that there was nothing seriously wrong with Tommy, but that I would have to change his diet—give him more solid foods. So I bought some from the government store, and the doctor gave me some medicine for him. . . . I'm really very much relieved."

"I'm very glad. . . . I was worried about him."

She gave Paul a searching look. "I appreciate that. . . . And yet it seems a little strange—you worrying about John Belmont's son."

"Louise, I don't really associate Tommy with Belmont—and somehow I don't think you do either."

"Maybe I should—more. . . ." Her voice was grave. "But Belmont seems to care so little for him—and they're so little alike. . . . I guess, I just try not to think about it, that's all."

"Louise, do you know anything about Belmont and Sister?" Paul said rather abruptly.

"Oh, have you found out that he—" she asked shamefacedly.

"Wess claims that Belmont went to Sister's room last night and stayed there. But Wess might be wrong. He heard them talking, but that doesn't prove anything."

"Prove what?" she asked blankly.

"That Sister may be married to him as well as to you."

"What—do you mean?" she asked, suddenly startled, her big eyes dilating.

"I mean that it's not uncommon in these parts for a man to have more than one wife—even though it's illegal, and the church is against it."

Suddenly, the haunting look of fear was back in her eyes. Paul divined that she knew much more than she would admit.

"I don't know anything about that," she said hurriedly. "But if you want to know *what* she is, I can tell you that. But . . ."

"I don't want you to get excited about it," rejoined Paul soothingly. "And there's no need either to worry about our conjectures."

"I wish I could tell you—everything. But I can't, until . . ."

"Until what?" queried Paul blankly.

Her cheeks bore red spots; her low voice suddenly rang.

"That's for *you* to figure out, Paul Manning." And before Paul could rally she left the room. Paul stared at his comrade.

"Wal, what air you waitin' fer?" ejaculated Wess.

"Waiting for . . . ? What do you mean?"

"You know what I mean, you dumb galoot. When air you gonna tell her you're in love with her?"

"How many times have I told you to mind your own business?" snapped Paul furiously.

"Pard, this *air* my business. An' if you don't do somethin' aboot it, *I* will."

"Wess, if you say a word to her, I'll—I'll shoot you, sure as my name is Paul Manning."

"Wal, it'll be mud, if you don't do somethin' soon," said Wess devilishly. Then suddenly the cowboy's mood sobered. "I got somethin' else to show you thet ain't so pleasant. Air you able to go oot?"

"Well, I'm stiff and tired, but I can get about okay. Is it about Louise?"

"Nope. I'll be back pronto."

Paul, pondering what new issue was involved, made short work of his breakfast. Kintell came back presently to take him out the back way, as they usually went when they were bound for the corrals. The cowboy was not communicative.

Black Mesa loomed bold and frowning under a hard bright sky. The black rocks high on the mesa glistened as after a rain. On all sides the aftermath of the storm showed in the drifts and bars and miniature dunes of sand left by the wind. Another time they would blow away and the contour of the landscape would again change.

Kintell led Paul behind the ridge to the protected space between it and the mesa, where the hogans of the Indians stood. Paul had walked and ridden past them often, but had never been in one. Kintell halted at the door of the second, a large mound of adobe mud plastered over a framework of poles. The door consisted of an upright rectangle of peeled cedar logs in which a blanket hung. Yellow, vicious dogs snapped and growled at the visitors. At Kintell's call a wrinkled Indian man emerged, and held open the blanket for them to enter. Paul followed the cowboy in.

The round space inside received light from a good-sized hole in the roof, which Paul's quick survey discovered to be a cleverly woven dome of cedar poles on the outside of which had been plastered the mud. A half-burned-out fire of cedar fagots had been built directly in the center of the circle under the hole, through which the blue smoke lifted. This smoke, or some quality of the air, made Paul's eyes smart. Two dusky-haired children clung to the skirts of a pleasant-faced squaw whom Paul recognized as Natasha's mother. She greeted him. A young brave, falcon-eyed, with dark clear skin like transparent bronze, rose from a box to speak to the cowboy. Paul then had his attention directed to the beds of sheepskins along the wall. And on the nearest, covered with a blanket, lay Natasha. Then Paul understood his misgivings and Kintell's somber silence. He hastened to kneel beside the Indian girl.

"Natasha! You are ill," he said solicitously, as he bent keen gaze upon her. There had been a shocking change in the girl. The rich, red-gold bloom had fled from her face. It was thin and pale. Her large, dark eyes did not shine with dusky coquetry this day.

"I'm better now," she replied weakly.

"Natasha, what was—the matter?" he asked haltingly.

"T.B.—my pard," Kintell snapped.

Natasha's plight struck Paul as more pitiable and hopeless than if she had been a white girl. She had been robbed of the heritage of the Indian; to have fostered in her the language, wants and habits of the white man, all to the bitter end of being victim of his disease.

"Natasha, can I do anything for you?" asked Paul.

"I don't know. Wess said you might want to." And she lifted somber eyes to the cowboy for confirmation of her words.

"Shore I did, Natasha. We'll see you through this."

"Natasha, you must have a doctor see you, and proper care, clean things, good food, pure milk. . . . Will you let me arrange for these?"

She nodded with a ghost of a grateful smile.

"Natasha, when you're well again you must get out of Bitter Seeps," went on Paul. "Where can you go? What can you do?"

"White man, this is the last time I shall speak your language," she replied. "There's nothing more for me but the hogans of my people. But I want to go far back in the canyons."

"You shall. I will help you. Have you anyone to go to?"

"Taddy here wants me to marry him. His people live far over under the big mountains. It is wild there. No roads! No traders! I think I'll go."

"Taddy?" queried Paul, and looked around to see the young Indian brave beside him. "Are you the boy?"

"Yes," he replied, in soft, guttural voice.

"Why do you want to marry Natasha?"

"We play—we go school—we grow up together."

"Have you any work?" went on Paul.

"No work. Bad year."

"Have you sheep, goats, horses?"

"Me poor. My people poor. But we take care Natasha."

"I will give you work riding for me until Natasha is well again."

Kintell slapped the Indian brave on the back. "There, Taddy. We'll make a cowboy oot of you."

"Natasha, do you like Taddy?" asked Paul, turning to the girl.

"We were sweethearts once."

"All right. Listen. While Taddy is working and you are getting well, Wess and I will buy you a flock of sheep and goats, some ponies, saddles, blankets, camp outfit, clothes, food, everything you need to start with. Then when you are strong again you can ride away to his people. To the lonely canyons you spoke of. . . . I'm very sorry about this, Natasha. I'd like to help you and Taddy. It will be good for me. . . . I'd like to think you were happy again, way out there in the sage—"

"I shall not forget you, Paul Manning," was her enigmatic reply. There were tears in her dusky eyes. Paul rose, seeing this as his reward, and he felt satisfied. Wess, still kneeling, put more questions to the Indian girl, but she did not answer. When Paul bade her good-by and still she did not speak again, he knew that she had used for the last time the alien language forced upon her.

"Wal, what's yore hurry?" asked the cowboy, joining Paul outside.

"I want to say something to Belmont while I'm hot."

"Okay. Let's rustle," drawled Wess, coolly.

Paul stamped into the trading post. Indians were present, as was the government farmer from the school and another white man. Belmont was trading with a squaw; Sister stood behind the counter like a watchdog, and at the moment Louise entered from the corridor.

"Belmont, I'm riled and I must get it off my chest," announced Paul, in a voice that stilled the talk.

"So?—and what about?" responded the trader, guardedly and slow, with speculative cold eyes on the intruder.

"I owe you thirteen hundred and forty-five dollars on our last deal."

"That is correct," returned Belmont, far from slow this time.

"I can't pay it now. I have about that in cash. But I want to use it to good purpose. And you'll have to wait."

"Manning, your good purposes may be all right, but they don't concern me. And this one is not good business for me. I'm registering a kick."

"Kick and be damned," retorted Paul. "I've obliged you, and I don't feel any compunction in making you wait."

The trader betrayed amazement and a growing resentment, but a restraint which proved him deep and resourceful.

"Natasha is ill. She's going away—to her people. I'm staking her and Taddy," said Paul.

"What? Thirteen hundred, forty-five dollars just for a red-skinned wench!" ejaculated Belmont, in strident, incredulous fury.

"That's the sum. And it's a damn little for what she's suffered. . . . You won't understand this, Belmont, because Indians are dirt under your feet. But it pleases me to prove to these Indians that all white men are not yellow skunks."

"You'll prove a hell of a lot, Manning. These same Indians will think *you* the skunk," rasped Belmont, his face livid and his corded jaw protruding.

9.

SPRING MERGED imperceptibly into summer. The sand blew no more. Heat veils lifted off the desert. And at noonday the sky took on a copper tint. Paul learned to know what it was to have the sun burn through his sombrero. He grew leaner and darker, yet daily stronger.

Bitter Seeps entered another of its desert phases. And parallel with it began an insidious change in Belmont and his fortunes.

After a torrid day the night was gratefully cool. Paul lay wide awake on his bed, listening as he had on other nights for Belmont's heavy tread. The tranquil days had been only too few. Human nature, like the desert, had returned to dark, covert moods.

A footstep outside brought Paul upright and quivering. It passed Louise's cabin, to enter the corridor. His door opened. Then Paul, in the moon-blanched room, recognized the tall form of the cowboy.

"I'm awake, Wess. What's doing?" he whispered.

"Slip on some clothes an' come oot pronto," was the low reply.

Kintell stayed by the door, listening. It took Paul scarcely more than a minute to join him. They went out together. A waning moon hung weirdly over the dark mesa. The night had worn on toward the small hours. Kintell drew Paul off the flagstone walk upon the soundless ground. Presently, as they got away from the post he whispered: "I been up for some time. Another of them mysterious wagons from across river. An' I was aboot to sneak around in front when I seen an Indian comin'. Thet wasn't onusual, but this fellar made fer my tent. It was Taddy."

"Taddy!" ejaculated Paul, astounded. "What does he want? I hope Natasha—"

"She's okay. They're in the Segi now. . . . But heah's Taddy. He'll speak fer himself."

The slim, dark Indian came out from under a cedar near Kintell's tent. He had a quirt in his hands.

"How do, boss," he said.

"Hello, Taddy. What brings you back?"

"I meet Indian—Shagonie—by Red Lake. He come across mesa. Indians tell Shagonie white men want help drive cattle. They say much pay. Indians no go. They know white men. Same who come with new herd sell Belmont. But no new herd. Them boss's cattle."

"Same white men!" burst out Paul indignantly.

"Yes, boss. Same Calkins," replied the impassive Indian.

"Wess, they're going to rob us again. Of all the nerve!"

"Wal, I'd say it was gall."

"We must be a couple of suckers. Does Belmont think he can get away with that again?"

"I reckon he's too slick. If Calkins is makin' another drive it'll be back across the river. . . . An' come to think aboot it, pard, only yestiddy I was wonderin' if our herd hadn't thinned oot some toward Solitude. You see we haven't rode oot there fer days. An' we jest cain't keep all thet stock under our eye at one time."

"You've got a hunch Calkins is already rounding up a bunch?"

"I didn't hev thet hunch, but I shore got it now."

"Taddy, when did you meet Shagonie?" queried Paul, turning to the Indian.

"By Red Lake yesterday."

"You didn't ride all the way here since yesterday?"

"Me ride all night."

"Pard, Taddy could make thet ride in six hours."

"Well . . . ! And when did Shagonie see Calkins?"

"Two days and yesterday. Three. They promise meet Calkins. But they no go. Tell Shagonie."

"Taddy, who and what are these cattle thieves?"

"Shagonie ask. Indians they know. White men from far over river."

"Wal, Taddy, you're shore sayin' a mouthful," interposed the cowboy. "Where's yore hawse?"

The Indian indicated a far point beyond the post on the south slope of the mesa.

"Pard, Taddy must not be seen heah by Belmont. We'll give him some grub an' set him rustlin'."

Wess went into his tent to emerge with canteen and bag. "Take the bag, Taddy. But drink an' leave the canteen."

"Good-by, Taddy. I sure appreciate this," said Paul, wringing the Indian's hand.

"We no forget," replied Taddy, and silently stole away in the wan shadows.

"We no forget!" repeated Paul musingly.

"Shore. You gotta hand it to these redskins. They have been cheated so by Belmont an' his kind thet it's hard fer them to believe white men decent. But you do one a kindness an' he'll not forget you."

"Wess, we are up against it good and hard," rejoined Paul. "And I can't understand why I'm not seeing red."

"Wal, fer one thing you're thinkin' of Louise, an' fer another it'd be no good. You're learnin' a heap, pard."

"But we can't let them get away with it."

"I should smile not. Go back to bed an' get some sleep. We'll take breakfast as usual, an' ask fer a lunch today. You tip Louie off thet we'll be oot late an' mebbe all night. . . . An' don't forget to pack yore gun."

Before sunset next day the riders had arrived at a rocky break on the north rim of the basin. They halted back out of sight in a shallow ravine where grass grew abundantly. While Paul rested after the grueling ride under a hot sun, Kintell took the glass and stole out among the rocks to reconnoiter. Paul had just about gotten cooled off and rested when the cowboy returned, his lean face stern and hard.

"Taddy gave us a swell hunch," he bit out. "Located big bunch of cattle first look. An' soon spotted the thievin' ootfit. Come on, pard."

He led the wondering Paul up among huge, brown boulders, and out to a break which commanded a view of that end of the basin. Paul crawled after Kintell to an advantageous position.

"Be careful how you stick yore snoozle up," advised the cowboy. "We ain't so damn fur away in a straight line. An' mawses have sharp eyes if these rustlers haven't. . . . Take a peep now. You see we ain't more'n a mile straight across to thet point where we found the cattle tracks come up oot of the canyon. But as we cain't fly we'll have to ride around the rim, an' fur back at thet."

"I see the cattle on that bench," replied Paul excitedly. "And I see smoke, too."

"Thet's from the camp. Now take a squint through the glass."

Paul had to search around to locate the smoke, and when he did he gave audible expression to his feelings. In a niche of the rimrock, at the back of the bench, he espied a camp fire, a man evidently busily cooking, packs and bedrolls scattered around, and two horsemen riding in.

"There they are, all right," he said, breathing hard. "Don't need the glass now I've located them. . . . Wess, what're we going to do?"

"Wal, we shore air goin' to bust up thet little rustlin' party," drawled the cowboy. "Gimme the glass again. I want to figger oot a way to sneak up on them."

"Tonight? The sun is setting. It'll be dark before we can get around there."

"Reckon we might wait 'til mawnin'." After a long, careful scrutiny of the camp and the lay of the land Wess added: "Pard, it's a lead-pipe cinch. We'll circle back of the rim an' get off at the haid of the break where they ride oot. Then we'll slip down. They'll be eatin'. It'll be dark an' we can slip right up on them."

"Tonight!"

"Shore. Right now. Let's rustle so we can have all the daylight thet's left."

"Okay. But tell me what to do."

"Foller me an' don't make any noise. Thet's all."

"You'll hold them up?"

"I'll say I will."

"And if there's a fight?"

"Small chance, pard. But I can tip you off to thet, if they're bad eggs. An' if I *do* tip you off, duck fer cover an' grab yore gun."

They returned to their horses and led them up the ravine. The sun had set when they reached the top. Mounting again they rode off over the plateau. Paul could see the break where the rim dropped off into the basin, and the ragged line of the canyon. All the western sky was dull red. Daylight lingered long. It was just succumbing to dusk when Kintell located the head of the draw.

"You see it's the right one," he whispered, dismounting. "There's the tracks of the herd we trailed. . . . Let's tie up in this scrub oak. Take off yore spurs. Tough on the ponies. No water. No grass."

Paul's state was one of suspense and watchfulness, but when he started down the draw behind the wary, slow-stepping cowboy his nerves began to string and his pulse to throb. Now and then Wess would stop to listen, and turn to see where Paul was. Once he whispered: "Step soft, you club-footed ham! This ain't no picnic."

After that most unflattering epithet Paul put one foot forward after the other as if he were fearful of stepping on dynamite. But he made no more noise. The draw deepened into a shallow canyon with splintered walls. Soon it grew so dark that he had to feel his way. The cowboy, however, appeared to have the eyes of an owl. The long slow approach augmented Paul's suspense. He had ample time to think, to prepare, but his sensations were paramount. The lonely black abyss below, the silence, the stealthy cowboy, the uncertainty of this adventure worked upon Paul's imagination. He did not want to kill a man, but he might be forced to in self-defense. He recalled that Calkins had worn a gun in his belt. If he attempted to pull it upon Kintell he would surely get shot. The draw deepened into a canyon. Then the left wall gave place to gloomy space. Wess kept close under the right wall, where, owing to rocks, the going was difficult.

All at once Paul's progress was blocked by the cowboy. "Heah's the bench we seen from above," he whispered. "An' if I figgered correct thet camp is close. But where's the fire?"

"We've been an hour in coming this far. Fire might have died down," whispered Paul in reply.

"Say, we haven't been a quarter gettin' heah. But I'm bound to admit the trail's gettin' hot."

They proceeded very cautiously indeed. Paul had never experienced such silence. The place seemed dead. It got on his nerves. Again the cowboy's iron hand stopped him. "There! I heah cows bawlin'. We was further away than I reckoned."

They rounded a sharp dark corner of rock to be startled by a bright camp fire some hundred rods or more distant. It threw a red flare upon the face of a red cliff above. Dark forms of men passed to and fro across the light.

"Doggone!" whispered Kintell, plainly baffled. "There they air. An' all open aboot heah! What the hell to do now?"

"We might go back and come out above them on that cliff," replied Paul.

"Don't like thet idee. I reckon I'll have to crawl. I see some rocks stickin' up. Some of them big enough to hide a fellar. If they was only in line . . . ! Wal, boss, you wait heah."

"I won't do anything of the kind."

"Huh?"

"I'm going with you . . . unless you think I'd impair your chances. Don't lie to me."

"Wal, pard, I'm shore glad to have you. It looks kind of skittish to me. An' I was only tryin' to look oot fer yore safety. . . . Come on. We *got* to move like mice now."

Stooping low, Kintell very slowly walked ahead until a good-sized boulder loomed up. Then he went down on hands and knees. Paul followed, feeling how strange it was for cold sweat to break out on his hot body. It seemed a long time before Paul looked up from Kintell's heels. The cowboy had halted behind the boulder. He peeped from behind it. Paul heard voices and a coarse laugh. Then Wess flattened himself on the ground and wormed his way to the right. Paul found imitation of a worm highly diverting despite its extreme discomfort. Again the cowboy turned, this time to line up behind another boulder, the first of several large ones near the camp. He had infinite patience. He crawled a few feet, then waited to rest or listen and look. Paul scarcely breathed.

The ground grew soft with thick turf, making this crawling performance very much easier. Nevertheless Paul did not breathe more easily. He feared his panting breaths might be audible. Probably Wess did hear them, for he halted until Paul's laboring breast eased. The voices became louder, almost distinguishable. Paul appeared aware of the shadowy cliff, of the star-lit dome on the left, of the lowing of cattle. Then Kintell crawled on, and this time did not halt until he reached his objective.

Paul peered out on his side of this big boulder. The camp fire lay between seventy-five and a hundred feet distant, and as luck would have it a larger rock rose almost in line with him. Manifestly Wess saw this, for he swerved from his side of the barrier to Paul's. After a careful survey of the foreground the cowboy put his lips to Paul's ear.

"Like takin' candy from a baby! . . . Now, when I

jump up an' yell you foller suit. Stay with me, but a little to one side, so if they shoot we'll be spread oot."

Without further words the cowboy entered the last lap of this tedious and nerve-racking approach. Paul kept his face almost even with Wess's heels. His mouth began to get dry and he swallowed with a constriction of his throat. The firelight flickered upon the seamed and cracked cliff. When Paul thought that he could not crawl another inch, Kintell stopped. They had reached the boulder. It was high and wide. Behind it Kintell stealthily rose, his dark gleaming face turned to Paul. His gun glinted as he drew it. Paul got up carefully and pulled out his own gun. They were so close to the fire that Paul smelled smoke and coffee and ham.

"Haw! Haw! Wot'n'll do we care if Belmont does find out?" rang out a loud voice.

Wess's left hand squeezed Paul's arm, an act which no doubt was prompted by the speaker.

"I told you I wasn't stuck on this job," replied another man, and he, Paul made certain, was not Calkins.

"Bloom has it straight," interposed a third, who undoubtedly was the leader of the trio. "If we can get this bunch across the river we are settin' pretty. We can sell and Belmont can't do a damn thing. He won't dare make a fuss."

"But thet new partner of his—what's the name, Manton . . . ?"

"No. It's Manning. He doesn't know he's alive. He's thinkin' too much about his health to bother any little deal of ours. Besides Sister says he's sweet on the girl."

"Haw! Haw! Then we might get Belmont to buy another bunch of his pardner's cattle."

"Sure, we might. But we don't want to. Belmont is gettin' stingy. His business is peterin' out. The Indians have no use for him."

"Aw, I'll bet Belmont is makin' money there."

"Yes. But not like at first. He won't last at Bitter Seeps. No trader ever lasted there."

"Then if this is the last smack we can take at him let's make it good. We could round up another fifty head tomorrow."

"No. We got more now than we can handle easy. And a long, hot, dry drive ahead of us. Once across the river we can take our time. . . . I sure didn't like that cowboy's eyes."

"Thet nut? Why, boss, he wasn't all there."

"Maybe he wasn't. But when Belmont told me he was from Texas I had a little jolt. Most Texas cowpunchers are *there* with bells on."

"Listen to my hoss," called one of the men, in a different tone of voice.

"Aw, he smells the ham."

"Bloom, better unsaddle and hobble them," added Calkins.

All this while Kintell had been peering from behind the boulder while Paul contented himself with listening to this most informative colloquy. But at this juncture Paul could not resist a careful glimpse. The heavy-set Calkins sat eating. Another of the group was in the act of throwing brush upon the fire. It blazed up brightly to show the whole circle distinctly. The third man had his back turned to his comrades and was looking at the two saddled horses.

Wess gave Paul a swift nudge. Then he leaped out with a stentorian yell: *"Hands up!"*

And as he ran forward his gun flamed red and banged. Paul held his own weapon ready and rushed into the firelit circle, where he lined up beside Kintell.

"Stick 'em higher, Calkins," Wess ordered harshly. "I won't miss you next time."

The dark-jowled leader lifted his hands as high as his head as he glared with controlled fury at his captor.

"Bloom, what'd I say about that Texan? Here he is," rasped Calkins sarcastically.

The man called Bloom, a tall rider with sharp features shaded under a sombrero, cursed loudly. The third fellow, round of face, turned a dirty yellow hue in the firelight.

"Caught with the goods, huh? You—cheap cow thieves!" rang out Kintell fiercely. "We heahed you talkin'. All about double-crossin' Belmont. Aw, no, he won't do a thing to you bums. Not atall!"

"You got the drop on us, Texas Jack," growled Calkins coolly. "What are you goin' to do?"

"Hawg-tie you an' drive you-all into Bitter Seeps."

"Is it worth anythin' to you to know Belmont—" Calkins began.

Then the crafty rustler made a lightning-swift dive for his gun. Wess shot a second before Calkins blazed away. Paul heard the sickening rend of bullets striking flesh. It terrified him to see Wess go down as if he had been hit by a club. Calkins swayed and sagged as he shot again, this time at Paul. A hot missile whistled past Paul's face. Then Calkins sank in a heap, almost falling in the fire.

The other two men rushed for the horses and leaped astride.

"Stop there!" yelled Paul, suddenly answering to anger.

But the rustlers plunged away, goading their horses. Paul emptied his gun at the swiftly moving riders. One let out a terrified scream. Then they vanished in the gloom. Frantically Paul wheeled to find Wess on his feet with smoking gun leveled. He had his left hand high upon his shoulder. Blood was flowing between his fingers.

"Wess, you're shot! My God—this is terrible!" gasped Paul.

"Shore I'm shot. An' I ought to got mad before," snorted the cowboy, striding over to Calkins.

Paul hastened after him, remembering despite his poignant excitement to reload his gun. Calkins was alive and conscious.

"Talk now, damn you, or I'll bore you again," called Kintell piercingly, and shoved his gun at the prostrate man.

"Don't shoot. . . . I'll talk," replied Calkins hoarsely.

"Belmont hired you to pull thet first drive of our cattle?"

"Yes."

"An' thet's straight aboot you double-crossin' him in this drive?"

"That's straight."

"Who is Belmont?"

"He's all kind of things."

"Hell! You said a mouthful. But you know what I mean?"

"Belmont's a Utah rancher an' trader. He fell out with some of his neighbors. An' he left Utah."

"Ah-huh. An' when was thet?"

"Before he came to Bitter Seeps."

"Is Sister his real wife?"

"I don't know."

"Then the girl is?"

"Reckon so. It's rumored over at Lund. But nobody knows which . . ."

"Where does Sister come in?" flashed Paul, as the man broke off.

"She's got some hold on him—but I don't know what it is. . . . Texas, I'll thank you for some whisky. I'm bad hurt. . . . There's a flask in that pack."

"Find it, Paul," said Kintell, as he picked up Calkins' gun. "Where'd I hit you?"

"Low down and center. I feel cold and numb. . . . Hurry."

Paul found the flask and helped the stricken man to drink. A bloody patch on Calkins' shirt augured ill for his chances.

"Pard, never mind aboot him. Come heah an' tie up this hole in my shoulder."

"Wess, is it very bad?" queried Paul, his hands trembling as they felt the warm, soapy blood. He pulled Wess's shirt wide open and down over his right shoulder.

"Hurts like hell. But I can't see fer blood . . . I can move my arm . . . Feel thet collarbone . . . Wal, I guess it's all right, too. If the bullet went clear through—"

"It sure did, Wess."

"Good. Then all I have to worry aboot is blood poisonin'. . . . There's some hot water, boss. Wash them holes clean an' then tie 'em up."

Calkins' groans aroused Paul's pity, but did not seem to reach the cowboy.

"Do you think he'll—die?" whispered Paul, as he worked over Wess's wounds.

"I reckon so—an' give us a hell of a lot more trouble," growled Kintell.

"We might square it with the authorities, but never with Belmont."

"We don't want to square it with him," protested Paul vehemently. "We're going to use it."

"All the same, boss, we'll not say a word aboot this fight onless thet fellar Bloom an' his pard come across first. An' thet's not likely."

"You mean they'll be afraid to incriminate themselves?"

"Exactly . . . ouch! Boss, you may be a swell writer, but

you're shore a bum doctor. Thet back hole is raw an' red hot."

"Sorry. I'm almost through. Then hadn't we better do somethin' for Calkins?"

"I'm afraid nothin' can be done fer thet *hombre*. But, Paul, I had to bore him. He drawed on me, an' if I hadn't spoiled his aim he'd have killed me shore."

When it came to an examination of the wounded rustler, Paul corroborated Wess's judgment. The bullet had entered just below the breastbone, and it had probably lodged in or against the spine. Calkins could not move. His talk grew incoherent and he lapsed into unconsciousness. Paul put a pack under his head and a blanket over him.

"Reckon you might as wal come an' eat. This beef stew is swell, an' there's no sense in yore starvin'," observed the cowboy.

Paul replenished the fire and made an effort to eat, but his appetite was lacking.

"Boss, I'm feelin' pretty rocky an' better lay down," said Wess presently. "Thet ride in the mawnin' will be aboot all I want."

"Wess, say you're not seriously wounded," implored Paul.

"Wal, I reckon not. But I bled like a stuck pig. An' I gotta be careful. You're elected to stand night guard."

Soon afterward Paul realized the incredible fact that he was in a lonely place with a wounded cowboy, who slept and snored, and a dying rustler. Paul felt that sleep was far indeed from him. He paced to and fro, he added a little wood to the fire occasionally, he took a reluctant look at Calkins, and hovered over Wess like a mother over her infant, and listened to the night sounds.

It was this abnormally sensitive faculty of Paul's that finally brought him up sharply at a real or imagined cry.

Whatever he heard, it pierced him to the soul. As he stood there shaking he gradually convinced himself that no wild bird or beast had uttered it, that no sound in nature could have affected him so acutely. And all at once, the first time for long hours, he thought of Louise. Had her spirit cried out to his? He had read of such strange things happening to lovers. Was Louise lying awake with that divining power of woman to see through walls and darkness? Would it not be more likely to be true that she had wailed out in anguish because Belmont had rendered her situation insupportable? In the darkness and solitude Paul fell prey to this, and all his fortitude, his hope, his reliance upon love and idealism were as if they had never been. Bitter Seeps held all its victims in a stark naked realism.

Paul recognized something crucial in the hour. And unable to define it he endeavored to grasp the physical and spiritual details of his enforced vigil. The blaze of the fire shone on Kintell's lean dark face, stern in the set rigidity of pain, on the ghastly visage of Calkins, so suggestive of the stamp of death that Paul feared to approach him. A ruddy, threatening shadow danced upon the cliff. The unguarded cattle, giving vent to frequent bawls, appeared to be working back down into the basin. Coyotes held melancholy festival out on the rocky benches, wailing and yelping with their keen, sharp, high, wild notes. From the grass and the thickets, from all around, arose the low, dreaming, incessant chorus of insects. And Paul projected himself into this scene, alone there with grave responsibility forced upon him, a party to the killing of a thief, at last cast upon his own resources of strength and endurance.

But this survey of visible things got Paul nowhere. It was thought, feeling, passion, with their attendant mysticism and limitless range, from which he could not escape. In this solitary environment the profound realities of life on the desert of Bitter Seeps fell with crushing force upon Paul's dreams, hope, love, faith, upon all he believed in. From that midnight hour he realized there would be a terrible strife between things as they were and things which he dreamed of. It would be a battle between the inborn romancer and the driving realist. He must never attempt to write any more about human nature until that battle was won. If he lost it to the materialism of the age, to the nemesis of hard fact upon his trail, to the failure of love and honor in himself and a brutal infidelity forced upon Louise, in his vain effort to prove how friendship could save a rolling stone like Wess Kintell, then indeed he would never write again and must abandon a career which had seemed so bright in prospect.

What a young impressionable fool he had been in all his association with that old life! Thought of Amy swept over him with astounding significance. Her shallow little nature had caused his first real suffering, which, compared to what gripped him now, seemed a pale flame of youth. She vanished, a ghost of the past, and he knew all that he had felt was only the stronger, the more unquenchable. What, then, about the forces which had united in his pity, his love, his passion for Louise Belmont?

Paul plodded across the bench to the rim of the ragged canyon. Far away, above a bold plateau, a strange moon had arisen to change the desert. He spent a bitter hour there. But neither the harsh, irretrievable facts of the present, nor the irrevocable ones which must follow, could quite kill the things that made life significant for him. In the end Paul could not believe in fatalism, in predestination, in atheism, in all those fetters of the free mind and soul.

"All that is in me!" said Paul to the star-studded sky with its dark-blue endlessness, to the magnificent reach of bold black horizon, to the shadowy abyss that yawned at his feet, breathing of eternity. He felt strangely strengthened and comforted while at the same moment more clearly conscious that he was only finite, only one atom of struggling mortality, only one man caught in a hard corner of the earth and fatally involved in the tragedy of a young woman and her child.

Upon Paul's return to the camp fire, which had burned down to red coals, he found Kintell sitting up.

"Howdy. I was jest aboot to yell fer you," he said.

"I was out on the rim. Wess, do you feel all right?"

"Don't you know it's cold?"

"I don't feel cold."

"Wal, rustle up the fire, anyway. An' take a look at Calkins."

Paul threw on dead sagebrush he had collected, and when it blazed up he hesitatingly approached the prone form of the rustler. Calkins' face was in the shadow, but it had a mask-like cast that alarmed Paul. Quickly he bent to lay hold of the man. The body was cold and stiff. Paul rose, recoiling.

"Ah-huh. I had a hunch he'd croaked," spoke up the cowboy.

"He's dead. . . . Been dead for hours, maybe. Poor devil! But we couldn't do anything."

"Throw a tarp over him. . . . Wal, it's comin' on mawnin' an' I'm gonna hug the fire till daylight."

They talked the short remainder of that night. Dawn disclosed the cattle once more down in the basin, working steadily to the west, and bawling for water. Kintell obviously favored his lame shoulder, but managed to help Paul get a hasty breakfast.

"What to do with Calkins is a sticker," said the cowboy. "He might dry up an' blow away heah without anyone bein' the wiser. His cronies won't ever come back. An' if Indians fell onto this camp they'd swipe the ootfit an' say nothin'. What do you say, boss?"

"We'll have to bury him, but we shouldn't try to hide his grave as that would arouse suspicion if anyone found it."

"Okay. Thet's sense. Mebbe we better think over tellin' Belmont. We can gamble he won't tell aboot it."

"But—how would you explain? What reason . . ."

"We ketched him rustlin' our herd, an' held him up. I shot him in self-defense. You seen it. An' I'll say I've got a couple bullet holes to prove it."

"We are safe, in any case, as far as liability is concerned. But Belmont's reaction . . . the effect on Louise. That worries me."

"Pard, you shore have cause to worry aboot her," replied Wess somberly.

Paul dug a shallow grave and wrapped the body in a tarpaulin before covering it. While this task was in progress, Calkins' hobbled horse came into camp. Wess found a bridle and put it on him.

"Must be water down in thet canyon," said the cowboy. "There's a bucketful heah. Boss, I'll lead the hawse an' you carry the water. We'll fill the canteen an' give our nags the rest."

The sunrise was gilding the eastern ramparts when Paul and Wess reached the head of the draw. They found the mustangs little the worse for an inactive night. And having changed one of the saddles to the extra horse and made the most of the water, they set out on the return trip. Alternately trotting and walking the horses they rode all day under a boiling sun. From noon on Wess showed weariness, but he did not sag in his saddle until they made the plateau slope above the post. Here Paul had to support the cowboy in his saddle.

That last lap of the ride was for Paul the hardest on body and mind. Kintell appeared in bad shape, his own strength was spent, and never had the aspect of Bitter Seeps struck him so repellently with its concentrated essence of all that was hateful and terrible in the desert.

The hard black rocks of Black Mesa gleamed with a cold grayness, suggestive of the bitter winter that had cracked them from the cliffs; the glistening green-faced bluff, with its many bright trickling threads of water and the great pale pool, like an evil eye, surrounded by its sinister bands of alkali; the raw sedge along the borders of the outlet; the weathered slopes of shale, the red bare ridges, the wide flats ghastly in the sunlight, the last bars of sand left by the storms, the roads like belts of hot bronze, from all of which heat veils lifted smoky and dark, and dust devils whirled along in yellow columns, and lastly the trading post, squat, rude, brooding with its dark secret, linked the lives of its inmates with the tragic power of Bitter Seeps.

Only Louise saw the arrival of the riders and Paul helping Kintell off his horse and into the tent. Before Paul had removed the cowboy's coat and boots, Louise entered, the same wide-eyed lovely girl, yet not the same.

"Oh, Paul! I saw you hold him in his saddle—help him off. . . . *Blood!* Oh, what has happened?"

"Pard, I'll tell—her," panted Wess. "Look to the hawses —an' tell Belmont—what we agreed on."

Paul had steeled his nerve for the return of that darkly fugitive terror in the topaz eyes of his beloved. He greeted her with his old smile, his old endearing pet name. And not to have saved Belmont's life would he have failed to kiss her then.

Outside again he took up the bridles to lead the horses toward the corral; and not all the dragging step, the blurred eye, the abated breath came from the last exertions of that arduous ride.

* * *

10.

THE TRADER came at once to see Wess, showing little trace of the fury which he had exhibited upon learning of Calkins' treachery.

"Kintell, are you bad hurt?" he asked, not unkindly.

"Can't tell. But I didn't reckon I was."

"Let me see the bullet hole."

Paul removed the blood-crusted scarf to expose the inflamed and angry wound.

"Clear through. And no splintered bones. But you'll need a doctor. I'll drive up to Walibu and fetch him at once."

"Much oblige', Belmont."

"You've done me a service. Calkins has been crooked before, but not with me. . . . Now, listen. Keep that attempted raid and the fight under your hat. Bloom and Spraull will be only too glad to keep their mouths shut. They know me."

"Okay, Belmont. Suits me fine. But we buried Calkins shallow, right where he fell, and left all his things. Some Indians or mebbe whites will find him sooner or later."

"Leave that to me. Just where is the camp?"

"Do you know thet end of the basin?"

"Every foot of it. And a short-cut trail."

"Wal then, it's a bench on the north side where thet canyon opens up. Their camp was in plain sight close to the red wall. You cain't miss it."

"I'll ride out there tomorrow. That's all. The incident is closed. . . . You both savvy?"

"We understand, Belmont. And unless we are accused we shall keep silent," replied Paul gravely.

"Shore I savvy thet, Belmont, but I can't get yore interest in me all of a sudden," added the cowboy with sarcasm.

"I don't want this news to come out," rejoined the trader gruffly.

"Ah-huh. Wal, my boss an' me have plumb forgot all aboot it. I was cleanin' my gun an' it went off an' bored me. See?"

"Good . . . tell the doctor that. We could handle this hurt alone, but if it became infected and we had to call him in, such a story would look queer. It might excite curiosity."

"An' I shore don't want no curiosity aboot me an' my affairs."

The trader rushed out, and while Paul sat on the edge of Wess's bed there came the clatter of horses' hoofs.

"Boss, I jest cain't see anythin' to it but thet Belmont doesn't want the limelight on him," said Wess finally.

"Assuredly. He's playing into our hands, Wess."

"I reckon, if the deal should ever come to court. But we don't want thet, boss."

"Why not, provided we get proofs of his selling whisky to the Indians? We'd have him on three counts."

"Because, you bonehaid, we'd hardly be able to get enough on him to put him away for keeps. An' when we tried it thet'd give away thet you an' Louie love each other. Then he'd kill her inch by inch."

"What's the good of finding out any more, then?" asked Paul hopelessly.

"Wal, it'll help us to bluff him," declared Wess thoughtfully. "But if he's really stuck on Louie—if he wants her more than Sister—then we shore are in a hole."

"Wess, I don't see how love as we feel it could be possible to his kind."

"Say, you look wuss than me. Brace up! When I said our name would be mud I didn't mean we was licked. We'll never be licked, pard. Louie loves you, man! An' thet *settles* it."

"Does it?" Paul returned tensely. "And how long do you think she can stand this? . . . Didn't you see that look in her eyes?"

"Wal, there's *one* way of doin' it if nothin' else works," said the cowboy grimly.

"No, Wess . . . one killing is enough—too many. This isn't the old West any longer. If you killed Belmont, they'd hang you . . . and that would break Louise's heart."

"But, pard, you seen that hell back in her eyes. . . . It raised another kind of hell in my heart."

"Killing him would only make it worse," Paul averred stubbornly. "And what about the baby? What would she tell him about his father . . . ?"

"Paul, *you're* gonna be thet kid's real father someday. . . . Mark my words."

"Not ever that way," Paul returned doggedly. "Wess, you must get this idea out of your head."

"Wal, you're the boss," said the cowboy resignedly, "but I ain't so sure you're usin' *your* haid about it."

"You'll have to leave that to me," said Paul shortly, and strode out into the dusk.

The night was warm and still. Crickets chirped under the cedars. An evening star blazed white over the dark rim of Black Mesa. His midnight vigil out on the desert over the black and solemn canyon returned with all its power to strengthen, yet to deepen his conflict. And he seemed to be rent by a violent shock that propped him bolt upright. The convulsion passed, leaving him with the thought that he must fight every hour, every moment for Louise's sake, to make his agony as if it were not.

Paul went into the kitchen. Sister sat at the table, eating with the Indian woman, Gersha.

"Sorry to be late, Sister," said Paul cheerfully, as he sat down beside her. "A cup of coffee and a biscuit will do me."

The woman directed Gersha to serve him.

"Wess accidentally shot himself," went on Paul, "and I had a devil of a time getting him home."

"Is it serious?"

"No. But he lost a lot of blood and the long ride tuckered him out." Paul ate and drank slowly, revolving in mind conjectures as to the reason for Sister's haggard face and sullen somberness. He connected these with the change in Louise. And the wild thought wheeled in Paul's mind—could he make an ally of this strong woman, could he so work on her jealousy that she would betray Belmont to get rid of the girl she believed had usurped her place?

"Are you ill, Sister?" he asked kindly.

"No."

"You look terrible. As though you had lost your last friend."

"I have no friends," returned the woman with bitterness. "I am an outcast from my people and my church."

"You are!" ejaculated Paul, his heart leaping at having broken through her reserve. "I'm sorry to hear that. You've never seemed happy at Bitter Seeps."

"Happy—in this Gethsemane!"

"Your allegiance to Belmont ruined you?" queried Paul, and as she appeared stunned he went on impulsively, "I know why Belmont left Utah."

"Who—told you—that?" she stammered.

"Calkins."

"Was he drunk?"

"I don't think so. It struck me that he was not very loyal to Belmont."

"What more did he tell you?" asked the woman, irresistibly propelled by fear and curiosity.

"That Belmont had sworn to rid himself of you—that he never wanted you, nor intended to marry you in the first place."

"Never—wanted me—" she gasped, while her hard visage went turgidly red.

Paul felt justified in adding to what Calkins had really said. It was war to the hilt now between Belmont and him.

"On account of the girl," added Paul. "He was mad about Louise. But still wanted to hang on to you."

"So that's the truth. . . . From Calkins—of all men!"

"Sister, I'd rather you respected my confidence. I hesitated about telling you. But you seem to be getting a rotten deal here. And Wess and I are your friends. We know your relation to Belmont."

The woman leaped up, white as a sheet. "What do you mean? I have nothing to hide. Belmont will drive you away for such—such vile suspicion."

Paul had no need to speak further. The woman reacted to her own consciousness of a suspicion she had repudiated. She wrung her hands and shook in every limb. It was a dethronement of faith, if not of love, in a frustrated nature. She would have roused pity in a far sterner man than Paul. Ashen gray of face, and staggering as one mortally stricken, the woman moved to leave the kitchen.

"Think well, Sister," warned Paul. "There is more to this. I'm not afraid to face Belmont. But will that help you or me?"

"No, it wouldn't. . . . God has failed me! But woe betide John Belmont!"

Paul hastened to catch her at the door, to whisper: "I'm your friend. You be mine!"

Whereupon he returned to finish his cup of coffee. Gersha served him a second. Paul relieved his concern by proving again that she could understand very little English. His agitation gave place to strong suppressed feeling. Had he gone too far? Had he responded to impulse or inspiration? Would Sister yield to her passionate jealousy or would she brood over his revelation? Paul concluded she would keep the secret for the present, finding in it the nucleus of a revolt against her position, and a plot to oust Louise.

The long corridor was as black as a tunnel. Night had fallen. Louise's neglect to light Paul's lamp, something she had never forgotten, was only another damning detail of her wretchedness. He passed by his door, and going out, he stepped naturally up on Louise's porch. Her cabin was dark. He knocked at the open door. Her step seemed too slow, and he called: "Louie!"

"I'm here," she replied in soft haste. "Oh, Paul, don't say Wess—"

He stepped over the threshold and she bumped into him. Then suddenly, before he could restrain himself, Paul seized her in his arms. "Wess is in pain. But he's all right. Belmont has gone after the doctor."

She made no answer nor a single movement. Paul heard a slight gasp as he drew her to his breast. There he held her, laying his cheek to hers, and waited as much to find the control he needed as to ascertain what she would do. Louise was not stiff, but nothing about her responded to his embrace. Still, as he waited, like a man possessed, he felt her cool cheek grow warm, and her breast slowly heave. A long sigh escaped her. Then he burst out: "Louie, darling, it was so good to see you again. It's so heavenly now to feel you. . . . Oh, we had a hell of a trip. I'll tell you some other time. But the more I have to endure, the sweeter it is to come home to you. . . . I just had to do this. I can't go on hiding it from you any longer. Louie! Give me your lips!"

"I—can't," she whispered.

"Don't you really love me?"

"Love you! Oh, dear God!"

With strong hands he pulled her face up and sought her lips in the dark and kissed her with loving tenderness, subduing the sick, bitter passion in his soul. That kiss seemed to run through her like a revivifying fire. She became instinct with life and fight.

"No—no, you mustn't. . . . Oh, Paul! *Stop.* . . . There's something I must tell you. . . . I—he—"

"Tell me nothing," interrupted Paul, in a whisper as passionate and earnest as hers had been wild. "I love you, Louie. I don't want to hear if anything has happened. I don't care for myself *what* might have happened. Nothing can make any difference, so long as you love me, want me, will come to me someday. . . . *He* cannot change you or degrade you or lessen your preciousness, not one little bit. Not in my sight . . . ! But so help me God, if you despise yourself . . . if you sicken and weaken . . . if you let your physical loathing for that beast blunt your spirit again . . . I will kill him!"

"Hush!" she cried poignantly. "I've been a—coward. Oh, my Paul, I did not know . . . ! You must *not* kill Belmont! They would hang you! I will be brave. I will stand it. But I am only mortal. Belmont loves me. My indifference has made him love me all the more. And it's been terrible. . . . But now, I promise, I swear—it shall be nothing."

"It shall be—it *is* nothing with me, too," replied Paul

huskily. "After all, Louie, you are Belmont's real wife. And until you are no longer his wife—we must endure. Think of the future. A home with me! I'll make up for all you've suffered. Don't *you* succumb to morbid thoughts—to a frenzy to be free, and kill him yourself. For freedom will come, Louise. I feel it."

"Paul, I will do as you say. I will live for you. . . . He shall not put out the tiniest spark in me."

Silently he held her, in one long breathless clash of possession, finding in her spirit, her vow, her kiss, the strength that he had pretended.

"Come. Let us go to Wess. I want to tell you and him what I said to Sister."

In five days Kintell's fever left him, and he was on the mend, up and around. But the strange gloom that had settled down upon him did not vanish.

During this anxious period Paul seldom left him for long, and Louise shared the nursing. Between them, and under the physician's instruction, they averted a serious illness for the cowboy. Paul expected that Wess would soon be his old self, but except for a smile for Louise now and then he was a stranger. Paul importuned him to "snap out of it"; he lectured him, and finally took to a humorous attack. This likewise failed to pierce the cowboy's aloofness.

"Say, what in the hell is wrong with you?" demanded Paul, at last exasperated.

"Bitter Seeps," replied Kintell darkly.

"Bitter Seeps?"

"It's got me, same as Louie an' Sister an' Belmont. . . . Same as it's gettin' you."

"Why, Wess," stammered Paul.

"An' I'm thinkin' aboot shakin' this red dust from my boots."

Paul had no answer for that, and went his way. But he

was stunned. Kintell had sickened of this bitter, evil, poison hole of dust and wind and heat. Paul could not blame him, could never have made one little appeal to hold him; yet he was amazed, and suffered another saddening disillusion. He thought he saw Kintell's point of view; at least he appreciated what effect a dangerous wound might have upon a wild cowboy's mind. What hurt him so cruelly was to discover that he loved this droll Texan, and might lose him. If there had ever been an obligation, Wess had paid it a hundredfold.

Saddling a mustang, Paul took to the plateau, his first ride for days. The cattle were strung all over the desert adjacent to the post, and as far out as the west end of the basin. So far that summer they were faring well. He rode around the herd, drove in the stragglers, counted the daily increasing number of calves, and in so far as his limited experience would permit, he conscientiously performed the duties of a cowboy.

By sunset he was riding down the slope under the ragged crown of Black Mesa, looking down on Bitter Seeps, hating the place as he had never hated anything, seeing it as a malignant octopus, with the gray post and the pale pool as menacing eyes of the beast, and the gullies and ravines twisting tortuously away from it, as grasping arms reaching to ensnare all living creatures.

But dark as was Paul's mind when he entered the court, he changed his outward self as if by magic. Louise heard his whistle, his light step, his cheerful voice. His smile, the pat of his hand as he passed her door were assurances of unfailing love, and they uplifted her from the worry and dread of a lonely day. Paul saw this as he had seen it before. And it made him strong, furious, indomitable, while it almost crushed his heart with the pathetic fallacy of it. As if he were omniscient! But Louise lived through his love and he felt that no man had ever had a greater burden, nor a nobler cause. But with it his impatience grew to find a solution to the problem that lay so heavily on his heart.

Thus the summer was ushered in on a blast of heat. Belmont complained of the Indians staying in their hogans or under their sun shelters. The old medicine men claimed they had not seen a hotter summer. It hurt Belmont's day business, but improved that of the night. The trader drank heavily. His bluff, hearty manner suffered an eclipse.

Kintell went back to riding the range. Though he never proclaimed it, he evidently preferred to ride alone. Paul did not intrude; indeed he had himself come to prefer solitude. Often he would see the cowboy silhouetted from a ridge top, or sitting motionless on his horse on the plateau rim, gazing down upon Bitter Seeps. What went on in Kintell's mind? It haunted Paul. He knew that Wess loved Louise and he believed it to be a loyal, brotherly affection born of the girl's sweetness and her hapless state. But after all Wess was only human, a lonely rider, a man of fire and passion; and it might well be true that his heart was breaking. Paul stifled the slightest infringement of jealousy upon his loyalty to his friend. And he fought to make himself glad that Louise was fond of Wess. But at the same time he began to wonder. Had the cowboy forgotten their plans for saving Louise? Still Paul refrained from broaching the subject to Wess, in the faith that his friend would provide an answer when the time came.

By midsummer, when the rains were almost due, Paul had taken to riding early in the morning and late in the afternoon. Inured as he had become to the outdoors and the hardships of the desert, he found the noon hours, when the copper sun poised straight overhead, to be insupportable.

At this period, day after day, and increasingly so, the red hole that encompassed Bitter Seeps grew to be a ghastly, shrouded furnace above which red clouds hung in the still air, and the heat veils rose like curtains of dark transparent smoke, and the infernal dust devils swooped down off the desert.

Paul could not avoid all of this enervating and wearing burden of the season, but learning from the Indians, and comforted by the assurance that Louise was doing the same, he slept through the worst heat of the day. Sleep, however, would not then have been possible for him had he not remained awake for half and more of each night. Paul had become a spy, a stealthy prowler in the dark, an insatiable seeker for the nocturnal truth about this trader. He went to the extent of wearing moccasins, a velveteen shirt, a silver-shielded belt, and a scarf around his head. He painted his face dark. If he ever ran afoul of Belmont or one of his accomplices he wished to be mistaken for an Indian. He also had been practicing drawing and shooting his gun during his rides out on the range. Kintell, who likewise was playing the spy, demurred at this disguise and activity of his employer's, all to no avail.

One night, long after midnight, the noise of the inevitable wagon attracted Paul to the cedars that lined the road. He encountered Kintell bent on the same errand.

"Playin' redskin an' packin' a gun!" ejaculated the cowboy. "Boss, have you gone daffy?"

"I know perfectly well what I am doing," replied Paul impatiently. "All the same I may be crazy, at that. But I'm getting sick and tired of waiting for something to happen. None of our plans have worked. We know Belmont is a crook, but we can't prove it. What are we going to do?"

"Now, keep yore shirt on, Paul," said the cowboy, soothingly. "Things ain't changed enough to do us any good yet.

But our time's comin'—never fear. . . . Of course you could just take Louie and light out."

"Sure—if she'd go. And what about the baby?"

"Take him along, too."

"In this heat! The boy has been failing again—he wouldn't last a day out in that sun. Besides, what about Belmont? He'd follow us and he has the legal right. . . ."

"Then you'd have to kill him," rejoined the cowboy bluntly.

"So—if I did—then they'd hang me. And then where would Louise be?"

"No wuss off than she is now," the cowboy said implacably.

"Then what would you have me do?" demanded Paul bitterly.

"Jest let me throw a gun on him, thet's all," ground out Kintell.

"I've told you time and time again—no! There will be no shooting as long as I have anything to say about it," Paul snapped fiercely.

"Then you'll jest have to wait . . ." was the cowboy's imponderable rejoinder, whereupon he strode off into the darkness.

Paul gazed after him despairingly, at the same time realizing that Kintell had forced him into a recognition that his own patience was nearing a break.

The sound of the approaching wagon fell on his ears, and suddenly Paul was struck with an idea. Why not climb up on top of the roof of the post and listen? Perhaps he could find out the purpose of these mysterious nocturnal visits.

He slipped back from the road under cover of the cedars, and gained the corner of the post at the back of his room. The ascent would be easy, aside from the danger of making a noise. Louise's open window was not far from the cedar tree by which he expected to mount to the roof. He might awaken her, but that did not worry him, for Louise was not the screaming kind. Carefully he ascended the tree to find that he had to make more of an effort than he had guessed. Not only did he rustle the branches of the cedar but he also detached a portion of earth from the roof, which slid off with a sound that to Paul's excited ears was loud enough to awaken sleepers at a distance. He crouched there in the starlight listening. He heard noises from in front of the post, and then a slight creak below. Peering down he made out a pale face framed in the blackness of Louise's window.

"Louie, it's me," he called in a shrill whisper.

"Paul!" she cried in a low, startled voice.

"Yes. . . . Ssh! Not so loud."

"What in the world are you doing?"

"That wagon is here again. . . . Don't worry."

"The wagon!—Oh, be careful! Belmont will . . ."

Paul, crawling along, passed out of hearing of her poignant whisper. The roof appeared as solid under him as the ground, and the weeds grew high enough for him to hide, if he lay flat. Moreover he could advance without the slightest sound. Thus emboldened and firing to this adventure, he crawled the length of the long wing to the main roof over the post. This had a perceptible slope up to the peak. Gaining that, he saw the dull flat in front of the post and he heard low voices and soft footfalls. Paul did not hesitate to proceed down the slant, crawling noiselessly and cautiously, until he attained a position scarcely a yard from the edge. He seemed actuated wholly by a bold daring. Rising upon his hands he peeped through the fringe of weeds to make out a small buckboard, at the back of which stood two men.

"I didn't want so much," Belmont was saying, almost in his ordinary voice.

"Take it or leave it," replied the other. "I'm not anxious to make that long ride often. Besides it's risky out here. Some of those government men might wonder why I got all this whisky for one small trading post out in the desert. They know how few white settlers ride through our range."

"So what? They can't hold you for it."

"Mebbe they can't. But it's still risky. If they found all this stuff here, they'd be snoopin' around all over for sure."

"Anybody been talkin'?"

"Bloom Burton gave me a hunch to lay off Bitter Seeps."

"So. . . . Have you seen Calkins?"

"No. He drifted off on some deal of his own, Bloom said."

"I reckon he did," replied Belmont gruffly. "All right, Bill. I'll take the load. Just heave it onto the porch."

Paul saw the men lift heavy cases out of the car, and one of them deposited his load on the porch with a distinct jar. His blood leaped. Belmont would not be having whisky hauled out in the dead of night without a reason—obviously to hide the amounts he was selling to the Indians.

"Careful, man!" whispered Belmont fiercely, from directly under where Paul knelt.

"Sorry. Jarred some dust off the roof."

"What the hell!" muttered the trader, as if mystified. After a trenchant moment for Paul he went on in quicker tone. "Bill, come here. . . . Listen!"

In the silence that ensued Paul's straining ears caught a very soft silky sound.

"Bill, do you hear anythin'?"

"Sure. It's dust fallin' off the roof."

"Dust? You're loco. There's no dust on the roof. . . .

Here it is. . . . Sand. A little stream of sand pourin' down!"

"I jarred it off," replied Bill.

"But that never happened before," muttered the trader.

Paul suddenly awakened to his perilous predicament. He distinctly heard the soft seep of sand falling beneath him on the porch floor. It was he, and not Bill's carelessness with the case of liquor, that had dislodged it. Moreover Paul detected a quivering of the porch roof under his weight, a staggering fact which had escaped him in his excitement.

"Bill, there's someone up there!" whispered the trader hoarsely.

"Aw, John, you're loco 'stead of me."

Cautious footsteps moving out from under the roof froze Paul's blood. His tongue cleaved to the roof of his mouth. He began to shake so violently that he increased the steady stream of sand seeping down. Next instant the burly form of the trader loomed up black. He saw Paul as clearly as Paul saw him.

"By God! I was right. It's an Indian!" burst out Belmont furiously. And he made the swift action of a man drawing a gun, only the gun was not forthcoming. Belmont plunged in under the porch. "Where's my gun? Gimme a gun!"

His low bellow of deadly rage and his heavy footfalls served to spur Paul out of his petrification. Wheeling, he crawled with all his might up the slant of the roof. He had just gained the peak when the darkness split to a red flash and a gun cracked like a thunderclap. A hot bullet zipped Paul's ear. He leaped up, bounded down the slope, and flew along the flat roof to the end, where he jumped sheer to the flagstone path below. It took but a few swift springs for him to gain his room. Softly he closed the door and dropped the bar in place. Then shaking like an aspen leaf, choking for breath, he sat down on his bed, to remove his disguise.

The disguise and the speed with which he had fled had saved him. His ear stung where the bullet had burned it. But no blood flowed. The coldness of terror fled to be replaced by a hot frenzy. What a narrow escape! Belmont had shot to kill. And in those waiting, panting, bursting moments Paul discovered what it was to have the old cave man rise out of the past to master him with elemental power.

Thudding footsteps came down the corridor. Hard raps from a metal instrument—a gun!—preceded Belmont's hoarse voice.

"Manning, are you there?"

It was a query, the sibilant doubt of which told Paul that the trader was suspicious, that he half expected not to be answered.

"Sure I'm here," replied Paul. "I was awakened by a shot. Heard someone running. . . . What the hell's going on?"

"Indian thief. He was on . . . I saw him—shot at him. Did he run down the hall, out this door?" replied the crafty Belmont, whose wits seldom failed to work.

"I don't know. Thought it was outside. Heard him flop."

Belmont strode on out. Paul stole to his open window. He was in time to see Belmont pound on Louise's door.

"Yes?" she called.

"Have you been awake?"

"Not long. I think I heard a gun. Then running steps."

"He got away, then. I thought I'd hit him," concluded Belmont, turning away from the door.

"Hey, trader, what's all the row aboot?" came in Kintell's cool drawl from the shadow.

"That you, Kintell?" called Belmont, plainly irritated.

"Shore. I'd have been heah sooner but I got cactus in my bare feet."

"I shot at a prowlin' Indian. He ran back this way."

"You don't say? Doggone if this Bitter Seeps ain't some place."

"It's a good place to leave, Kintell," returned Belmont with significance.

"I'll say. I wonder if *thet* fellar leavin' hell-bent fer election is yore Indian thief."

The inspiration for this cryptic speech of the cowboy's came from the rattle of the wagon and galloping hoofs up the road. Paul saw Belmont make a gesture of passion. He stood a moment, head like a hawk, listening to the swiftly receding wheels of the buckboard.

"Belmont, I heahed thet fellar go by my tent not long ago," said Kintell curiously. "He was sneakin' along easy. But he shore opened her up on the way back. What's it all aboot?"

"I don't know any more than you," replied the trader testily. "Probably there were two wagons."

"Ump-um. Thet one goin' north is the same one thet came from the north."

"Kintell, you seem pretty much interested in what goes on around my place," said Belmont, bitingly cold.

"Shore do. It's the queerest place I ever seen."

"Queer? What do you mean?"

"Wal, it's a spooky place," drawled the cowboy. "An' a blisterin' hell hole of a place. . . . An' a poison water hole of a place. . . . An' a place where nobody sleeps an' a lot goes on at night."

"Kintell, you and Manning are as queer as anythin' or anyone else around Bitter Seeps."

"Oh, yeah?"

"I'm sick of your bellyachin'!"

"Belmont, you've got the bellyache yoreself," retorted Kintell sharply. "An' you can bet yore sweet life it doesn't come from yore alkali water."

"That'll do. You're fired."

"You cain't fire me, Belmont."

"I'll see that Manning does."

"Like hell you will," replied Kintell tauntingly, as he moved away in the gloom. "Like an old lady who keeps tavern oot West. . . . Haw! Haw! Haw!"

11.

THE DESERT of Bitter Seeps, all stone and baked earth, retained the heat into the fall. Each succeeding day grew drier, hotter, fiercer. The corn, melons, hay in the Indian gardens burned to a crisp, as brown and wrinkled as leather. Cattle far out on the wasteland died in their tracks. The humans had reached the limit of endurance in body and mind.

Kintell rode the range alone. During the little part of daylight that he showed himself at the post, he appeared a gaunt, piercing-eyed, burdened man. He ate in his tent, meager meals like those of a poor Indian. When spoken to, he was sharp and brief. At last even Louise no longer addressed him.

Paul, too, was wearing to a disastrous break. He realized it, but could not check the overpowering forces of the place, the time, and whatever terrible climax seemed imminent. Belmont's quarrel with him over his refusal to discharge the cowboy had widened a considerable breach. Apparently the trader welcomed it. Belmont, too, was plotting. His deep and gloomy thought resembled the brooding of the wasteland. The subtle, almost imperceptible change of the last few weeks now stood out palpably. Belmont was under a tremendous strain, the havoc of which he did not suspect. His greed and lust and love of the bottle seemed to have united with the disintegrating influence of Bitter Seeps.

Of them all Sister expressed most markedly the effect of the maddening heat and the appalling situation. She never left the store or her room. Seldom did she speak and then only to the Indian girl. At any moment of any hour of the day or night her white face might appear at her window. She watched with eyes that Paul dreaded and would trust no more. Hate dominated that thwarted soul—hate of Louise, of her new-found and ineradicable friends—and love for Belmont that was also hate. She watched for what Paul at last divined—for some act that could be interpreted to Louise's dishonor.

For this all-potent reason Paul had to cease his little attentions to Louise, and the precious moments for the interchange of that love which had upheld her marvelously, and nourished her beauty.

Louise did not understand. Her great reproachful eyes drove Paul wild with his impotence. He wrote her a long letter, but dared not risk delivering it that day or night. Belmont had ordered Gersha to take care of Paul's room and he had ordered Louise not to type any more of Paul's manuscript. Louise's passionate remonstrance he waved aside with the explanation that he would not let her work during this hot weather.

Finally in desperation Louise waylaid Wess, who for the first time failed her. He too had become alive to Sister's spying. Paul, as watchful even as Sister, saw the girl and the cowboy together, saw her turn away disconsolate. Wess had spoken harshly; like a wolf in a trap he had snapped at what hurt him. More than any preceding detail of this miserable affair, Wess's inexplicable affront to Louise dismayed and tortured Paul. He had relied upon the cowboy, and seeing Louise importune Wess he had been racked by a hopeless hope. Now Wess had failed him. The whole thing was maddening. His pity for Louise made him ache until he was numb. Yet he was driven by this still-ineradicable sense of honor to reject the thought of violence that now beckoned to him so appealingly. His rage at Wess, at himself, at that ghoul-eyed Sister, at the implacable and forbidding Belmont, knew no bounds. He yearned to rush to Louise and beg her to ride away with him, but this same, now inexplicable bond held him back.

The baby, too, showed the marked effects of the terrible heat. Paul saw him seldom, but his feverish wails during the days attested to his misery. Often, Paul wondered whether or not Louise's crooning little comforts to him were that or her own weeping. From the thinness and gauntness of his little arms and legs, and the red splotched skin, Paul could see that Tommy was failing. If this heat lasted much longer, it would be the end for him—perhaps for all of them, Paul thought gloomily.

Dark night was welcome. Paul stretched out in the hammock, his fevered blood slowly losing its boil, his brain the pressure as of a hot steel band. The night was still, hot, melancholy. Stars shone out of the blue dome above. Somewhere an Indian was chanting. It was so silent that the faint seeping of the water down at the spring reached Paul's ears. The slow, soft thuds of Kintell's steps as he paced his beat under the cedars were sounds equally significant. That strange cowboy who had hated to walk now kept unflaggingly at it.

Then another and a different step disrupted the chance

for peace and slumber that Paul was wooing. Belmont! He thumped out of the corridor onto the flagstone walk. His step struck Paul as that of a man whom it would be perilous to meet upon a narrow trail where neither could turn back. Belmont would stride on—he would brush aside friend or foe alike. Paul had heard this step often, and now as always, it seemed to crush his heart. Belmont strode heavily on to Louise's porch. He fumbled at her door, which evidently was locked.

Paul's deadened heart leaped to acute and palpitating activity. And his spent body answered. But slowly he sank back upon the hammock.

"Louise," called the trader in a decided but low voice.

No answer! He rattled the door and cursed under his breath.

"Louise!"

At this louder call the soft footfalls of the cowboy ceased. He too heard, and no doubt stood stiff and cold in the shadow.

"What do you want?" Louise replied.

"I want in."

"You can't come in. Must you be told that a thousand times?"

"Are you sick?"

"No."

"Well, you let me in, then," he demanded impatiently. As he received no answer he pounded on the door. "Open, I say."

"No!" cried Louise ringingly. There was no weakness, no fright in her.

"You damned little cat! I won't stand this any longer."

"Belmont, you're thick of understanding, or you'd have known long ago."

"Louise, I'll break the door in."

"Go ahead. But if you do I'll either kill you or myself."
He could be heard fuming his amazement.

"That's a bluff. You have no gun."

"Indeed I have."

"Where'd you get it?"

"Paul gave it to me."

"That cursed, interfering dude again! Listen. Sister has been hintin' at things I wouldn't hear. If you're not careful, she'll put ideas into my head."

"Impossible! Animals cannot receive ideas."

"Hell's fire! What's got into you, girl?" he burst out furiously.

"You can never come to me again, John Belmont."

"I'll not stand for bein' stalled off this way," he blustered. But he was impressed.

"You'll have to stand it."

"But why? Louise, haven't we argued enough? You know I love you," he went on in a lower voice, husky and eager, betraying how her revolt had fanned his desire. "I'll be better to you in the future. I've come to love you terrible hard."

"Love? Bah! Go to Sister," cried the girl in passionate scorn.

Belmont kept silent for a long moment.

"I'm through with her," he whispered hoarsely. "Truly. I'll get rid of her. And I promise I'll make it legal this time."

"Will you? If I know that woman, you will most decidedly not."

"So that's your reason?" queried the trader, in a pondering return to the will that brooked no obstacle.

"That's one of them. Another is—I loathe you—you beast!"

Belmont uttered a stifled curse of rage and pain, and he beat against the door in a convulsive tattoo of strong, nerveless hands. Thick as his hide was, that ringing assertion of this wife at bay—the unutterable contempt that tried to find expression in the vile epithet—pierced the sordid man to the quick.

"Louie, for God's sake—take it back!" he implored, in a voice so unlike Belmont's that Paul could not but feel his torture. It seemed such a ridiculous paradox that this rum-selling, hardened trader, with his amours, could be victim to anything like deep and all-persuasive love. Yet Paul felt the bitter truth of it and gloried in the man's misery.

"Never! I am through, John Belmont," cried Louise passionately. "I hate you! I hated you in Utah after what you did to me and Tommy. But your Bitter Seeps has filled me with something more terrible than hate. . . . If you come near me again I'll kill you! If I fail—and you touch me—I'll kill myself!"

Belmont stumbled away from the door, out upon the path, with a sobbing intake of breath. He had not yet made the corridor when Sister shrieked from her window.

"I heard every word," she screeched.

"Shut up! Don't nag me now, woman," replied Belmont thickly.

"Nag! I'll invoke the curse of hell on you—unless you cast out that white-faced slut!"

"Sister, I warn you—"

"You fool! She loves a younger man. That is why she denies you——"

"Hellcat!" roared the trader. "Take that!"

Paul heard a cracking blow on flesh, and then a sliding scrape of chairs, and a sodden crash. Dead silence ensued. Paul waited a moment with bated breath and charged suspense; then he glided away from the post to cudgel his stunned wits into realization that the blighting damned-up passions of Bitter Seeps had burst.

Kintell's stealthy quick step sounded behind Paul. He turned to make out the cowboy's tall shape in the gloom. The two stole away toward the cowboy's tent.

"Man, did you heah him sock her?" whispered Kintell, profoundly stirred.

"I should say I did," returned Paul with a deep breath.

"At thet I don't blame him so awful much," went on Kintell. "Thet dame is a terrible pill. But she must have rights."

"For putting up with Belmont—and how," muttered Paul.

"Shore. . . . Holy mackili, but this is too much fer my pore haid. . . . Pard, you heahed Louie?"

"If I hadn't would I be bursting like I am . . . ? Wess, that girl has guts."

"She shore has. This has happened before, Paul. More'n onct. . . . By Gawd, I begin to have a hunch that Louie never let him in since she came oot here."

Suddenly, a light seemed to burst in Paul's brain. He caught the cowboy's arm excitedly. "Wess, do you remember what he said, about getting rid of Sister—that this time he would *make it legal?*"

"I heard him—but I didn't make anythin' out of it. But say, thet could mean . . ."

"Sure. You remember what Calkins said. He said it was rumored up around Lund that Louise was Belmont's wife —but that he didn't know. And he didn't know about Sister, either. . . ."

"An' you mean . . . ?"

"He can't be married to both of them, legally. It's possible that Sister is his real wife, and that he never really married Louise at all!"

"But pard, she wouldn't have let him . . ."

"Wess, you underestimate Belmont. He has friends and

influence over the line, some of whom would agree with his ideas. . . . He could easily have faked a wedding ceremony, and even a marriage license, figuring that if he got Louise here she would never find out that she had been tricked. Or he might never have divorced Sister before he married Louise."

"An' she found out. . . . Thet's why she hates him so. Paul, I could kill thet dirty —— right here and now!" Kintell rasped. But Paul grasped him with an arm of steel.

"Wait, Wess. *No.* . . ." A great hope was soaring in Paul's breast. "Don't you realize what this means? If we can prove Sister is his real wife, *he no longer has a claim on Louise—or the baby.* His marriage to Louise would be invalid. We can protect her legally. . . . Wess, you've got to ride to Utah . . . now . . . tonight, and find out the truth of this."

"Pard, you hit the nail on the haid. . . ." the cowboy muttered. "Shore, now I wonder why I didn't think of thet before. But it's not too late. I'll find thet rustler Bloom an' his pard. I'll buy them to tell. Men like thet will do anythin' for money. If I have to shoot a laig off of one of them to make him squeal—okay, I'll do it. . . . Paul, dig up some money. Plenty of the long green, pard. I may need it. . . ."

"Here's my wallet. Go as far as you like. . . . Wess, this is our big chance. I'm counting on you."

"Don't you worry. Ha! I'm gonna do it, pard. Paul, from the very first somethin' struck me deep heah. An' I'm a son-of-a-gun if we're not on the right track at last."

"Then get going—at once!"

"Right now. But Paul, remember yore job will be to watch Belmont, day an' night. Keep him away from Louie, absolutely. Do yu savvy?"

"Don't you worry. I will, Wess."

"If you have to kill him! But I reckon thet'd be a last

card. Stay close to the post until I get back. And keep a close watch on Louie. Mebbe things are beginnin' to look up at last."

In the gray dawn Paul plodded to and fro under the cedars. Although a great load seemed lifted from his shoulders, he was still not free of the gnawing uncertainty of inevitable conflict and climax. But it was a blessing just to hear a mocking bird, to feel the cool desert air, to see the marvelous beauty of the sky before sunrise. Nature was relentless and inevitable. She had no concern for the souls of men. She kept busy at her own ends, which were inscrutable. Glorious dawn, loveliness of earthy things, melody, color, a silence and peace that seemed to come from eternity—with these she met stricken mortals as if to mock them with the mighty life they saw. Paul could not lose his weariness and sense of uncertainty, yet the greatness of nature rallied him.

But this hour was brief. Before the sun topped the mesa, sky and atmosphere and the rock-ribbed earth presaged another and even more torrid day. Heat and drought would endure, and man, with his inexhaustible resources, might survive them, but not always the devastating passions that they engendered so mercilessly.

Paul shunned even the Indians. His breakfast consisted of an apple and a biscuit, sustaining and tasteless food that he had to force down. He wandered out on the desert, where there was no shade. He could not stand the heat for long, but he was too restless to stay indoors.

He drank at the spring. Cold clear sparkling water that slaked thirst and sustained life. The leaven of Bitter Seeps! The insidious medium through which the desert permeated blood and tissue and brain of living creatures, to work its mysterious alchemy for evil. Paul saw that hard, bitter, evil eye peering at him from the transparent depths. Yet this day the water did not taste bitter. Paul marveled at that.

It struck him so singularly that it remained in his mind. At supper time he addressed a query to Belmont that was sincere and had no subtle inquisitiveness, such as had many of his remarks to the trader.

"Belmont, does this Bitter Seeps spring of yours always taste the same?"

The trader gave a queer little start that Paul would have missed had he not been looking squarely at him.

"Wha-at . . . ? Why do you ask?" countered Belmont, looking up from his plate. His eyes held a hard steely penetrating look. Paul sustained an inexplicable shock.

"Why . . . ? Well, I drank from the spring a little while ago," replied Paul, trying to respond casually. "And the water didn't taste so bitter. It was almost good."

"Ahuh!" grunted the trader, his gaze going back to his plate. "I've noticed that once in a while. Reckon there's a weaker flow of mineral at this season, before the rains come."

"What kind of mineral?"

"Some kind of salt. You've seen the white mark of alkali along the edge of the water?"

"Yes. Looks like frost," returned Paul shortly, and his gaze reverted to his plate. He did not speak again during the meal, which he rather hurriedly finished.

Once in his room Paul gave free rein to a roused train of thought. He had received an amazing and strange intimation about Bitter Seeps. He traced it to the gleaming look in Belmont's eyes. And if he were not at the mercy of a vivid and morbid imagination that look had resembled the cold green evil color of the waters of the spring. Paul could not rid himself of this impression. The longer he pondered over the matter, the surer he grew that the evil of Bitter Seeps bore a direct and sinister relation to the evil in Belmont. How remarkable to have stumbled across the fact that Bitter Seeps was not always bitter! Why was it not? Paul remembered what had been told him about the Navajos, the Hopis, having lived upon that water. They still used it from necessity, but sparingly. Paul's observation was that they never drank it any more. They bought pop and ginger ale openly at the post store, and certainly hard liquors in secret. Therefore, it was greatly to Belmont's advantage to have the flow of mineral strongly present. In regard to the trader Paul had a suspicious mind. He wondered if it could not be possible for Belmont to assist nature in this peculiar dispensation of nature's minerals. The thought flashed through Paul's dark mind like an illumination. He could not dismiss it. The suspicion would not down. Belmont might be capable of any villainy.

No doubt Paul's hope was father to the thought. He was tremendously keen to obtain definite proof of the trader's crookedness.

Paul searched around among his effects for a couple of small bottles. These he emptied of their contents and rinsed out. Analysis of Bitter Seeps water would be interesting in any event.

When he left his room, dusk had fallen. There was a copper glow over the western horizon. Stars shone faintly out of a hazed sky. Heat still lay like a heavy blanket over the desert. As Paul stole by Louise's cabin he noted that her door was closed. She did not leave it open even in this sultry weather. A light shone from her window. Paul went out the back way, down by the hogans and across the gloomy flat to the spring.

As he neared the pool some wild animals, probably coyotes or foxes, scurried away into the darkness. Cattle were drinking from the runway below the pool. Paul went directly to the flat rock, where he knelt to drink. The water was not bad at all—just a little alkaline. All the water in that desert was like that. Paul's next move was to fill one of his bottles. Then he walked along the edge of the pool to find a place where he could hide and watch unseen. The dark bluff from which the water seeped dominated the scene. Toward the cliff not even a moving object could have been distinguished. But by crossing the runway to the north side Paul calculated that looking toward the south and the low horizon in that direction he might see anything coming from that direction. Wherefore he found a comfortable seat just above the level of the pool and composed himself to wait.

He was gambling on one chance in a thousand. He felt he was laboring under one of Kintell's hunches. An uncanny sense of something about to be revealed gave him a grim zest. And he began to attend to the task with all the power of the acute sensorial perception the desert had developed in him.

Cattle wandered away from the spring and others came. Paul could not see them because the background behind the runway was black. When Indian squaws came, however, and slouched with soft unoccasioned tread out on the stone platform, Paul made them out clearly against the pale southern sky. They dipped their gasoline cans and plodded away in the gloom.

As the night wore on the heat haze cleared, allowing the stars to shine somewhat brightly. Their faint glow beamed upon the pool. A cool breeze came down from the mesa to fan Paul's heated brow. Under the black cliff the shadows were impenetrable. The strange silky seep of the waters came from there, and it seemed a sound of mystery. Paul's feeling of the brooding mystery and melancholy of Bitter

Seeps intensified during this lonely vigil. In fact, all the characteristics of the desert seemed intensified. The wail of distant coyotes struck mournfully upon Paul's sensitive ears. Wild, haunting, lonely, poignant desert cries! The rim of the plateau stood up bold and dark along the whole of the western horizon. An Indian rider came loping down the road from Walibu and his chanting song sounded like a lament. An Indian dog yelped at the coyotes. But after a while all sounds ceased save the seep of water and the rustle of leaves.

The immensity of the desert bore down upon Paul's spirit. It seemed no different there from where the wilderness of canyons yawned.

Night and silence fitted the looming plateau and the star-crowned mesa. But they stirred a strength in Paul. There was something in man that this barren world of rock and sand could not kill.

At a late hour when he was about to abandon his vigil for that night, the stillness was broken by footsteps. They came from the direction of the post. A man of forcefulness, wearing boots, was approaching. Presently the red eye of a cigar shone in the blackness. In another moment Paul recognized Belmont's walk. The trader came down hard on his heels. He was decisive, energetic. Still he did not appear to be walking with his usual bold vigorous stride. If it were possible for Belmont to saunter, that was what he was doing then.

Paul hugged the ground, suddenly prey to hot and tingling sensations. Suddenly a tall stalwart figure showed blackly silhouetted against the pale southern sky.

Paul recognized that figure and a strong shuddering passion burned out the coldness of nerve and vein. The pool was about fifty feet wide at that point. When Belmont walked out upon the stone platform, all his form down to his knees could be plainly distinguished. He stood there a moment with the moving alert head of a listening deer. Then Paul heard a rustle of paper. Next a slight splash on the water broke the portentous silence. Belmont had thrown something into the pool. Again! Paul saw his arm move with an underhand sling. There came another little splash, this time in the center of the pool.

It had been made by a small hard object. Paul lay there, rigid externally, with his vitals palpitating, a cold sweat breaking out all over him, while the trader pitched eleven more objects into different parts of the great spring. Then followed a sound of the crushing of a paper bag. The man thrust it in his pocket. He puffed on his cigar, which again showed a ruddy light. Expelling a deep breath he turned away and disappeared in the gloom toward the post.

Paul crouched there, the cold clammy wetness of his skin succeeding to a burning sweat. His premonition had been absolutely true. Belmont was poisoning Bitter Seeps. There could not be any other explanation for his midnight visit to the spring. He was using some mineral or chemical that was, no doubt, soluble in water. The effect, no doubt, lasted until the substance completely dissolved, which might take days or weeks.

Paul whispered a curse of wrath: "I should have shot his leg off with that bag in his hands . . . ! Wess would have done it. . . . But he must pull that rotten stunt often."

Stealthily Paul made his way back to his room, where he lay wide awake for another long and pondering hour. Next morning after breakfast he strolled down to the spring, as was his custom, and making sure no eye watched him at the moment he bent to take a mouthful of the water. Again it was nasty and hard. He spat it out in disgust. Then he filled the second bottle, after which he got up to stand a moment peering into the pool. It appeared the same. He could not distinguish any new objects on the vague green bottom of the depths.

....

12.

THAT DAY was hot. Paul kept to his room most of the time, brooding, thinking, plans revolving in his mind, to use the knowledge he possessed, and what he hoped Wess would bring back from Utah. He believed that an analysis of the two bottles of spring water would establish Belmont's guilt. But that would take time. Government investigators would be slow and dilatory. In any event, if the trader saw he was liable to be convicted of being a cattle thief and a poisoner of Indian waters, he would take Louise and hide somewhere in the wilds of Utah. Paul doubted the wisdom of bringing action against the trader solely on these grounds.

Meanwhile, he could only wait for the cowboy's return. He lay down dressed as he was. He slept awhile, only to awaken, wet with sweat. Then he went outdoors and walked under the stars until he was tired. The night seemed mysterious and promising with its whispers. Paul could not doubt the ominous presage of the desert. If he could only contain himself!

Next morning it was late when he awoke. The day already bore indication of being like its predecessor. This period was the early hot spell common to the region. It would not last long. Paul felt better able to stand the heat than the loneliness and uncertainty. He avoided direct contact with Belmont and Louise, and kept to himself, although he watched her cabin closely. Most of the time all of them were indoors as well, so there was little need for close surveillance. In this way three more nightmare days passed. The weather grew hotter. On the fifth morning Paul had to get out in the open. He walked miles. Upon returning he passed around the post toward the wing he occupied. But the wide-open door of the wool room invited respite from the sun and he entered.

It was a huge, long room, irregularly floored with flagstones, and lined on each side by stall-like bins for the storing of wool. It smelled strongly of sheep. Paul sat down on a bale of wool near the door. He fanned himself with his sombrero. And he gazed out at the red valley, hazed with heat, ghastly with the smoky veils and shrouds of dust.

"God-forsaken and forlorn," muttered Paul. "That is the curse of Bitter Seeps. . . . If only Wess would return . . . how long can I wait? Another day of this—"

Swift, soft footsteps that he would have recognized among a thousand pattered on the hard ground outside. Louise! She had seen him—there was no escape. Like a bent sapling he sprang erect.

In another moment she stood in the wide doorway, the sun glinting from her bronze hair, white-faced as the white, flimsy clothes she wore.

"Paul!"

She moved toward him, and he thought of something he had once read about an army approaching with banners. She was magnificent. He no longer wanted to escape. His heart knew this to be the crucial hour, though his brain could not divine how.

"Louise!" he replied, as a guilty man who craved forgiveness.

She moved straight into his arms and looked up at him. All that was glorious in life, and human in her, and terrible in Bitter Seeps, shone from her lovely eyes.

"Don't you love me any more?" she asked mournfully.

"Oh, Louie!—you child!"

If he had been stone she would have fired him; if he had been dead wood she would have quickened him to feeling.

"Don't you?" Her clinging hands were hot; her hot breasts burned through her thin clothing.

"Love you? How can you doubt it?"

"But you have been—oh, so cruel!"

"I am afraid of Sister. She watches. She means to destroy you."

Louise clung to him as if to make their bodies one. "Paul . . . ! I thought I could endure. . . . But when you avoided me—oh! I feared you despised me. . . . I refused Belmont. He can never have me again. I'd rather die. . . . But darling, I am yours—yours . . . ! For God's sake, take me away from this hell—before it is too late!"

"Louie, I—I will," he quavered.

It was then she loosened the clutch on his sleeves, and swept her bare arms around his neck, and with tears streaming from under her closed eyelids, she sought blindly for his mouth. Her lips, like sweet live fire, burned away the horror of the hour. And he was soaring to the heights of bliss, to the oblivion of dream and enchantment, to the deathless hopes of love, when an awful voice dragged him down to a consciousness.

"There!" shrieked the woman, dreadful in her triumph. "Shameless Magdalene that she is . . . ! Sneaking to this storeroom to be in the arms of her lover!"

Violent and aghast, Belmont thrust Sister out of his way, and advanced with slow and heavy steps. Paul drew Louise to his side and held her, as she sank quiveringly against him. After the shock, his first sensation was one of profound relief.

"Manning—what's this mean—you kissin' my wife?" demanded the trader, thickly, out of suspended breath.

"I should think that was obvious," replied Paul coolly. The thing he had feared, the secrecy he abhorred, ceased to exist.

"You playin' with Louie?—flirtin' with this girl?"

"No. I am the farthest removed from that."

The woman let out a laugh which held nothing womanly in it. She lined up beside Belmont, a stronger mind at the moment, possessed by a thousand devils of hate, and strangely betraying her exultation at the proofs she had long broodingly watched for. It was she, and not the dazed trader, who struck cold terror to Paul's heart.

"You love her?" queried Belmont with incredulous amazement.

"Yes. I love her, Belmont."

The trader made a swift gesture, as if to thrust away an extraordinary and disturbing fact not to be accepted.

"You meet her—in my empty storeroom, where no one comes? You enticed her here, for your—love-makin'?"

"No. We met by accident," returned Paul hurriedly, feeling a shock pass through the slender form encircled by his arm. "I had been walking on the desert. I felt hot, dizzy, and I stepped in here to get out of the sun."

"But how come *she* happened in?"

"Belmont, you fool!" interposed Sister. A large discolored bruise, swollen and angry, almost closed one eye, and with its contrast to her pallor, and convulsive workings of her face, rendered her hideous to behold. "They met here on purpose. But what if it was accident? Didn't you see them in each other's arms, kissing so they never heard us?"

The inexorable logic and passion of the woman seemed to penetrate Belmont's obstructed intelligence, and he lurched out of his slack posture to vibrate visibly. But Louise cut short his attempted utterance.

"Our meeting here was neither accident nor design," she said, with a calmness unnatural for that strained moment. "I saw Paul come in here. And I followed."

"All right, Louise. But why did you follow him?"

"Because I wanted to. . . . Paul has avoided me for days. I had to see him."

"Ah-huh! And why, woman?" burst out Belmont. Sister had been unable to destroy his faith in Louise. Eagerly he sought something that would refute Sister's accusation, and anything that would explain the discovery of her in Manning's arms.

"Because I love him," cried Louise ringingly.

"You—love—this dude?" gasped the trader.

"Yes. Yes! I love him!" she blazed passionately, as if her honor and womanhood had been questioned. And the little bronze head rose proudly upon Paul's shoulder. "I worship him. I live for him. It was he who kept me alive."

With a snatch that tore her blouse off her shoulders Belmont took her from Paul and drew her, like an empty sack, up close under his baleful eyes. The girl did not resist. She did not shrink or tremble. He had no more power to terrorize nor intimidate her than if she had been a bag of his own wool.

"You love him? Say it again!" This was the last desperate gasp of his failing faith.

"Yes."

"Then—that was—it?" he choked, in gathering might of passion.

"What?"

"Why you've been different since he came?"

The woman interrupted: "Aye, John Belmont. I told you. She is a brazen thing!"

"Speak!" thundered the trader. "That's why you—"

"Yes. I might have given up hope—and accepted the lie you forced on me, and my baby—but for him."

"You never—loved me?" he rasped, shaking the beads of sweat from his brow.

"Whoever said I did, John Belmont? I always feared you —despised you. I came here only because of Tommy— Where else could I have gone! And you ask me *now*? God in heaven, but you are inhuman! I loathe you! Let me go. Your touch is contamination."

The exceeding strength of her spirit, the magnificent truth of her abhorrence broke Belmont's grip upon her, and likewise the last weak hold he had upon himself. The fierceness of his thrust spun her around and would have sent her prostrate but for Paul's intervention. He caught her, steadied her; and then hand in hand they watched the madman in his eclipse of all that was sane. For a moment Belmont's frenzied muscular convulsion was that of a man hanging by the neck. He turned black in the face. Tremendous energy possessed his breast, but only strangling, spitting hisses escaped his lips. These passed as swiftly as they had overcome him. Then Paul saw that the trader had been affected solely by her searing scorn, by the inescapable truth of her hate, by the irretrievable fact of his loss. Presently he would recover to be seized by the animal in him, and he would be likely to rend and slay. Paul gazed about for a weapon to defend Louise and perhaps save his own life. And all the while bewilderment possessed him.

"Manning is—your lover," asserted Belmont, lowering at the girl.

"No!" flashed Louise. "You can't understand honor, nor his love for me, nor his consideration."

Belmont quailed again under the piercing quality of her words, their stinging justice, their stripping naked his ghastly sophistry and the monstrosity of what he called love.

"Belmont," interposed Paul, his voice icy, "you insult her. Have you no sense of decency?"

"Belmont, he lies," interrupted the woman wildly, seeing in the trader's blunted force a failure of her plot in its fullness. "They both lie. . . . Look at the false-faced doll! Look at the angel eyes, so proud, so clear! Yet all the while they have looked upon Paul Manning to lust after him."

"Take care, woman, that I do not kill you," growled the trader ominously.

"She is the one you should kill," cried the woman. "I sacrificed wealth, home—everything for you—and you lied to me. . . . You promised to get rid of her. You have never listened. . . . Listen to me now . . . ! They are lovers. They have deceived you. I have seen him go into her cabin—and not come out till dawn! Time and time again!"

"Oh, you lying wretch!" whispered Louise in horror.

"So now we've got down to it," said the trader, in a calm that boded catastrophe, as he strode forward to confront Paul.

"Belmont, it's not true," shouted Paul, coming out of his stupefaction. "This woman is vicious. She hates Louise . . . I swear to God that she lies."

The woman could not be shaken of her victory. Jealousy, the terror of all emotions, had seized Belmont's mind. Her beady little eyes glittered. She was no lunatic but a woman getting rid of a rival.

"Belmont, their brazen embrace—that we saw through the door—was nothing to what I can tell you. . . . I have listened at her open window . . . her cries of bliss . . . their kisses . . ."

Belmont loomed over Paul, like a hairy giant with roll

ing ox eyes and distorted visage, his ponderous fist uplifted.

"Liar!" he bellowed, and struck with all his might.

A stunning shock and blinding flash preceded Paul's
hurtling back, clear off his feet, to fall with such force that
had he struck stone instead of bags of wool it would have
killed him. He alighted in a sitting posture and lay there
helpless, dazed but still conscious. His sight seemed to
come out of a blackness which had darkened a thousand
bursting stars. He saw the trader, hair up like the mane of
a lion, dripping froth from yellow fangs, his legs planted
wide, his huge fists waving. And for Paul Manning that
instant saw the sweeping away of all instincts save murder.

"I'll smash you!" roared the trader. "I'll beat you to
death!"

The woman tugged at his ponderous arm. She checked
his stride. "Let him go! If you must kill—kill her!"

Belmont flung her aside with a frenzy which betrayed
that what he meant to wreak on Manning he might mete
out to her. She fell heavily against a bin and lay there
moaning. It was Louise who rose to block the madman's
advance. She screamed as she thrust him back with incredible strength.

"Don't you strike Paul again! *I will kill you!"*

Her voice, terrible to hear, galvanized Paul's thoughts.
Death was in the air. It stalked in that bare, torrid room.
Death was the solution. And suddenly Paul felt master of
himself, with a fixed and immutable power. Ice ran along
his hot veins, to the burning core of his bones. He gath-
ered nerve force for the expenditure of a tremendous muscular effort. He would leap up, seize the heavy iron wool-
sack hook that hung within reach, and brain this degen-
erate devil.

But a clinking step outside, a shadow at the door blocked Paul's spring.

"What the hell's goin' on heah?"

"Wess! Thank God you've come!" cried Louise, spent and faint.

The cowboy's query, like his entrance, changed the tension of the situation. It was as if the death which four desperate hearts had separately decreed had stalked in from the heat-hazed, ghastly veiled inferno outside. Kintell did not need to ask. His gaze that had the glitter and the point of a dagger translated the scene in one flash. He took long strides over the flagstone floor. Belmont backed instinctively from that menacing figure, from the wagging gun at its hip, from the gray eagle face.

"Hold on, Kintell. . . . No mixin'—of yours," called the trader, shaken.

"Hell you say? Wal, spit yore story pronto, or—" Kintell had no need to finish that threat.

"Sister led me here. We found Louise in Manning's arms. They're lovers."

"Shore. But Paul is no more what you mean, Belmont, than am I."

Paul had risen shakily to his feet, the blood still salty in his mouth. He pointed to Sister: "Woman, you swore to a vicious and damnable lie," he cried.

"Ah-huh. Pard, come across with yore story," the cowboy said.

"I told the truth. You know that. Belmont might have believed in Louise's innocence but for Sister."

"An' what's the lie she swore to?"

"Kintell," replied the trader huskily, "Sister saw Manning go into Louise's cabin night after night."

"Thet's a damn lie! Heah, you hag!" The cowboy whipped out his gun, and sidling away from Belmont to ward the woman, with his left hand he reached down to clutch her by the throat and drag her to her knees. "Talk, you heathen! Or I'll beat yore lyin' brains oot!"

"Don't kill me!" she begged in abject terror, and would have sunk down but for that powerful hand.

"Woman, take back yore lies an' be quick aboot it," ordered the cowboy in cold passion.

"You—choke—" she gasped. "Yes, I—I lied—God help me! I never saw Manning go into Louise's cabin! I never saw anything—but that today in here."

Kintell released Sister with a shove, and sheathing the gun he drawled contemptuously: "Wal, Belmont, did you get thet? I hope you did. Come, you got a lot more to get!"

The trader's answer, like his spent fury, was directed upon the unfortunate woman.

"That finishes you with me," he shouted, again black as a thundercloud. "I'm expectin' Shade to drive in today. When he goes back, you go with him."

Whatever this meant, it spelled utter woe to Sister, who in her defeat, excited even the pity of Louise.

"Belmont, think," implored the girl. "She has given up everything for you. She must have meant something in your life . . . and you will need her now."

"Belmont, I'm gonna have a swell time talkin' turkey to you," went on Kintell tantalizingly. He had something sure back of his cool effrontery. "Aside from yore rottenness to these pore women, you air shore a scurvy *hombre*. I haven't figgered yet all you was across the river. But Calkins told me you'd got run oot. Heah on this range. I shore got you figgered. You cheat the Indians. You air a hawg. Wuss than thet, you sell rum to them. Believe me, trader, thet's no little crime on this desert."

"Blah! Cowboy, you're some on talkin' yourself. But

you can't prove a word of all that," interrupted Belmont

"The hell I cain't! We can prove it all. We saw the liquo packed oot of thet wagon, an' heard you talkin'. It wa Manning you shot at thet night, an' no Indian. I knov where you hide thet liquor. . . . More'n thet, we knov you air a cattle thief. You hired Calkins an' his ootfit t steal your own stock. Two hundred sixty haid of cattl which you sold back to Manning. I guess maybe we cain' prove thet."

"Rant and be damned, Kintell," replied the trader, bu his face was ashen, his voice weak. "You can't scare me You never have seen me sell any liquor to the Indians an you can't prove the cattle deal. Besides you killed Calkin I hid his body where you'll never find it. If you bring sui against me, I'll accuse you of murder."

"Yes, and how about poisoning the spring," broke i Paul, hard and fast. "I *saw* you at that trick—and I've go water samples to prove it."

"All lies, lies . . . you can't prove any of it, and yo know it," shouted Belmont, the color returning to his fac But his eyes were still riveted on the menacing figure o the cowboy, with his hand clawlike at his side, his eyes th color of grey steel.

Paul decided on a last chance at mediation. "Belmon what'll you take to give up Louise and the baby?" he sho out.

"What'll you give?" slowly queried the trader, in craft surprise.

"I'll give you my share of cattle, and all the cash I hav banked at Wagontongue—about ten thousand dollars.

"Huh! You sure hold Louise cheap. . . . Listen, yo conceited Easterner! You haven't money enough to bu her. I wouldn't sell her for all the cattle and all the gold i the West."

"But she hates you. She'll never be your wife again. . . . And besides you have no real legal claim on her anyway. . . ."

Belmont shot him a sharp, surprised look. "The hell you say . . . and where did you get that wild idea?"

They were interrupted by the entrance of a tall man at the back door. He carried his coat over his arm. He was dusty and hot, and wringing wet with sweat. His hurry and the expression of his florid face and keen blue eyes betokened an arrival of importance.

"Here you are, Belmont. I just got in."

"Howdy, Shade," returned the trader.

"I'm butting in on a mess, I see," replied the other, his bright eyes taking in the actors in this evident drama. "But I've great news for you. Perhaps it will help."

"News!" ejaculated Belmont with a start, his heavy features lighting.

Shade took from his coat pocket a large envelope, which he handed to the trader with officious ceremony.

"I've got you reinstated," he said authoritatively. "You can go back to Utah!"

Belmont's big hands shook as he turned the envelope over and read the address. His ox eyes rolled from it to Louise as if there were no others present. And suddenly he became vibrant with new force, new passion.

"Louise, you're goin' back to Utah," he boomed.

"Never—alive!" whispered the stricken girl, and she sank down in a faint. Belmont picked her up and held her in the crook of his elbow.

"Manning, our partnership is ended," he said. "I'll settle with you tomorrow after I return from Black Canyon."

As he started to turn away Kintell spoke in a vastly different tone.

"Let her down!" With the cold command the cowboy

strode forward to jam his gun into Belmont's stomach.

"Hyar!" yelled the trader hoarsely as he let the girl slide to the floor like an empty sack. His red visage turned an ashen gray and his big eyes protruded. "Take that gun away. It might go off!"

"You're damn right it might," snapped Kintell grimly as he backed away with the menacing level gun. "Belmont, I shore been playin' with you. Wanted to heah you talk. Wal, I reckon yore Utah pard there fetched you some good news. Now listen to some bad news. I've been over in Utah. I've seen Bloom an' forced him to talk. I shore got yore number."

"Bloom?" ejaculated the trader, his chest appearing to cave in.

"Yes, Bloom. Paul was right—you ain't got a legal claim on Louise, cause she ain't even yore wife."

"You're lyin'. . . . You can't prove that," gasped Belmont, staggering back, as if dealt the one blow that could fell him.

"Am I?" shot back the cowboy. "Wal, Bloom talked an' he talked plenty. You ain't married to Louise *because Sister is yore real wife,* an' a man cain't hev more'n one wife at a time any more—even though there's some around here still thinks they can get away with it. Now get oot of heah. Yore gig is up so far as this girl is concerned."

Ghastly of visage, Belmont whirled and seizing hold of Shade, he lurched out of the wool room. The crushed and haggard Sister followed them, turning to gaze back fearfully.

"Wess, you got here just in time—to save me from God knows what. . . . I would have killed him, or been killed myself. . . . I was at the end of my rope," said Paul shakily.

"Wal, killin' him wouldn't hev been much loss. . . . But

say, you took a fierce poke. Split yore lip . . . you feel all right?"

"Sure, Wess. A little dazed, that's all. . . . Help me with Louise."

"Shore . . . pore kid . . . she's comin' to all right." Suddenly Kintell seemed himself again, the old soft-voiced, cool and easy Texan. "Let's get oot of heah."

Together they helped the faltering girl to her feet. Then half carrying her, Paul made his way across the heat-seared ground to her cabin. At the entrance Louise faltered again, and sweeping her into his arms, Paul entered her cabin and placed her gently on the bed.

Although occupied with his ministrations to the fainting girl, Paul was conscious that this was the first time he had been inside her room. The interior of the tiny cabin was neat and well kept, with ruffled curtains at the windows and spotless though well-worn furniture. From the far corner of the room, Tommy stared wonderingly at them from over the top of his crib.

With water from the small kitchen at the rear of the cabin, Paul bathed the pale golden brow with a hand that shook despite himself. Louise's heavy eyelids fluttered and opened. Paul knelt over her, almost transfixed, mute above her yearning eyes of fear and love.

"There, Louie," said Kintell in a deep voice. "You've come to. . . . We're heah, an' everythin' is gonna turn oot all right."

"Oh, Paul—you look so terrible. . . . Your mouth is bleeding." She made an effort as if to rise, but Paul restrained her.

"It's nothing," replied Paul strongly. "Everything is fine now. But you must rest. Wess and I will watch outside. When you feel better, we'll come and talk to you. But remember, above all, Belmont will never take you away from us again!"

With a little sigh of relief, she lay back on the bed, her eyes wide and lovely, with the haunting fear gone.

Paul left her, quiet and resting, and joined Wess who had gone out onto the steaming desert. They picked a shady place under a tall cedar facing the door of Louise's cabin and sat down to talk. Paul was literally bursting with curiosity. "What did you find, Wess? I know that it was plenty, from the look on Belmont's face when you braced him with it," he said eagerly.

"Wal, it's good, an' then mebbe again it ain't," replied Kintell as he wiped his wet brow and brushed back his damp hair with a grimy hand. "I found Bloom on a ranch near Pink Cliffs. He sure spilled his guts . . . after I threatened to shoot a laig off him. He says Sister was sure married to Belmont, all right—but he doesn't know where or when. As far as he knows there was no divorce. . . . But then nobody 'round these parts pays much attention to thet, as you know."

"Is that why Belmont left Utah?"

"Wal, only partly. He was mixed up in a gold-mining deal . . . sold a lot of stock his partners thought was wuthless. They was gonna put him in jail fer it . . . so he lit oot. Then they discovered silver an' the charges were dropped. Thet's what Shade came over here to tell him aboot."

"But you said this was only partly the reason why he left."

"Shore. He was worried thet if they started lookin' 'round, they might poke into his married life too . . . an' the mood his partners were in they'd hev hung him for anythin' they could get on him."

"Wess, that man has diabolical luck as well as cunning.

. . . But this time, he won't get away with it," said Paul stridently. "He *knows* we've got the goods on him about Sister. This time, I don't think he'll interfere."

"Wal, I ain't so sure," muttered the cowboy. "He shore turned all shades of green when I told him Bloom had spilled . . . but he's slick. He'll come up with somethin' yet."

"I know. But we won't take any chances. Tomorrow morning, I want you to ride up on the mesa. . . .Watch for Belmont leaving for Black Canyon. I'll have horses saddled, ready. As soon as you get back we'll be on our way —toward the *Utah* line."

"Utah! But boss, thet's where he says *he's* goin'!" the cowboy ejaculated amazedly.

"Sure. But after he thinks this out, even if he suspects that's where we've gone, he'll not follow us there. He knows we'll be out to prove that he's married to Sister. . . . I think he'll give us a wide berth."

"Pard, you've got it. Thet's the ticket." Kintell slapped his thigh resoundingly. "An' this time mebbe we've got John Belmont's number. . . ."

They were interrupted by a call from the cabin.

"Paul, Paul . . . where are you? Oh, there you are." Louise had come out on her porch, a little pale and unsteady, but composed and more lovely than Paul had ever seen her.

He rose and came forward to greet her anxiously. "Are you all right? You should rest more, and stay out of this heat."

"Paul, I'm a big girl now," she said with a ghost of a smile. "It was silly to faint, right in the middle of things. But I'm all right now."

He took hold of her arms. "Louise, I—we both know all about Belmont and Sister. . . . Wess found out when he went across to Utah . . . but why didn't you tell me this before?"

Her gaze dropped. "Paul, I was so afraid—and ashamed. I was such a child," she said hesitantly. "He swore that she was nothing to him—that they were in business together, and that she had put up the money to start his cattle business and the post here. . . . Oh, I was such a fool. But I was lonely, unhappy . . . for a while he was good to me. Then, one night after we had come to Bitter Seeps, I heard them quarreling, and she threw it up to him. When I faced him about it he lied. . . . He swore she was not his wife, but I could see it in his eyes, that he was lying. . . . That was the end of him as far as I was concerned." She lifted her eyes to gaze out over the ghastly heat-veiled expanse of desert. "I wanted—oh, so much—to tell you, particularly when I knew you were holding back . . . that your sense of honor forbade you to make love to me. But I was a coward—I was afraid you would hate me for having let myself endure this situation so long. And then there was Tommy. . . . I couldn't bear to tell anyone that he was nameless, and that I had . . ." Her voice broke.

Paul shook her gently. "You silly, foolish, wonderful child! Don't you realize that Tommy is not nameless— that the onus is not on you but on Belmont?" he said with deep emotion. "No court in the world would deny him his name under the circumstances. You have acted honorably —you have nothing to be ashamed of. . . . But that's all over now. Tomorrow morning, as soon as Belmont is gone, we are leaving. And you and Tommy will never be troubled with him again."

Her response was to lean forward against him, the tears flowing now. He stood there, with the slender, trembling form in his arms, conscious of an exaltation he had never known before that seemed to transcend all the dark, terrible moods that had ever assailed him at Bitter Seeps.

Presently he was conscious that the cowboy was at his elbow. "You kids better break it up jest now. I think you both should lay low too fer the time bein' an' get some rest . . . jest in case. Tomorrow'll be a big day—fer all of us."

13.

WHEN PAUL awoke to a hot sun streaming in his window, he realized suddenly, with a start, that it was late in the morning. He had only planned to sleep for a few hours in order to be on guard when Wess left for Black Mesa, but he realized that he had overslept. Quickly he rose and dressed, but did not bother to shave. His mouth was stiff and sore, but at the moment he hardly felt it.

Kintell's tent was empty. At the stable, Paul saw that both the cowboy's and Belmont's horses were gone. There was little time to waste. He ran back to Louise's cabin, which at this moment seemed strangely silent, almost as if deserted.

He knocked on the door. "Louise, are you awake?"

"What is it, Paul?" her voice sounded strangely muffled.

"Are you dressed, and ready? Belmont has gone!"

"Ready—for what?"

"To leave. . . . You must be packed and ready by the time Wess comes back. Remember what I told you last night?"

"Paul—I—I—I can't. I'm not going."

Frantically he rattled the door. "What's the matter! Can't you let me in! What has gone wrong?"

"I can't let you in. I'm not dressed."

"Then put on a robe and come to the window. . . . I must talk to you."

"No, Paul. I can't. It's—it's all over. . . . I can't go with you."

By this time he was beside himself.

"Has *he* been here, since I last saw you?" he demanded.

"No—it's just . . . well, I was rash. I lost my head yesterday. For Tommy's sake—and for all of us—I must stay."

"You're lying. Let me in, or I'll break down the door," he shouted in a frenzy.

At length the key turned in the lock and Louise appeared. She was fully dressed. Her face was white and drawn, her eyes two great haunting gulfs.

Roughly he seized her arms. "Tell me, what did he say—what did he *do* to you?"

She strained to twist free. "Please Paul—let me go. . . . I told you. Belmont was not here." Her voice was cold, dead. "I was just carried away yesterday. Now I know it's impossible. . . . You and Wess must leave here before there is more trouble."

"If you don't tell me the truth—*I'll find him and kill him myself!*"

This aroused her at last. "Oh, no—no, Paul. . . . Please. Oh, not that!" There was terror in her voice.

"What about your love for me—your kisses . . . what you have said to Belmont—your imploring me—begging me—'take me away from this hell, before it's too late,' you said."

"Don't Paul. . . . Oh, please—don't." She was sobbing now. "Let me go. . . . Just leave me—alone." She twisted away from him and darted into the cabin, slamming the door behind her. Paul, his heart turned to lead in his breast, could hear the sound of violent weeping.

Stunned and dazed, he stumbled down the porch steps out into the blazing sun. Oblivious to the withering heat, he stood there, blinded, crushed, and sickened.

Suddenly he heard what seemed to be a step behind him. He whirled and looked in all directions. There was nothing there but the cluster of tall cedars, rippling in the slight breeze that blew down from the mesa. He ran to Kintell's tent. A quick glance into the cowboy's tent disclosed that it was still empty. Then suddenly he heard the clatter of horses' hoofs in the direction of the stable. As he burst out of the cedars he saw a tall figure on horseback disappearing down the trail around the south side of the mesa in a cloud of reddish dust.

"Wess! Wess! *Come back*," he called in stentorian tones. But the cowboy was gone.

For a moment, Paul stood there, his brain somehow too dazed and confused to comprehend what had happened. Then the light burst upon him. Wess had come back in time to overhear their conversation. True to his nature, the Texan had divined what had happened, and was on his way, even now, to Black Canyon and a fateful rendezvous with the trader.

Black Canyon was a deep gulch in the heart of the great mesa, and at its upper end, ten miles or more to the westward, there was a little settlement of Indians with whom the trader did considerable business. He made infrequent visits up this canyon, always alone. The trail was rough and perilous. Paul had traversed part of it. How easy for a spirited horse to make a misstep on a narrow ledge! The grasping Belmont would make one more trip to Black Canyon, bent on collecting debts, perhaps to dispose of his last consignment of liquor to the Indians, or sacrifice his cattle to the white trader there. Whatever his motive, it was the blunder such men made once at least in their lives.

At that moment Paul Manning's ordeal ended. His mind was now, suddenly, crystal clear. Quickly, he ran back to his room for his gun. Buckling on the heavy weapon gave him a queer hot little flush of elation, which, even as he gloried in it, surprised him. Where was the doubt-ridden, fearful Paul Manning now? At this moment he knew what his inevitable course must be. He must reach Black Canyon before the cowboy did. He could not allow his friend to sacrifice himself for a cause that was not truly his own.

As his horse pounded up the long slope west of the mesa, Paul went over in his mind what somehow he knew inevitably would be the cowboy's own plan. Wess would follow the southern trail and then cut across the lower end of Black Mesa toward the eastern rim of Black Canyon, and try to intercept Belmont somewhere along the narrow, rock-walled trail that wound through the steep gorge. In order to reach there ahead of the cowboy, Paul would have to climb to the top of the mesa somehow from the west slope and ride straight across to Black Canyon. There were no trails up that side, but Paul had seen several draws which cut through the sheer black cliffs, one of which he had fancied on his previous rides could be ascended on horseback.

As Paul galloped along, it seemed that nature itself presaged a break in the mood of Bitter Seeps. Black Mesa had showed no scarlet flush of sunrise that morning. The east was dark. No hard copper hue tinged the blue of sky. Far to the north the pink cliffs of the Segi sheered up into clouds as dense as purple ink. Ropes of lightning zigzagged down into the canyons and the low rumble of thunder rolled along the ramparts and the mountain walls. A storm hung in the drowsy, sultry atmosphere. Still the heat veils rose from the gray rocks and the red earth, and in the distance that ghastly gray haze shrouded the desert. The roasted earth would not soon relinquish its fire.

A half hour of hard riding brought Paul to the mouth of the draw. Without hesitation he plunged up the steep and dusty bottom. The going, at first, was easier than he had expected, but gradually the way became steeper, and choked with scrub brush and boulders. In the intense heat both horse and rider became bathed in sweat. Several times the roan slipped and pawed on loose rocks that tumbled down into the draw, almost losing his footing, but each time he recovered precariously and went on. Paul marveled at the endurance and agility of the horse, and urged him on with friendly words.

Twice they were blocked by what seemed impassable cliffs, but each time they worked around them, until finally, spent and almost blinded with sweat, they gained the top of the mesa.

At the top, while his horse was briefly resting, Paul bent a gaze, now keen and searching, on Bitter Seeps, a tiny straggle of dark trees, with the little humps of buildings beside them. His gaze had in it the element of farewell. Perhaps this would be the last time he saw it, and what it held for him. But at this point he had no choice. His ordeal had ended when he had faced John Belmont in the heat-steeped gray shade of the wool room.

Louise's wan face, her wide eyes that looked to be emptying her soul in vain and stark oblation; Belmont standing like a bull, red-eyed and lowering, about to charge; and the cowboy, gray-faced, steel-eyed nemesis holding the trader at bay—all these and thought of the torturous conflict within himself had been the all-potent factors that had made him the protagonist in this tragic drama of Bitter Seeps.

Grimly now, he recalled how for days on end—these awful blasting days that boiled the brain and sizzled the blood—he had fought the temptation to beg Louise to run off with him—and then even the terrible urge to close his eyes to the dark and bloody purpose in Wess Kintell's mind —and above all, in these last hellish moments, the urge to rend and to slay the trader himself.

But he had loved his friend, even as he had loved Louise. Their love had saved him from himself, and even from the rashness of word and deed they would have inflicted upon themselves. He knew now that he would follow this wide-eyed girl to the ends of the earth, and that whatever her fate, it would be his fate also. He could no longer hesitate to do what seemed necessary, regardless of the consequences to himself. He was no longer afraid of himself nor for himself, and in this moment he realized that he was finding the victory over Bitter Seeps he never would have dreamed was possible. Then Paul addressed himself to the task at hand.

As its name indicated, Black Mesa was as flat as a table. A gray expanse of sage, spotted by cedar trees, extended far to the east. Paul scanned this expanse with the eyes of a range rider searching for a favorite lost horse. This was the summer grazing ground for Indian stock. He did not intend to be seen by shepherd or hunter or rider. To this end he made certain of his prospect before advancing.

"All to the good!" he muttered, and that soliloquy was addressed to the black storm cloud in the north and the low rumble of thunder. Before he turned back on this trail, the elements would have combined to protect him. Nature had signified its intent to hide his tracks. Bitter

Seeps had had enough of John Belmont. So Paul Manning pondered as he rode swiftly across the mesa toward a clump of cedars. From behind this he again surveyed the mesa top. A lonely hawk soared low over the sage. Jack rabbits bounded away from before him. He saw no other living creatures.

A singular impression of being alone in an utter solitude added a final strength to Paul's conviction that the gods of chance, justice, freedom were his allies. And with his exultation mingled another feeling, too vague, too remote from memory, too strange to have been experienced before. Yet it had to do with something familiar. He had never been on top of this mesa, yet it seemed that he had. Never had he faced as flat, as universally gray and monotonous a stretch of wasteland. Nevertheless there dwelt with him a sweet, vague sense of having roamed over this forlorn tableland.

The sun cleared the purple cloud bank in the east and poured its white-hot rays, like molten metal, down upon the earth. Soon the sage-flat reeked with transparent veils. Paul knew the sweat streamed off his body, but he did not feel the heat.

At last the gray level broke in a wandering line of black. This was the far rim of the canyon that he sought. He urged his horse to a gallop now, for it was imperative that he lose no time in reaching the section of trail he had chosen.

Presently Paul stood among the stunted cedars on the rim of Black Canyon. A ragged, many-faceted rent in the rock yawned beneath him. At that point the gorge was deep, narrow, precipitous. No green softened the glistening, tumbled floor far below. Leaving his horse hidden in a clump of trees, Paul started at once to work his way down the almost perpendicular angle on foot. In an ordinary hour he might have found this descent hazardous and exceedingly difficult; but now he combined the judgment of a savage and the agility of a goat. He reached the trail, carrying a short, heavy snag of dead cedar.

Paul peered back down the canyon, where in sections and for a long way he could mark the line of the trail. Up the canyon the narrow track soon turned a jutting corner of wall. His next move was to creep along, bending to search for the hoof marks of Belmont's horse. Bare rock showed the white cuts of iron shoes, but these did not satisfy him. Farther on plain tracks in a thin layer of dust caused the hot gush of blood to leap along his veins. They were fresh; they were headed north; they had undoubtedly been made by Red-Eye, Belmont's half-wild sorrel stallion.

A sullen roll of thunder entered into Paul's deductions. He gazed aloft. Half the sky was dark. On the edge of the blue half the sun had begun to lose something of its whiteness. Before long it would be obscured and the heat spell broken. Belmont had passed this point several hours before. By this time he would have transacted his business and would be far on his way back. The storm would hurry him. There were two bad sections of trail in this upper part of the canyon. Paul was between them. The less dangerous lay up the canyon a quarter of a mile or more. Belmont, being a Westerner and in a hurry, would ride this section of trail. But he would dismount to lead his horse around the other. Neither action should be attempted after night or in the dark fury of a desert storm.

Paul planned to intercept the trader when he rode around the narrower corner.

When Paul reached this point he experienced grim satisfaction in his memory. The picture in his mind had been perfect. The black gorge narrowed and boxed; the wall above the trail sheered precipitously several hundred feet;

below was a frightful void, straight down everywhere except just under the perilous corner, where a black slant of rock jutted out. The trail around this corner was solid rock, two feet wide, slippery and far from level.

Paul had learned much about trails and horses in these past months. The gentlest and safest horse could be frightened and slip off this trail here. Red-Eye would plunge high and paw the air and go hurtling into space. But what then? Paul had in these moments become somber, thorough, implacable. He peered down to see what chance a rider had for his life going over that precipice. None! He would strike the jutting slant, then slide and fall into the abyss, to be crushed far below. This was the place.

He selected a covert some rods from the corner of the wall, from which he could see up the canyon and a little of the trail as it turned. There was a possibility of an Indian coming along headed north, and a remoter one of meeting the cowboy here before Belmont arrived. But Paul discounted both. By his calculations he had gained ten miles on the cowboy by using the short cut; and with the impending storm, the Indians would not be likely to be on this trail. This was the most crucial and inevitable time in the lives of four persons.

The moment Paul concealed himself and composed himself to wait, he suffered the bane of inaction and fell prey to his powerful feelings.

"I must not fail," he soliloquized, and gazed with vast absorption at the gray cedar snag he gripped so tenaciously. It was not like a bludgeon or a mace or a savage war club. It was a snag from the dead top of a gnarled and stunted cedar, one of those bleached trees that reached out with weird and writhing arms.

A shadow passed over him. The white light faded, and the cessation of heat was like withdrawal from a fire. Still the rocks burned through his clothes. A murky cloud, like a blanket, had come between him and the sun. The change to sky and canyon seemed communicated to the waiting figure. To the south the strip of blue sky appeared to be rapidly receding; to the north the dark canopy overhead grew purple and then black and at last a dead ebony hue. Ropes of lightning ran up and down this densest bank. The rumble and roll of thunder grew loud and detonating.

Paul gazed aloft and backward. The clouds had passed him, swelling, mushrooming, moving ponderously to swallow up the blue. But in the canyon it was hot, windless, smoky. The gleaming black rocks had lost their shine.

Gradually the sky was blotted out. Flashes and flares of lightning illuminated the clouds above, and thunder rolled across the heavens. The forked streaks and reverberating booms marked the center of the approaching storm. Darker grew the canyon until it appeared under the spell of a waning, sunless afternoon.

Suddenly his frame corded stiff. Far up the canyon a horse and rider had come around the corner. His eye strained to prove familiarity of gait and size and hue. It was Belmont.

Soon horse and rider, coming at a trot, passed out of Paul's line of vision. This was the signal for him to leap from his covert. He took one sweeping glance down the canyon. The trail seemed as lonely as if no savage had ever passed along it, and none ever would. Then he ran to his last stand.

The place had been hollowed out by winds and water, by the gods of the canyon elements, that through the ages had destined it for ambush. Paul leaned behind the corner of wall. One step to the trail! With his left hand he drew his gun, muttering: "If there's a hitch I'll use this. But there will be no hitch."

Allowing for Belmont slackening Red-Eye to a walk at the narrow places Paul calculated it would take him fifteen minutes to reach this end of the box canyon. All his force of brain and muscle concentrated on the issue. Never had his senses been so keen.

The storm was almost overhead. Presently a lightning bolt would rend the ink-black cloud. In the stillness between the rumbles of thunder Paul listened for the roar of rain. All he could hear was a faint moan of the wind in the cedars on the rim. The drowsy heat persisted. Flares grew continuous until the twilight of the canyon brightened to a weird supernatural glow. Thunder boomed. A breath of hot air wailed down the canyon and passed, leaving a faint smell of brimstone. Seconds, age-long, dragged out to minutes. He leaned motionless against the hot rock, his body tense, his nerves cold, his ears like the strung wires of a harp.

All the peculiar physical characteristics of place and time seemed magnified momentarily. That canyon became a sepulcher. The grotesque arms of the dead cedar snags on the rim waved for the storm to rush on, for the specters below to dance, for the evil spirit of Bitter Seeps to leap from under the black walls. Particles of dust, infinitesimal sparks, glittered when the lightning glittered. And the smell of sulphur permeated Paul Manning's quivering nostrils.

Clip-clop! Clip-clop! Clip-clop! The metallic hoofbeats of an iron-shod horse, nervous and driven, smote Paul's understanding ears. He moved clear of the wall, his strung right arm high, his hand clutching the billet of wood. *Clip-clop! Clip-clop!*

The lean red nose of a horse, with dilating nostrils, pushed past the corner of wall. Paul poised himself to strike. Then, suddenly, acting on a motive that, for the moment, he could not comprehend, he stepped out from behind the ledge to confront the trader.

The red horse, emitting a piercing snort, reared high with wild eyes. Belmont bawled in fright.

"*Whoa!* Whoa Red. . . . Steady there old boy!"

It was a narrow escape for the trader. The horse almost went over the cliff. But he crashed down, one hoof half over the edge, and stood shaking in every muscle.

Then Belmont saw Paul.

"Good afternoon, Belmont. I figured I'd find you about here." A cold ring, edged with sarcasm, gave a cutting edge to Paul's greeting.

"Man-ning . . . *you?*" the trader rasped out, his bold eyes rolling. "What the hell?"

"Yeah, that's what—hell!"

Belmont's gaze took in the gun Paul held in one hand and the club in the other. His swarthy visage changed to an ashen hue. One flash of light confirmed a reason for that strange encounter. Belmont could neither back nor turn the horse on that narrow ledge. He could only go forward.

"My Gawd, man!" he whispered hoarsely.

"If you had a God, it would be too late to call on him, Belmont."

"But Manning! Wait—listen. . . . I'll give Louise up. I'll pay you back for your cattle. . . . Let's talk. . . ."

An icy calm had descended on Paul. He saw that he was at once the master here, and he meant to play it to the fullest.

"Sure, Belmont. . . . And what else can you offer? Make it big!"

"Hold on, Manning! I'll quit the post. . . . You can have it. And I'll show you my marriage license to Sister. . . . I didn't burn it like I told Louise. Let me get off this hoss, walk ahead of you . . . on the square—I swear it!"

"Sure, now. Wouldn't I be a sucker now to lose this chance? Well, Belmont, where you're going, you won't have much chance to talk your way out."

"But you got the drop on me. . . . It ain't fair."

"Fair! Have you ever been fair to anyone in your life?" Paul's voice was utterly contemptuous. "I'm no gunman, even though I've been practicing—and you know it. . . . But neither are you. You wouldn't have a chance with Wess Kintell. He'd shoot you before you could lift your arm. But I'm going to give you that chance." With a swift motion he flung away the club and shifted his gun to his right hand. Then he sheathed it.

"All right, Belmont, here's your chance. *Now go for your gun!*"

In a flash, the trader had grasped the inevitableness of that moment. A crafty gleam appeared in his eyes. Instead of trying to draw his gun, he suddenly kicked back mightily with his spurred boots with stentorian yell. But the frightened horse, instead of plunging forward to sweep Paul off the ledge to his death, reared high with a shrill neigh of terror. The left knee of the wildly careening animal struck Paul in the shoulder and threw him down against the wall. As Paul fell, he saw Belmont collide with a projecting corner of wall and go hurtling out of the saddle. The horse came down on grinding iron-shod hoofs almost on top of him, slid precariously, but recovered to go clattering down the trail.

Paul leaped up, his hair standing stiff at his narrow escape. He stared down. Belmont had hit upon the slant of rock below the rim and was slipping toward the precipice. His nerveless fingers failed to hold. A bloody blotch appeared on the right side of his distorted visage where the sharp corner of stone had cut like an ax. But he was conscious. His great eyes fixed on Paul, malignant and fierce. His legs slipped over the edge of the rock. Then flat-handed he halted his slide to his doom for a moment, in which a consciousness of the end changed the hellish fury of his eyes to a ghastly terror. His hold loosened. His body slid over the rim, then his awful face, then his upflung clutching hands.

Paul stood there stunned. He listened. After what seemed long seconds a dull crash came up from below—then another crash quickly smothered by the cracking and rolling of rocks.

"Belmont, to hell with you!" Paul leaned over the abyss, his jaw wobbling, his mouth dripping, every atom of flesh and bone retched by a sickening glory. A dazzling blue-white streak of lightning illumined the canyon to unreal light and a splitting clap of thunder filled the still air with a tremendous volume of sound. He leaped up as big drops of water splashed about him. A gray wall of rain came roaring down the canyon. Sheathing his gun he ran toward the rock that marked his descent from the rim above.

Before he reached it the torrent of rain overtook him, the gray wall receded in black gloom, the ropes of lightning blazoned intervals of blinding brilliance, and the continuous crash of thunder heralded the end of the world.

14.

PAUL RODE his horse at a sharp trot through the roaring gray curtain of rain across the lower end of Black Mesa toward a side trail that led down to the south slope. All at once he was weary, but grimly triumphant. Twice he had

had the opportunity to kill John Belmont, and twice he had stayed his hand. Now fate had intervened to save him from being a murderer. He had given the trader a fair chance to draw on him, but Belmont had been afraid . . . and that fear had been his own undoing. Whatever the outcome—and at this point Paul did not care—he had no regrets. He was also aware that the rain would wash away any telltale tracks that he and Wess had made toward Black Canyon. Perhaps no one save he would ever find out the secret of that dark and perilous trail. Perhaps they would—and Louise's saving might become her tragedy. But he had no fear about facing whatever such a future might bring.

The storm had spent its strength when Paul reached the edge of the cedar grove behind Bitter Seeps. Rain still fell, but it was lessening. In the west the black clouds had broken to let out rays of gold and silver, and a pale rainbow, like the lunar one visible by moonlight, glimmered with its eternal promise and was gone. Paul dismounted and watched with careful eyes for several seconds before he led his horse into the stable, unsaddled it and turned into the corral. He noticed that the cowboy's horse was still missing. Paul smiled a little to himself at the thought that the cowboy would by now be puzzling as to what had happened to the trader. Then his smile vanished, as the thought struck him that if Wess were gone until late that night, he might be suspected if Belmont did not return at the proper time. But it was also a possibility that those at the post might expect Belmont to stay overnight at the settlement, rather than chance the perilous trail in the storm. In any event, nothing could be done now but wait.

A roar of many waters greeted Paul's ears as he trudged down through the cedars from the corral. He waded boot-high in a torrent that ran down under the floor of Kintell's tent and down its way to the post. Streams were pouring off the mesa.

He halted for a moment to listen to the sound of running water. How strange and pleasant! Bitter Seeps was in flood—the most heartening sound he had ever heard here.

"Well, that should wash the poison out of you for good," he soliloquized, as he slipped down through the trees to the edge of the clearing.

There was no sign of life about the post, or the cabin, as Paul cautiously stole up to his door. Once inside, he drew a sigh of relief, which was followed by a gasp of amazement and consternation. There were still six inches of muddy water on the floor of his room, and the dark reddish stain showed where the flood had run much higher. His precious possessions! Paul set about attempting to salvage those which had not been damaged. As he worked he realized with a queer thrill that they were somehow unimportant now. He had found himself, in the dark and bloody crisis through which he had labored. He could look at the future unafraid.

Fortunately his bed was still above water and, after changing to dry clothes, he lay down with a sigh of weariness. Almost without realizing it, he fell asleep.

When he awakened from a sleep of utter weariness, the sun was shining brightly into his room. He smelled the dank mud. A mockingbird sang outside in a cedar. He felt giddy and buoyant. He dressed with nervous fingers. Hurrying out he went to Wess's tent. The desert appeared drenched, cleaned, transfigured. Red gullies lined the soil. Already the sand had dried out.

Finding Wess absent, Paul, now a little worried, hurried back to the post. He had slept late. Kitchen, living room, the store were all vacant. But on the porch and the square outside appeared more Indians than usually visited the trading post at one time. Indians always conversed in low guttural tones, so that such talk meant nothing to Paul, nor their somber visages, nor their collection in groups. Mustangs stood at the rail and on the flat.

To his great relief, Paul espied Kintell talking to the visitor Shade and the government farmer from the school. An Indian rider, muddy and wet, stood near them, holding the halter of a tired pony. This Indian seemed passive and inscrutable, as all the Indians were to Paul, but there was a trenchant air about him. The government farmer was gesticulating. Shade's face looked grave and troubled. The cowboy listened with eagle head bent low. Paul did not have to look a second time to know what had happened.

Somehow, at the moment, Paul did not want to face this group of men. He turned and strode back through his room and out to Louise's cabin. Stridently, he knocked on the door.

"Louise, let me in. Something has happened. Belmont has not come back," he said.

After a moment of silence, the door swung open. Her pale face was still set in that haunting mask that wrenched Paul's heart. He longed to tell her in a flood of words that her agony was at an end, but restrained himself with great effort.

"It has—indeed—if Belmont is not back," she replied dully.

"I didn't ask, but I know he isn't. . . . There was an Indian rider, wet and muddy. The government farmer is there with Shade. Wess is talking to them. Shade looked pale and upset, and I heard Sister weeping in her room."

Louise placed a trembling hand on her breast, as if to still her heart. She stared at Paul with slowly dilating, darkening eyes. "What does this mean, Paul?" she asked haltingly.

A step on the porch outside froze Paul's lips. Someone strode to the door and knocked.

"Louie, how air you? An' where's thet pard of mine?" came in the familiar drawl.

"Oh, Wess! He's here. Come in."

The cowboy entered. Paul felt that he would drain his eyes from their sockets. Wess came in with his slow step, and halted to light a cigarette.

"Howdy, friends. Shore is a peach of a mawnin' after the storm," he drawled in his careless easy way. Whatever had happened, he appeared as if it had not concerned him particularly. "Louie, you look like a peach, too. Gosh! I'd like to kiss you."

"You may."

"Wal, sometime when Paul cain't see." His lean tanned face wore the smile Louise always inspired when he was his old self. Paul had never seen it so beautiful. The cowboy was absolutely the cool, provoking, lovable Wess of months before this tragic period, except, Paul thought, there appeared more of a piercing light in the gray eagle eyes when he looked at Paul.

"Tell us!" burst out Paul, rising. "Belmont has not come home. Sister is weeping. Why?"

"Pard, I reckon thet little proposition I had to make Belmont won't have to be made."

"Why?" said Louise wonderingly.

"Funny, thet hunch of mine. You know, aboot Gawd Almighty never would let Belmont get away with it. . . . I shore do have swell hunches. . . . Louie, I have one more thet you're gonna be the happiest girl in the world."

Louise's face had gone pale, her eyes like dark velvet.

"Pard, I don't want to break the sad news to you an'

Louie all too sudden," the cowboy went on. " 'Pears Belmont is some incapacitated. His hoss Red-Eye come in last night riderless!"

"He is dead," intoned Louise solemnly. "The instant I saw you—I knew."

"Wal, you're some guesser, Louie. . . . Belmont has gone to square his long account."

Paul put an arm about Louise. "Then, it's all over, Wess," he said soberly.

"Tell us," whispered Louise.

"Wal, it seems Sister was worried last night aboot Red-Eye comin' in alone," replied the cowboy. "An' this mawnin' early she sent Indians ridin' oot to look fer Belmont. Thet buck oot there, Kishli, I think they call him, seen Belmont's red hawse on the canyon trail. He went up Black Canyon an' found the trader down on the rocks, daid as a doornail, his haid all smashed, an' every bone in his body broke. . . . Kishli seen where Red-Eye's iron hoofs scraped the edge of the trail. . . . Thet's a bad trail, so our government farmer says. An' it never should have been rid in a storm, much less on a mean hoss like Red-Eye. I reckon Belmont wanted to get home pronto. . . . Wal, he's home now in hell—where I hope he'll burn forever!" At this moment, the cowboy's eagle eyes were on Paul. Paul returned the gaze, and his wonderment grew. How much did this shrewd cowboy know? But if he knew anything, Wess gave no sign of it.

"Strange how sometimes things happen," Paul muttered awkwardly. "But at least we're free of him now."

"Paul, his death does not touch me," whispered Louise. "I can't be sorry."

Paul tightened his arm around her, but did not speak.

"Wal, my pard an' yore ladylove, I cain't be very sorry aboot it myself. An' I'm a tender-hearted cuss," drawled the Texan. "But it's over. Right heah we ferget. You savvy? Now, what air yore plans?"

"I think we should get out of here—as quickly as we can," said Paul. "What do you say, Louise?"

At her murmured assent, the cowboy went on, "I think we can get Belmont's wagon. But what do you want to do aboot the post, Louie? You an' yore boy have a claim to it, an' half the cattle."

"Let Sister have it—all of it," Louise was quick to answer.

"Ump-umm. Not if little Wess is on the job. I've spoke to Shade—he'll take over our share of the herd if Sister won't. . . ."

"At least let her have the post," said Louise soberly. "Whatever she tried to do to us, it was only because, in her way, she loved Belmont. I think she's paid enough of a price for that."

The cowboy left, to busy himself with his preparations. Once alone, the girl looked up at Paul.

"Oh, Paul, I hated myself for what I did to you yesterday," she said hesitantly. "But I was frantic. That night before, Belmont sneaked up behind my cabin and told me that if I didn't go away with him, he'd kill you and the baby. He also said that we could never prove that he was married to Sister because the courthouse had burned down in the town where they were married—with all the records. He said he had destroyed his own marriage certificate, and that Sister would never testify against him. . . . Oh, I was so afraid, and hopeless. . . ."

"Hush, child. . . ." said Paul gently, placing his finger on her lips. "It's all over now. From now on, you and Tommy are in my care. And we'll be married as soon as we reach Wagontongue—that is—if you're willing."

"Oh, Paul . . . as if you didn't know!" She clung to

him, her kisses all the sweeter in the glory of her acceptance.

"We'll go back to my farm," he said at length. "We'll sell it. Meanwhile Wess can be looking for a ranch with trees and water—far from here. . . . Nope—on second thought, we'll take Wess with us. I'd like my sister Anne to meet a real fire-eating cowboy. Perhaps, we'll all come back West and find that ranch together."

"What a dreamer you are, Paul—but wherever you want to go is all right with me."

They left before noonday, and not even Wess, who was at the reins, looked back at the weathered post, the drooping cedars, and the muddy pool under the foot of Black Mesa. Paul sat next to Louise in the back, while she ministered to the baby, whom she was trying to coax to take a nap. Although the boy was irritable and restless, he already looked less sickly with the end of the hot spell. Finally he dozed off fitfully, and in a little while Louise's dark head nodded beside him, the havoc gone from her face. Paul, with a somehow inexplicable sense of gladness, looked down at the sight of mother and child sleeping there together. Beauty of nature, of woman and child, part of the restless, ever-changing movement of life. And he had been responsible for bringing peace to the face of this young mother, who as yet had not really ever been a wife.

Paul climbed up on the seat beside Wess. The usually loquacious cowboy was quiet, but he kept the horses moving at a fast clip. Paul gazed out over the desert.

The red ruin of cliffs south of Walibu sloped off into the dunes of the Painted Desert. The storm had left the desert bright, fresh, like a burnished mosaic. Mounds of blue, domes of purple, peaks of saffron—endless dunes in endless hues, blazed golden under the sinking sun. The cowboy never looked back. But Paul could not refrain from casting one last long glance the way they had come. The bold, dark bulk of Black Mesa was bathed in a yellow glow that was turning to red. The cedars at its base were hardly more than a dark speck at its base. Bitter Seeps was out of sight now, and with it all but memories that would be swallowed up so soon in the all-encompassing future.